his
first wife's
secret

BOOKS BY EMMA ROBINSON

his first wife's secret

emma robinson

bookouture

Published by Bookouture in 2021

An imprint of Storyfire Ltd.
Carmelite House
50 Victoria Embankment
London EC4Y 0DZ

www.bookouture.com

ISBN: 978-1-83888-790-2
eBook ISBN: 978-1-83888-789-6

For Keith Houghton
English teacher and legend

PROLOGUE

Nothing can prepare a mother for the way she will feel about her baby. How she'll fall in love so hard and so deep that every murmur, every sigh, plays on the strings of her heart like the notes of a familiar song.

To his mother, this baby is the most beautiful thing she has ever seen. The blue of his eyes, the lengths of his fingers, the softness of his skin: every tiny part of him is another discovery of perfection. In that moment, she knows for certain that she will never, ever love another as much as she loves the child in her arms.

I have felt this before – the all-consuming passion of love and care and protection – and I didn't expect to ever feel it again. This time it's more complex. I want to slow down time, to hold each moment in my hands and squeeze every ounce of joy from it. Because I know how precious it is. How transient. How fragile.

Is this my second chance? To be trusted with her most precious thing in all the world?

And what happens if I don't deserve it?

CHAPTER ONE

CAROLINE

SIX MONTHS EARLIER

Caroline had perfected the art of spending time alone, which included stretching the most everyday activities to fill the acres of time she had to spare. She dangled the teabag in the hot water, watching the liquid darken. It was possible to waste at least five minutes this way. And this was her second cup since she'd got in from work an hour ago.

This particular mug was her favourite. *If it's not one thing, it's your mother*, written in dark blue across the front. Jamie's idea of a joke. She only washed it by hand these days, scared that the dishwasher might fade the letters.

At least there were biscuits. Chocolate digestives from yesterday's trip to Tesco. By walking up and down every aisle, she'd managed to make *that* last over an hour. An hour and a half if she included the trip to the café. She'd bought a gossip magazine to hide behind while she drank a latte, still unable to concentrate for long enough to read a book. It was a waste of time; the magazine was full of celebrities that she didn't recognise. She watched the wrong kind of TV to know who they were.

Once the tea was ready, she took the unopened packet of biscuits through to the lounge. There wasn't even any housework to do: the room was immaculate. Even the cushions on the cream sofa – which they'd waited to buy until Jamie was safely out of the sticky fingers and crayons stage – were fully plumped. Tea on a coaster on the low glass coffee table, biscuits open, television switched on. Usually, she'd take three biscuits from the packet and put them on a plate. Having the whole packet within easy reach was dangerous. But it was Friday night: time to go wild. She'd only just flicked onto Netflix and started to scroll through American sitcoms when the doorbell rang. *Who could that be?*

At the door, her neighbour's son Robbie smiled at her sheepishly, his breath visible in the cold January evening. 'Only me. Guess what I need?'

Caroline pretended to consider her answer. 'Well, it won't be my classical CD collection or fashion advice, so I'm guessing the spare key?'

He laughed, in the way you do when you're eighteen and a friend of your parents makes a lame joke. 'Yeah, I went out without mine this morning and Mum and Dad aren't back from work yet. I'd wait, but I think they're going out for dinner. It's *date night* apparently.' The quotation marks in the air and poked-out tongue made it clear that any romance between his parents was a cause for mockery.

It was what he did next that really did it. He scratched the side of his head, just behind his ear. A small movement but it hit her in the stomach like a fist. He looked just like Jamie.

Her face must have given away her shock because Robbie frowned. 'Are you okay, Caroline?'

She squeezed a smile back onto her face. 'Yes, sorry, I'm fine. Just remembered something is on the cooker. Wait a sec, I'll get your key.'

Robbie's door key was in a small pot in the hallway cupboard. A pottery bowl which Jamie had made in his Year Eight art class. Creative arts were not his strong point and the memory of him

presenting it to her and suggesting she was more than welcome
to give it to her worst enemy for Christmas made her smile. She
hooked out the key and was handing it to Robbie when Pete
pulled up outside. As he unfolded his lanky frame from behind
the wheel of his shiny sports car, she glanced at her watch. It was
early for him to have left the office.

'Cheers, Caroline.' Robbie waved the key at her. 'I'll drop it
back later.'

'All right, Robbie?' Pete covered the length of the gravel path
in three strides. It was his long legs that had first attracted her to
him in their third year of university. The novelty of a boyfriend
who was actually taller than her. He stuck his hand out to shake
Robbie's. 'Still forgetting your key?'

'Yeah. Don't tell my mum. She's already been on at me about
being more responsible when I go off to uni in October. She
doesn't think I'll cope without her.'

Of course. He was off to Exeter this year. A-level results
permitting.

Was Pete thinking the same thing as her as they both watched
Robbie hop over the low fence into his own front garden? She
poked him in the arm. 'What are you doing here at this time?
Have you been sacked?'

Pete grinned. 'Very funny. I wasn't in the office. I had a
meeting on the other side of Vauxhall. Anyway, let me in. I've got
something to show you which might make you smile.'

He was already undoing the top button of his pinstriped shirt
when she stood back to let him in. His suit jacket, she knew, would
be hung up over the back seat of his flashy car so that it didn't get
creased. The backdraft of his aftershave smelled expensive and too
strong to have been applied long ago. Was that for her benefit?

As he passed her, he shook a small sachet of some kind of
granules in her direction. She peered at it. 'What the... What
is that...?'

'It's Space Dust. I was in a shop today and they had it on the counter. I couldn't help but think of that time we bought it for Jamie. Do you remember?'

How could she fail to remember? He'd been about four. They hadn't told him it was popping candy; he'd had no idea what to expect. The look on his face when it had started to explode on his tongue had been absolutely priceless. Even now, it made her laugh. 'As if I could forget that. My poor baby boy. He looked like something terrible was happening and you couldn't explain it to him because you were laughing so hard at his face.'

Pete sat in his usual place and ripped open the packet. 'You can talk. Anyway, as soon as it wore off, he was holding his hands out for another hit.' He raised an eyebrow at her and held out the packet. 'How about it?'

She sat on the sofa next to him; they were both creatures of habit. 'Are you serious? You bought that for us to eat?'

Pete waved the packet. 'Are you chicken?'

She shook her head at him. 'That was the same line you used on me twenty years ago when you forced me to go on that awful roller coaster at Alton Towers.' Still, she held out her hand.

Pete chuckled to himself as he tipped a small pile onto her hand.

She brought her palm to her lips and poured the Space Dust onto her tongue, wincing as she did so. The taste was definitely worse than she remembered. A manufactured strawberry tang with enough additives to pickle an onion.

Pete watched her. 'That bad, eh?'

It started to pop and fizz on her tongue. 'Your go.'

Pete straightened out the packet and held his head back as he tipped the entirety of the rest of the contents into his mouth. His eyes widened and he moved his lips to vary the sound of the crackling candy, making the clicks and cracks louder and quieter.

Caroline couldn't help but laugh at him. He'd always been such a big kid; it was part of his charm. When they'd married nearly twenty-five years ago, he'd been the joker of their group and he hadn't changed at all. Even once they'd had Jamie, he'd been the one all the kids wanted to play with. Maybe that was why he still looked younger than his forty-eight years: his childlike enthusiasm.

Twenty-five years. A quarter of a century. How could it possibly have been that long ago? If you'd asked her a few years ago if she felt any different from that wide-eyed twenty-two-year-old with long blonde hair, she would have shaken her head. People always said that she looked younger than her age, too, but the last couple of years had changed more than her hairstyle.

Pete crushed the packet in his hand. 'I'll stick this in the bin. Then shall I make us a drink to get the taste out of our mouths?'

Despite what her friends thought of him, he was still kind and thoughtful, not just funny. When he arrived, he could lift her mood. 'Actually, I've already got one here. I'd just made it when Robbie knocked.'

There was no need to be in the kitchen with him to know how he was making his drink. He always mixed the instant coffee and the milk together before adding the boiling water, citing some theory about not scalding the granules. Years of marriage limited the number of surprises. Well, almost.

Changes in a marriage happen imperceptibly. You can't live like you're on your honeymoon forever, of course. For one, it would be exhausting. But when do you start taking each other for granted? Not noticing if your wife has cut her hair or your husband has stopped giving you a kiss before he leaves for work? How far do you go down that path before you look back and realise that you are closer to being roommates than lovers?

Pete was already drinking his coffee when he walked back in. Spotting her mug, he pointed at the slogan with a grin. 'I'd forgotten that cup. Do you remember the one he bought for me? "You're one of my favourite parents."' He laughed and it was like watching Jamie. Dark blue eyes. Wide grin. 'He was such a funny kid.'

They would always have this, though. These shared memories. Stories about Jamie when he was a child and they were exhausted but proud parents. No one else would remember how beautiful he was when he would finally give in to sleep. How funny, dancing to the *Teletubbies* music in his romper. The first joke he told them about the fairy who hadn't taken a bath.

This was what she couldn't give up. What she tried to explain to her friends when they told her that she shouldn't let him in. That she needed to move on.

Because Pete didn't live here anymore. He was with Emily now. And Jamie was gone.

CHAPTER TWO

EMILY

The decor of the Priory House toilets was as tired as Emily herself felt. Whereas the offices and corridors were sleek and modern, the walls of the ladies' toilets – which were shared by all the companies who rented space in the block – looked as if they'd been lucky to see a lick of paint in the last five years. Clearly the company that owned the building were more concerned with impressing prospective clients than they were with the comfort of their existing tenants.

Emily leaned in towards the mirror and checked her teeth. The hard ginger biscuits she'd been nibbling to stave off nausea had a habit of sticking to them. Her puffy face looked back at her. She undid the top button of her blouse. Maybe a bit of cleavage would distract people from the extra weight she was carrying. Then she buttoned it up again.

The door to the bathroom opened and Amy rushed in. 'Don't talk to me. Don't talk to me. I'm bursting.' She slammed the door of the cubicle shut.

Emily laughed. 'Better now?'

Amy's voice came through the cubicle door. 'Much. I couldn't get the customer off the call. I've been jogging from one foot to the other for the last ten minutes.'

Emily knew how that felt. She didn't pass a toilet without going in these days. Always better to be safe than sorry. She turned to the side and appraised her body. Fourteen weeks in and there was still no bump. Instead, she had just thickened from the boobs down. She felt like an overfilled sausage.

The toilet flushed and Amy joined her at the basins. 'I feel like I haven't seen you in ages. We're all going for a drink tonight after work. Are you coming?'

Just the thought of the beery smell of the Admiral Nelson made her queasy. 'I don't think I can make it tonight.'

Amy flicked water at her. 'Come on. We miss you. It's not half as much fun when you're not there making us laugh. If I have to listen to Katie from finance talk about her wedding video one more time, I am going to hurt her or myself. Do you know she still refers to her friends as "my chief bridesmaid" or "Paul's best man"? We know you're married, Katie sweetheart, you don't need to keep reminding us.'

Emily laughed. She related hard to Amy's irritation. One of the reasons she'd decided to leave Ipswich and move to London was because all her friends back home seemed to be in a race to get married and pop out babies before they hit thirty-five. She'd been certain that a change of scene and friends who still wanted to go out and have fun would be a good idea. How ironic.

Amy stopped rubbing her hands and looked at Emily via the mirror. 'Oh, no. Please don't turn into one of those girls.'

Emily frowned. 'What girls?'

'The ones who get married and then never see their mates again.'

'I am not.' It wasn't her husband who was stopping her from wanting to go to the pub. It was hard to suppress a smile just thinking that sentence. Her husband. She had a husband. She was a wife.

It had all happened so quickly that if not for the platinum band on her finger, she'd feel as if she'd made it up. Just her and Pete, three weeks ago, with Pete's friend Steve and Amy for witnesses. They'd all gone out to lunch afterwards at an insanely expensive restaurant in Chelsea. For a moment, she'd considered asking friends from back home, but that would have meant another level of organisation that she didn't want. Plus, they would have been confused by the lack of fuss and frills. Wouldn't have understood how romantic and exciting it had been. At the restaurant, when she hadn't been able to choose her dessert, Pete had ordered every single one on the menu and asked the waiter to box up the ones she hadn't eaten. That night, they had taken them to their bedroom and used them as sustenance into the early hours of the morning.

Still, she did feel guilty about flaking out on trips to the pub. Before she and Pete had got together, the group from Priory House had been her whole social life: they were the only people she'd known in London. She and Amy had got quite close after bonding over fishbowls of Aperol Spritz and Emily's pitch-perfect impression of her bombastic managing director at the news agency. Amy had been a good friend during the ups and downs of the last few years, which was why she felt guilty that she hadn't yet told her about the baby.

According to the forums she'd found online, there was divided opinion over when you should tell people about your pregnancy. Generally, there seemed to be a consensus that it shouldn't be announced to the wider world until after the first scan at twelve weeks. As soon as they'd had that first scan and everything was okay, she knew that she should have told Amy. One of the upsides of not having a very noticeable bump was that she'd been able to put it off up until now. But she needed to tell someone. Otherwise, it just wouldn't feel real. 'I don't want to come to the pub because I can't drink at the moment.'

Amy narrowed her eyes. 'Is there something wrong? Or are you on one of those Paleo, keto diet things?'

Maybe if she made her laugh, it wouldn't be so bad? 'Kind of the opposite of a diet, really.' She splayed one hand on her stomach and the other on her lower back and did the stereotypical pregnant pose. Raised an eyebrow.

Amy froze. 'You're pregnant?' It was a millisecond wince and then it was gone. 'Congratulations. That's amazing news. I didn't even know you were trying; you kept that quiet.'

Damn. The jokey pose had been a bad call. Emily wasn't about to stick her other foot in her mouth by telling Amy that she hadn't been trying for very long, but she must have sensed her hesitation.

'Oh my God, was it an accident? You lucky cow.' Her eyes were shining.

Emily could have slapped herself round the head. Now what should she say? Which sounded worse? That she'd got pregnant quickly or that they hadn't planned a baby at all? 'Oh, Amy. Don't cry. I'm sorry. I'm so sorry that…'

Amy waved her apologies away while rummaging around in her bag to find a packet of tissues. 'Don't be silly. I'm made up for you, really, I am. Maybe if I follow you around for a bit, it might be catching.'

Emily opened her arms to wrap her in a hug, but as she leaned forwards, Amy shook her head. 'Don't. Or I really will start blubbing. Tell me how you're feeling.'

That was a trickier question.

She'd done the first test on her own, thinking that there was no point freaking Pete out unless she was definitely pregnant. After seeing the two blue lines, she'd waited another two days before telling him, nervous about what he might say.

As soon as the words were out of her mouth, he had jumped up from the sofa and whooped. His utter joy had been infectious. *This is going to be so wonderful, Em. A baby. I can't believe it.* This was something they would share: a happy, bright new future for them both. Even after Pete's unexpected proposal, their whirlwind registry office wedding and the regular scouring of Rightmove for a house within their budget, it still hadn't felt as if this was real. Once they had a child of their own, though, he would really be hers.

Family was important to them both. Pete had been through so much unhappiness. For so long, the loss of his son Jamie had cast a long, unmentioned shadow over any plans. She understood that, of course, and she loved him for his big heart. But moving into the future with her didn't mean he had to forget Jamie. She'd lost her mum three years ago and still thought about her every day. If anything, she missed her even more now, with the baby coming.

The marriage proposal had been a genuine surprise. Having been through a divorce, she'd assumed that Pete would be in no rush to walk up the aisle again. But he'd been adamant. The next few weeks – finding a dress, booking the registry office, trying on rings – had passed in a wonderful dream. A week after their frosted January wedding, they'd had the first scan and seen black-and-white proof of their healthy baby. She'd even allowed herself to start looking at pushchairs and cribs. But the last few days, something had changed. It was difficult to explain, but she had this sense that something wasn't right. Physically, she was fine, but she couldn't shake off the feeling that something was about to go wrong. That maybe this hadn't been such a good idea.

But how could she say any of that to Amy? 'I'm really good. We're very happy. Tell me about you. How are things going with your new role?'

Although they worked in the same building, she and Amy worked for different companies on separate floors. Amy blew her nose then nodded. 'Yes. It's good. I'm working long hours to get everything up and running but I'm enjoying it. Stuart isn't that impressed.'

Emily had only met Amy's boyfriend Stuart a handful of times but couldn't understand what her friend saw in him. 'Oh, really? Missing you at home?'

Amy shrugged. 'Missing his dinner on the table more like. I think I spoiled him during the gardening leave at the end of my old job. He got used to me making moussaka and lasagne and generally waiting on him hand and foot.' She smiled, but it wasn't much of a joke.

Emily had to tread carefully. Any criticism of Stuart put Amy on the defensive. She attempted a jokey tone. 'Maybe you should sign him up for a cookery course, then he could make dinner for you.'

She rolled her eyes. 'Never gonna happen. I'm lucky to come home to half an Indian takeaway. Anyway, I've been trying this new diet to increase my fertility. My acupuncturist told me about it.'

It made Emily's heart hurt how hard Amy was working to get pregnant. Acupuncture, herbalists, reflexology: she was trying everything. Stuart refused to see a fertility expert and didn't want Amy to either. He seemed to think that they hadn't been trying long enough to resort to that. Emily had her suspicions that he didn't want a baby at all, but she'd learned to bite her tongue. 'Oh, yes, what's that?'

'Oatmeal, beans, veggies. No red meat. No pasta. I've got vitamin supplements too. Obviously, I shouldn't be going to the pub either, but I really need just one glass of wine.'

Emily couldn't hold back any longer. Here was her beautiful friend, turning herself inside out to have a baby. 'Have you thought any more about going to see your doctor? There might be something really straightforward that would help.'

Amy avoided Emily's eyes by looking at her own reflection. 'We're going to give it a few more months. See what happens.'

It was so difficult to reconcile her bright, ballsy friend who was so successful at work with the person in front of her who was happy to hand over the reins to her boyfriend about her own body. 'If that's what you want.'

She turned back and nodded. 'It is. Things have been a bit… difficult lately. I don't want to rock the boat.'

'What do you mean?'

Amy was very loyal. It was one of the things Emily loved about her. 'Stuart seems a bit down. He's struggling to get work.'

Stuart was a freelance graphic artist, and he worked from home – although the few times Emily had been back to their house after work, he seemed to have packed up for the day, playing something on his PC which involved headphones and a lot of swearing. 'I see.'

She shrugged again. 'Just a rough patch, I guess. It'll all work out.'

Did the rough patch refer to his work situation or their relationship? 'You can talk to me about it all, you know. I'm here for you.'

'I know that. Now, come on. Tell me about your baby plans. Are you going to find out the sex?'

She and Pete had had that exact conversation last night. They would have to wait another few weeks for the next scan to find out, but they were torn. Pete was desperate to know. She thought a surprise would be better. Even thinking about it made her smile. 'We haven't decided yet.'

Maybe finding out the sex would be a good idea. If she could picture the baby as a boy or a girl, even give it a name, maybe these nagging doubts would go away and she could go back to that initial excitement she'd felt when Pete had held her close and whispered into her hair, 'This will be good for us, Emily. We will be our own little family.'

CHAPTER THREE

CAROLINE

Icons Café on Duke Street was getting more and more popular, but Caroline had been meeting her friends here for over five years and they thought of it as their place. This Saturday morning, it was packed with people carrying large shopping bags and bundled up into thick coats to ward off the icy February air. Caroline had to shuffle sideways to their regular table in the corner, where Gabby sat beneath framed black-and-white photographs of Audrey Hepburn and James Cagney. In front of her was a huge cup of coffee and a plate of three mini muffins.

Reaching over to kiss Gabby, she nodded at the tiny cakes. 'Morning. Are we on rations?'

'Hello, darling. I couldn't decide if I wanted a muffin or not, so I thought we could share.' Gabby pushed the plate towards the middle of the table. 'Spread the calorie load.'

Insomnia had raised its ugly head again this weekend and Caroline had been awake since 4 a.m., so she'd been up and eaten breakfast before she got here. 'I'm fine, thanks. But I don't know why you're worried about calories, there's nothing of you.'

Gabby shook her wavy blonde hair. 'It's all right for you with your five feet and eight inches to hide the biscuits in. When you're five foot one and a half, every spare pound counts triple.'

Caroline shook her head, but she knew there was no point arguing. 'Where's Faith?'

'On her way.' Gabby raised an eyebrow. 'I don't think she slept at home.'

Caroline clapped her hands. Faith had been through a messy divorce a few years back and she had just started having some ropey dates in the last few months. 'Good for her.'

As if announcing her arrival, the bell over the café door rang as Faith pushed it open. Her smile reached them before she did. Everything about Faith was big: her voice, her body, her heart.

It was impossible not to return that huge smile. Caroline pulled out a chair for her. 'Well, good morning, dirty stop-out. Have you been home or is this part of your walk of shame?'

Faith broke out her deep, booming laugh, which made the people on adjacent tables turn and grin at her. Spending time with Faith was like balm to the soul. Her ex-husband was a complete fool. 'Can we still call it the walk of shame at our age?'

Gabby folded her arms and pretended to frown. 'I don't know. What are you kids calling it these days?'

Faith hooted again. 'I prefer the stride of pride, I think. If you're really good, I'll give you all the details later. Including the fact that he has just invited me to go away for the weekend.'

Caroline smiled at the mock-nonchalant expression on Faith's face as she rearranged the salt and pepper pots on the table. It was so good to have something to celebrate. 'That's fabulous. We need details. What's his name and where are you going?'

'His name is David and his friend has got a boat on a canal somewhere. He's letting us have it for the weekend.'

Gabby pulled a face. 'Not you, too. Trevor has just announced that he wants to skip our week in Gran Canaria and get a boat on the broads next summer. He's been watching YouTube videos of some bloke banging on about it and got himself all excited.'

'Don't knock it till you've tried it. We did a couple of those when Jamie was young. We loved it.' Maybe it was nostalgia, but all Caroline could remember was moorings outside country pubs, Ploughman's lunches and Jamie toddling around with a baby fishing rod.

Gabby shook her head. 'I want to be lying around a pool with my Kindle, not in a floating caravan with Captain Trevor.' She groaned. 'You know he's going to make me call him that, don't you?'

Caroline joined in with Faith's laughter. Gabby might complain about Trevor, but their marriage was as solid as a rock.

The frazzled waitress flew past their table. 'The usual lattes, ladies?'

'Yes, please,' Caroline called after her.

Faith picked up one of the muffins and sniffed at it suspiciously. 'What is that stuff on the top of it?'

Gabby looked over the top of her glasses. 'Weirdly, it's popping candy. The waitress said they're from a new retro sweets range. The other two came with a mini Wham Bar and a Fruit Salad, but I picked those off and ate them before you came. Can you believe that the sweets we had as kids are now *retro*? Just scrape it off if you don't want it.'

Caroline grinned at the coincidence. 'That's funny. I actually had some of that last night. Pete turned up at the house with a packet he'd picked up somewhere and…' She trailed off as she realised the two of them were staring at her.

Faith paused with a generous pinch of muffin halfway to her mouth. 'He came over *again*?'

The look Faith gave her was as sharp as a pin. Caroline knew that neither of them approved of her seeing Pete so often. They were pretty convinced that he didn't deserve to be allowed into the house, to still be a part of her life. When Faith's divorce was final, she had packed up every single thing that her husband had left in the house, put the boxes in the garage and told him that he had a week to collect them or she was going to give them to charity. But Pete still had crates in Caroline's loft that he said they didn't have room for at his place. Though, in his defence, the house was still half his. They'd agreed that in the divorce.

Gabby reached out and squeezed her hand, her kind face full of sympathy. 'It isn't fair of him to keep popping over to yours. I know you don't like to say no, but he hasn't got any right.'

Faith's face, on the other hand, was thunderous. Her generosity of spirit didn't stretch to ex-husbands. 'I don't know how he's got the nerve after walking out on you.'

Caroline had tried to explain this to them a thousand times, but they wouldn't believe her. 'He didn't walk out on me. I asked him to leave.'

The first weeks after Jamie's death were a blur now. From the moment they'd got the call from his university, she had moved in slow motion. To begin with, she'd allowed Pete to comfort her. To put his arms around her and hold her close. But after the funeral, she had felt as if the rest of her life lay open before her like an abyss. There was nothing to hope for. Nothing to look forward to. Just an empty darkness.

There were many days when she couldn't get out of bed. Pete had tried to encourage her, suggesting walks and dinners out and even holidays. But how could she enjoy anything when Jamie was not in the world? Why would she want to feel better when even thinking about the future felt like betrayal? Pete got pushy. *It's for your own good*, he kept saying. *I'm doing this for your own good.*

Three months after Jamie's death, she'd asked him to leave. Told him she didn't want him in the house for a while. That she needed a break from him. *She* had asked *him* to go. Though would she have done that if she'd known that – ten months later – they'd be divorced?

Gabby patted her arm. 'We know that, Caro. But we also know that you weren't expecting it to be permanent.'

When you'd been friends as long as they had, and been through the tough times they'd seen, you got to be brutally honest. It had been Gabby and Faith who had taken it in turns to spend the night with her for a month after she'd asked Pete to give her some space. They'd just sat with her in her misery. Made her food, which she ate in tiny portions. Endless cups of tea – some she drank; others were left to grow cold.

When she could face going outside, it was Faith who had driven her to the doctor's surgery, collected the prescription for antidepressants, ferried her to counselling sessions every week for six months. Gabby would take her for coffee and, later, for glasses of wine. The fact that she was here at all was testament to their love and care.

So she could understand their anger towards Pete. Understand that they didn't want him even over the threshold of Caroline's home.

Gabby broke into her thoughts. 'Actually, I wasn't sure whether to mention this, but I saw them together yesterday. Pete and that woman.'

'What? Where?' Caroline had only seen Emily once, by accident. She and Gabby had almost bumped into them in a coffee shop. Caroline had been surprised by how much younger than Pete his new girlfriend was. She was shorter than Caroline – although not as diminutive as Gabby – and she had that kind of golden skin that always tans well. Her dark hair was long – Pete's penchant for long hair was one of the reasons Caroline had cut hers short once they'd filed for divorce – but she wasn't the stiletto-wearing, perfectly made-up supermodel of Caroline's imagination. She was pretty, yes. But ordinary pretty. At the time, Caroline hadn't been sure if that made her feel better or worse.

Gabby leaned forwards conspiratorially. 'They were in the new Waitrose near me. They didn't look very happy. She had a right miserable look on her face and,' she held up her hands as if she was about to be arrested, 'I know this is not very "sisterhood" of me, but she has *definitely* put on some weight.'

Faith coughed a sarcastic laugh. 'That woman wasn't very *sisterhood* when she shacked up with Caroline's husband.'

Much as she was guiltily enjoying this, Caroline had to point out the facts. 'That's not really true, though. We were already going through the divorce when he met her.'

Normally, she wouldn't be defending him like this, but things had changed in the last few weeks. Gabby and Faith had been fantastic, but she couldn't call them in the middle of the night when she woke up from a dream. Couldn't keep asking them to give up time with their own families to spend time with her. With Pete it was different. The way things had been between them the last few weeks had been… well, she realised that she'd missed him.

The waitress arrived with their coffee. When she'd gone, Faith carried on where they'd left off. 'You're right, of course. It's not her fault. It was Pete who couldn't wait five minutes to jump into bed with someone else.'

From anyone else, that would have sounded cruel, but Faith's anger came from loyalty. The old adage about scorned women wasn't quite accurate. In truth, it should have been 'hell hath no fury like the best friends of a woman scorned'.

But if Caroline was reading it right – Pete dropping by increasingly frequently, bringing her small gifts of things he knew she liked, the odd comment which suggested that all was not well between him and Emily – there was a chance that he could be back in her life again, and that meant she needed to start paving the way with her friends. 'He's not a terrible person. He was a good father.' This was true. Pete had always been the fun parent. The one who had scuba-dived on holiday, ridden the scariest roller coasters. She had always been the one holding the coats. Maybe that's why she'd acquiesced when he'd told her to leave Jamie alone. Not hassle him for contact once he'd left for university in Essex. A decision she had regretted every day for the last two years.

Faith interrupted with a tap on the side of her mug with a plastic stirrer. 'Anyway, I've had some good news. I talked to Lorna about my idea to employ an outreach worker. Someone to go out into the community, give our families support at home. She thinks it's a great idea and is going to help me explore some opportunities for funding.'

Faith worked at a children's centre running groups to support parents and pre-school-age children. Since she'd been there, the place was thriving and growing. That's why she'd been able to get Caroline a job in the back office when she didn't want to go back to work in social care.

Caroline knew how much work she'd put into pitching this idea to her line manager, Lorna. 'That's great, Faith. I'm so pleased for you.'

Faith's huge smile was back. 'Yeah, well. We're not quite home and dry yet. You know how slowly things move in the public sector and it'll be quite a lot of work to write the bids to get the money. And then I'll need to find the right person. Ideally someone who can hit the ground running. Maybe even someone with experience in social work?'

Gabby and Faith were so pointedly *not* looking at her that Caroline knew they'd had this conversation before today. 'I know what you're trying to do, Faith, but I haven't changed my mind. I like being in the office now. I've got everything organised the way I like it.'

Gabby waved her hand in the air. 'You might *like* being in the office. But you used to *love* being a social worker. You were so good at it.'

Caroline spooned the froth from the top of her latte. 'Not anymore.'

In her peripheral vision, she saw Gabby shake her head at Faith, telling her not to push it. Caroline *had* loved her job as a social worker, especially when Jamie had got older and needed her less and less. But it was emotionally demanding and she didn't have the resources to deal with it these days. Or this outreach job, for that matter.

Gabby unpeeled the casing from the third muffin. 'Well, what I *really* want to talk about is your birthday this autumn. We need to start thinking about what we're going to do to celebrate. You wouldn't let us do anything last year, or the year before, so I'm putting my foot down.'

Gabby loved any excuse for a party. *Why should the kids get all the fun?* Caroline groaned at the thought of Gabby stamping her small but insistent size threes on the ground. 'I don't want to be a killjoy, but that's the last thing I want to do. I'm not in the mood for any kind of party.'

Even the thought of a celebration like that without Jamie made her heart hurt. Gabby obviously realised that. 'I don't mean a party. It can be something low-key. Dinner at a ridiculously expensive restaurant or something. We can't let another birthday go past without any kind of celebration at all.'

Letting it go past was exactly what she wanted to do. Life going past was the best she could hope for, really. But the two of them were looking at her expectantly and she didn't want to let them down. They had been so good to her. 'Okay. But no cake or any razzamatazz.'

Gabby had her phone out of her bag already and was thumbing through to look at restaurants. 'Great. I was thinking Oblix at The Shard. But it gets booked up, so if you fancy it, I'll reserve a table now for the night of your birthday. Just the three of us? Or is there anyone else you'd like to invite?'

Caroline hesitated then tried to sound as casual as she could. 'Actually, book it for six. You can bring Captain Trevor, Faith can bring this new man who we will know intimately by then and, who knows, I might have someone to invite by then.'

Gabby looked as if she might burst with happiness at Caroline sounding so positive. Would she look so pleased if she knew that Caroline was hoping Pete might be back home by then and she would want him to be part of their special night out? Jamie would always be a huge hole in her life – in both their lives. But maybe it was possible for them to heal. Together.

CHAPTER FOUR

EMILY

Monday night, Emily stared into the kitchen cupboard, hoping for inspiration for dinner. As they'd had a Chinese takeaway yesterday and Pete had taken her out for dinner the night before, they probably should try to eat at home tonight. Half a packet of pasta and a tin of coconut milk stared back at her, along with a collection of spice jars still in their plastic wrapping from when she'd first moved in and been more optimistic about her culinary abilities.

Pete still wasn't home. Although their offices were down the road from each other, they travelled to and from work separately. She enjoyed her job as the receptionist for the news agency, but she was always out of the door at five thirty whereas Pete's hours were more erratic. He also had plenty of off-site meetings which – from time to time – ended up spilling into the evening.

Nothing in the cupboard inspired her, so she opened the fridge. Milk, cheese, an open packet of ham, some yoghurt: nothing that screamed dinner. Maybe she should call Pete and ask him to go to the supermarket on his way home. She wasn't bothered for herself, anyway; she'd had no appetite all day. Cheese on toast would be enough.

She should have asked Amy to go for a coffee after work tonight. They'd not seen each other since Emily's announcement in the toilet on Friday and she wanted to check that they were okay. The last thing she wanted to do was lose the only real friend she had around here. Especially as she hadn't done a great job of keeping in touch with her friends from home. Maybe she *should* have invited some of them to the wedding. It hadn't only been the speed of it all that had stopped her. If there had been familiar faces from home, her mum's absence would have been even more painful. How could she call them up now and announce she was married and pregnant and not expect them to feel she'd cut them out?

Sometimes she wondered if moving here so soon after her mum died had been the best idea. At the time, she just couldn't cope with being in the house alone. It was easier to sell up and start again somewhere new. Anyway, her mum would definitely have pushed her to make the move. *Grab life, Emily. Take your opportunities.* Plus, if she hadn't, she never would have met Pete.

Meeting Amy tonight would also have stopped her fidgeting around the flat and watching the clock. It didn't used to bother her when Pete worked late. She used to be quite happy with her own company, had loved that – with the large deposit from the sale of her mum's house – she could just about afford to cover the mortgage on this place on her own. When Pete had moved in, Amy had congratulated her but hadn't been able to hide her surprise. She'd nudged Emily. 'I hope that doesn't mean we won't see you anymore now you're shacking up with your older man?'

'Of course not,' Emily had assured her. 'I'm still me.'

But Pete had needed her. Sometimes he would cry at night and she would hold him close, kissing his face, telling him that everything was going to be okay. Both the end of his marriage and losing his son had left him raw and vulnerable. From their earliest conversations, she'd recognised the grief in him and shown him her own. Their honesty had brought an intimacy that had helped them both to heal.

Gradually, Pete had come back to life and then it had been him taking care of her. The kitchen in the flat was tiny, so they often ate out or jumped in the car and spent the weekend in a hotel in Bath or Cambridge or Brighton. For the first time since losing her mum, Emily felt as if she belonged to someone and that they belonged to her. When – a week after finding out she was pregnant – he'd proposed in a beachfront restaurant in Bournemouth, it hadn't felt fast; it had felt right. Married, a baby on the way and Pete's name added to the mortgage: they were family.

She'd been staring at a carton of eggs for the last five minutes. Maybe she could make an omelette? Even her limited repertoire included that. Or Pete might cook. Rustle up a pasta sauce or something. He liked to make a song and dance about it, flourishing a spatula like a conductor's baton. She would sit on the kitchen counter with a glass of red wine and laugh as he kissed his fingertips in appreciation of his gastronomic genius. What would she give to be allowed a glass of Rioja right now? It might stop her feeling so unsettled.

She walked into the lounge as she dialled Pete's phone again. The flat-screen TV on the wall reflected her frown back at her. She still wasn't used to it, or the host of other gadgets that Pete had gradually moved in. Their expensive blinking was more than a little incongruous amongst her second-hand sofa and the cheap vintage mirror draped in fairy lights.

Straight to voicemail. This wasn't unusual if he was in a client meeting – the world of software solutions never sleeps, he used to say – but he'd been in the office today. She called his desk phone for the fourth time, counted eight rings before hanging up. Where was he?

She sank down onto the sofa and crossed her legs in front of her. In a minute, she'd tidy the pile of bills on the coffee table and their mugs from this morning. The carpet could do with being vacuumed too. She hadn't had the energy to do very much around the flat the last couple of weeks. It was a small place for the two of them, but at least that meant less housework. When he'd lived with his ex-wife, Caroline, they'd had a cleaner, apparently. Mind you, their home would have been an awful lot bigger than this one. Much as she loved this place, it felt smaller with Pete's things here too.

And soon there would be three of them.

Emily hadn't been one of those women who'd always wanted a baby, but since finding out she was pregnant, she'd enjoyed imagining herself and Pete, sitting on this sofa with a little one in between them. If she was honest, she always pictured them having a little girl. Perhaps because it had been just the two of them for so long, she and her mother had been fiercely close. Whenever she'd needed her, for whatever reason, her mum had been there. *A mother will sacrifice anything for her child, Emily.* She wanted that with her own daughter one day. If only her mum could be here to see it.

She called up to the Echo Dot, which was Pete's new favourite toy. 'Alexa, what's the time?'

'It is 8.33 p.m.'

Surely, he should be home soon? A wave of exhaustion washed over her. Was it normal to still be feeling this tired all the time? Maybe she should go for a lie down on the bed. At least that way she would have a little more energy if Pete suggested they go out to eat instead of cooking.

It wasn't many steps up a hallway to their bedroom. It had been bland and neutral when she'd moved in but she'd spent many weekends looking at wallpaper and trying out paint samples. She had loved the bright yellow she'd chosen. It had seemed hopeful and positive. Now she would have preferred something more restful. Blue, maybe. Or grey.

She kicked off her shoes and lay down on her back. It wasn't just Pete's regular late nights that were nibbling at her mood. After the initial excitement about the baby, it was as if something was off-kilter between them. She'd begun to feel that the rug beneath her feet was being gently tugged at by the past. Was the reality of the pregnancy reminding him of Jamie, of what he'd lost? She'd tried to talk to him about it, to ask if he was okay, but he had told her that they should just focus on the future, that she wasn't to worry about any of it.

At last, she heard his key scrape in the lock and the door scuffing the thick new rug he'd paid for.

'Hi, Em! I'm home.' His voice was bright and studiedly normal. He hadn't come straight from the office, she was sure of that, but where had he been?

'I'm in the bedroom.'

He was already pulling off his tie as he came in and perched on the end of the bed. 'Everything okay? Are you just tired?'

'Yes, I'm fine. How come you're so late?'

He unlaced his shoes and pulled them off. 'Oh, I had a presentation I needed to get finished. It had to be sent off tonight. Sorry, I should have called.'

When they'd first moved in together, he would rush home to see her as soon as he could, bringing work back with him if he had to. He'd sit on the sofa with his laptop and she'd tuck her feet under his thigh while she read a book or watched a film with the cordless earphones he'd presented her with for that very purpose.

'I called you. A few times. On your mobile and your desk phone.'

'Did you?' He pulled his mobile out of his pocket, frowned at it then held the screen up to show her. 'I forgot that I turned it off. I was trying to focus. And I wasn't at my desk. I took my laptop to the conference room where it was quiet.'

Everything he said was completely plausible. Was she being unreasonable? Paranoid? That was the last thing she wanted him to think of her. After all that Caroline had put him through, she wanted to make his life easier, not harder. She held out an arm to him. 'I just missed you, that's all.'

He lay down next to her on the bed, propped his head up on his hand, reached over to brush her hair away from her eyes. 'If I'd known you weren't feeling great, I would have come home earlier.'

She frowned. 'I thought you said it was important? The work you had to get done?'

'Yes, it was. But you're more important.' He leaned over and kissed her on the top of the head. She felt tears start at the corners of her eyes, and before she could stop it, one rolled out and down onto the pillow.

Pete looked concerned. 'You're not okay, are you? What can I do?'

Love me, she wanted to say. *Love this baby. Love us best.*

CHAPTER FIVE

CAROLINE

She heard the child's screams before the door was even open.

Tuesday mornings, there were several mother and baby groups at the children's centre, but one of the things Caroline had stipulated when she took up Faith's offer of a job was that she would be back office staff only. She did *not* want to be in contact with parents and children. She was still too raw for that.

Michaela, the receptionist, had left the office door open while she popped to one of the playrooms with a message, so Caroline heard the clunk of the front door as it opened and then watched as the poor mother rattled the pushchair over the threshold. She was white with exhaustion, her eyes staring and glassy.

Caroline flicked her eyes back to the spreadsheet on her computer screen. If she got up to shut the door, the mother would see her and she wouldn't be able to avoid going out to help. Better to keep her head down. Except the plastic clack of buggy wheels made her glance up again. The mother had turned the pushchair around so that she could drag rather than push it; the whole thing nearly toppled with the weight of the bags hanging from the handle. The child's crying bore into Caroline's brain and simultaneously reached into her chest and pulled at her heart. She squeezed her fingers into her palms. Where was the damn receptionist? This woman needed help.

Now Caroline couldn't take her eyes off her. Her whole body seemed deflated; her dark green coat skewed by the buttons being in the wrong holes. Somehow, she managed to pull the chair to one side of the reception area and pull off her hat and gloves before reaching into the pushchair for her child: a furious little girl who looked to be around two, with strands of hair stuck to her cheeks by teary frustration. Jamie had been a horror at that age, hands into everything, tantrums when she would extricate a pen or a plug or a piece of something sharp from his sticky fist.

'Please stop crying, Shani.' Grey-faced and tight-lipped, she tried to set the little girl down on her sturdy legs but Shani curled them up and around her mother, clinging on like a monkey.

There was nothing else for it. Caroline couldn't watch her struggle alone any longer. Glancing up the corridor in the hope that the receptionist might reappear, she leaned onto the counter of reception. 'Can I help?'

The mother turned towards Caroline, bringing her daughter's angry red face into full view. 'Is there any way we could use your toilet? I'm trying to potty train her and I've forgotten the potty and I don't know where else to go.'

Potty training had been a world of pain with Jamie too. There hadn't been enough plug-in air fresheners in the world to cope with the smell of urine in their downstairs toilet. 'Of course – the baby changing room is behind those doors and there's a child-sized toilet in there. Go straight through. Take as long as you need.'

Now the woman looked on the verge of tears. 'She won't sit on a toilet yet. I don't suppose you have any potties? I know it's a lot to ask but—'

'No problem at all. There are some in there. Leave it in there when the contents have been tipped away and I will make sure it gets cleaned.'

Her gratitude was on a par with Caroline saving her life. 'Thank you. Thank you so much.'

As soon as the baby changing room door banged closed behind them, Caroline breathed out in the way her counsellor had shown her, trying to settle her heartbeat. Nearly two years on and still moments like this had the power to make it hard to breathe. Her memories were precious, but they brought a tail of pain with their pleasure.

Behind the door, the little girl continued to cry. Her protestations at using the potty were spiralling, getting louder and sharper. 'Nappy! Nappy! Me nappy!'

Her mother's voice was pleading. 'Please, Shani, use the potty. No nappies. You're a big girl.'

Caroline's shoulders were up by her ears. She wanted to open the toilet door and yell in to the mother, *Just stick a nappy on her. Why are you doing this to yourself?*

Watching the parents come through the centre had made her realise just how much pressure they put on themselves. Looking at one another's children, trying to judge whether their child was where they should be. The right height, weight, whether they could crawl or walk or use the potty. All these milestones became sticks they could beat themselves with. *It doesn't matter,* she wanted to tell them. *I was you. I tried to do everything right. But it's all just a waste of precious time.*

Like the poor woman in there, beating herself up because she couldn't get her daughter to sit on a potty. She'd probably read one of those authoritarian parenting manuals which say that once you've started you can't go back. Can't. Don't. Must. Should. Words like hailstones on the head of a parent just trying to get it right.

There were piles of leaflets about toddler groups and parenting classes on the reception desk. Without realising, Caroline had screwed one of them up into a ball in her hand. She dropped it into the bin. She couldn't take the sound of the child's cries any longer. There were a couple of small toy bears underneath the counter wearing T-shirts advertising a brand of baby wipes; they'd probably come as freebies with a large delivery. She plucked one of them up as she left the desk and made her way to the toilets. 'Your time has come,' she muttered to it.

Taking a deep slow breath to the count of four – more advice from her counsellor – before gently knocking on the door, she made her voice friendly and light. 'Are you okay in there? It's Caroline. We just spoke at reception.'

The lock clicked and the door opened slowly. Looking defeated, tears running down her face, the poor woman held out her hands. 'I don't know what to do. She keeps asking for her nappy, but I don't even have any.'

'I can get you one, but I wondered if there was a little girl in here who might like to take this bear home because he needs to learn to use the toilet.'

Though little Shani continued to cry, there was slightly less conviction to her sobs as she eyed Caroline with suspicion.

Straight away, her mother understood what Caroline was trying to do and changed her own tone to make it brighter, even if there was still a wobble to her voice. 'I don't know. Do you think you could teach the bear to use the toilet, Shani?'

Caroline could practically see the indecision crossing the little girl's face. She reached out. 'Bear. Want bear.'

Caroline turned the teddy bear's stitched mouth to her ear. 'What's that, bear? You don't know if this little girl can teach you?'

In a heartbeat, the little girl plonked herself onto the potty. Caroline winked at her mother. 'Well, what a grown-up girl you are.' She passed over the bear but didn't let go as Shani's pudgy hands closed on it. 'You must remember to teach him, though. Can you do that when you get home?'

Shani nodded, tears still drying on her face.

Once they were back outside and little Shani was strapped into her pushchair, chattering to the bear, her mother came over to thank Caroline. 'You really saved me. I'm a bit embarrassed now. You probably think I was totally overreacting. It's just, she didn't sleep last night, and we had to go shopping, which was hideous and—'

Caroline held up a hand to stop her. 'Honestly, don't explain yourself to me. I know what that can be like.'

When Shani's mother smiled, her whole face lifted. 'Well, thank you. You were amazing. Clearly you have great talent with kids.'

Caroline shook her head. 'I'm not. They always do more for strangers than they do for their mums. Like when you tell people you can't get them to eat any vegetables and then they pick up a handful of broccoli and stuff it in with relish to make you out to be a liar.'

The mother laughed. 'Well, you impressed me. You must be such a great mum. How many children do you have?'

Boom. There it was again. This was why she shut herself behind the office door. 'I don't. I don't have any children.'

She didn't want to explain to this woman that she had had a child. A much-loved child who she missed desperately. It would serve no purpose but to make them both feel bad. The truth was stark – she did not have a child – and there was no brief and easy way to explain what she was. When you lose a husband, you are a widow. When you lose your parents, you are an orphan. But when you lose your child, your only child, what are you then?

You are nothing.

After the mum had left – still professing her admiration for Caroline – she sat at her desk and stared at the screen. Nothing was going in. Moments like this didn't just affect her emotionally; they hit her mentally, leaving her unable to think about anything else. Sometimes the effect was even physical: trembling hands, a painful throat, even the inability to stand. Every time she thought that she was coping better with life, something like this would happen and throw her back to where she'd started. How long would it take until she could handle telling a stranger that her son was no longer with her?

In a couple of weeks, it would have been Jamie's twenty-first birthday. She and Pete would go together to lay flowers on the memorial bench they had paid for on the Colchester campus, where he'd spent the last months of his life. Although it was always hard to go there, it surprised her how much she was looking forward to spending the day with Pete. There was comfort in the familiarity of him. Away from the house, perhaps Pete would open up a bit more about what was going on with him and Emily. He might be living with her, but it wasn't as if they were married or anything. Surely it wasn't really serious? Either way, Caroline needed to know if she had been reading him right. Whether he was feeling the same as she was. Maybe together, they could start to properly heal.

CHAPTER SIX

EMILY

Everyone with a busy life sometimes finds they've arranged too much to do and then wishes on the night that they hadn't made plans; Emily had felt like that many times before. But this was different. There was no sense of 'you'll enjoy it once you get there', although that was exactly what Pete had said, as well as, 'You always do this. You know you do. Just get your make-up on and you'll feel different.' It didn't matter how she felt, though. Since she'd told Amy about the baby six weeks ago, they hadn't had a chance to get an evening out together: she had to do this.

Though she still hadn't needed to buy maternity clothes, anything with a zip or buttons in her wardrobe was now off limits. The middle of March was the wrong time to buy anything new anyway: she needed something warm right now, but didn't want to buy something that she wouldn't want to wear when the weather started to heat up. She pulled a long navy Lycra dress over her head and stood to the side in front of the full-length mirror. At least now that she finally had a discernible bump, the close-fitting dress made it obvious that she was pregnant rather than still carrying too many Christmas pounds. It wasn't just her appearance; Emily did feel different, but not in a positive way. More in a 'my limbs are heavier than lead and I just want to lie down' kind of way. At twenty weeks, wasn't she supposed to be in some kind of 'blooming period' right now? She wasn't feeling sick anymore, at least. For the first three months, she hadn't even been able to clean her teeth in the morning without gagging. But that had stopped.

Now she just felt tired. The less she did, the less she wanted to do. And that just wasn't like her. Where was the girl who would go out dancing until the early hours and still get up for work the next day? Originally, she and Amy had planned to go to the pub straight from work tonight, but when Emily had had to leave early for a blood test, Amy had kindly suggested they meet somewhere closer to Emily's flat. She'd also warned her that the partner she worked for had a meeting he wanted her to attend and she wasn't sure if it might run over. All good reasons for them to rearrange. Oh, how she wished they had.

The bar was full when Emily arrived, but Amy had texted her to say she'd reserved a table. The young girl at the bar gave her a bright smile. 'It's all ready for the three of you. That one by the window. You're the first.'

She was halfway to the table that the girl had indicated when she realised what the girl had said. *The* three *of us?* Emily's phone buzzed in her pocket: Amy.

Train delayed. We'll be there in 15.

Emily's skin prickled. She'd thought it would be just her and Amy. Who was *we*?

She squeezed through a group of men who were watching the football on a small screen in the corner and sat down with her glass of soda and lime.

On the next table sat a woman with a round bump – twice the size of Emily's – a smiling face and a cascade of blonde hair. 'Busy in here, isn't it? I'm glad I haven't got to stand at the bar. My feet are killing me. How are you finding it?'

She'd hoped to avoid talking about pregnancy tonight. 'I'm okay. A bit tired, but okay.'

'Lucky you. I was sick as a pig in my first three months. Second trimester is definitely easier. Apart from the extra weight on my feet, obviously.' She stroked her bump.

Did this woman think that Emily was in her first trimester? 'How far along are you?'

'I'm in my twenty-second week. You?'

She was only two more weeks pregnant than Emily. 'Twenty. I've got my scan next week.'

The woman glanced down at Emily's tiny bump. Emily knew what she must be thinking, but she was too polite to say it. 'We're about the same, then. Have you felt any movement yet?'

'I think so.' It was hard to tell. Was the bubbly feeling the baby or nerves? 'It's faint at the moment.'

The woman hesitated. 'Yes, it is in the beginning.' She placed a hand on her bump. Was her baby moving now?

Sitting with another expectant mother who was stroking her bump was not the way she wanted Amy to see her, but that's what happened. Amy was not alone either. Beside her was a beautiful woman Emily hadn't met before.

Amy stood behind Emily's chair and leaned around her to give her a hug. She smelled of the rain and Jo Malone. 'Sorry I'm late. Let me get a glass of wine and then we can catch up. Are you…'

'Drinking alcohol? Sadly not. Feel free to get me another lime and soda.'

'Coming right up.' She looked at the goddess beside her. 'Usual for you, Bets?'

'Yes, please.' She stuck out a hand towards Emily. 'Hi, I'm Betsy. I've heard so much about you from Amy.'

Amy turned her head back towards them. 'Oh, I forgot you hadn't met before. That's crazy. I feel like you've been around for ever.' She laughed and carried on towards the bar. It wasn't clear which of them she'd been talking to.

Betsy took the chair next to Emily. 'Hi, I'm Betsy,' she said again. 'I've started working with Amy. We've had quite a day of it. I've earned my vodka this evening. How are you feeling with your pregnancy? You're not going to make us put our hands on your stomach to feel some elusive kick like my sister used to do, are you?' She laughed and Emily tried to join in.

'No, you're all right. You can keep your hands to yourself.'

It was supposed to be a joke but it didn't come out quite like that. They were saved from the awkwardness by Amy returning from the bar with the drinks and a plate of nachos, which she pushed to the middle of the table. 'Something to soak up the spirits. I'm planning on a fair few tonight after that meeting.'

Betsy held up her drink. 'Hear, hear.' She took a sip and then grimaced. 'Ugh. Who took the vodka out?'

Emily held hers to her nose, the unmistakable tang of alcohol. 'I think we have the wrong drinks.'

'Sorry! That's my fault. Do you want me to go and get you another one?' Amy offered.

'No, it's fine.' She slid Betsy's drink to her in exchange for her own. 'You haven't got anything catching?'

'Only my irrepressible spirit.'

Amy laughed and nudged her. They were like a couple. Emily felt like a gooseberry. A third wheel.

As the evening progressed, more and more alcohol put the two of them in great spirits. It was unbearably boring to be the only sober one in a group. Despite her assurances that she wouldn't talk about work, Betsy kept reminding Amy of hilarious things that had happened at the office that week. Emily was surprised they'd got any work done with the amount of hilarity that had gone on. Either she was completely at a loss as to what was being said, or Betsy had to explain it to her as if she were talking to a five-year-old.

Eventually, Amy drained her drink and banged it down onto the table. 'I don't know about you two, but I'm starving. Shall we go and get a curry?'

Emily's heart sank. She had been hoping that Betsy would leave so that she and Amy could have a proper catch-up. She wanted to see how things were going with Stuart and with trying for a baby – although the amount of vodka Amy had sunk tonight probably answered that question. Emily definitely couldn't face eating spicy food this late, or sitting around the table with the two of them. 'I think I should head home actually.'

If Emily expected either of them to persuade her otherwise, she was disappointed. Amy picked up her bag and said, 'Okay. Do you want me to get you a cab?'

Emily waved her mobile. 'No, don't worry. I'll get an Uber on Pete's account.'

'Okay. Well, you order that and I'll walk you out when it comes.'

Betsy finally took the hint. She plucked her jacket from the back of her chair. 'I'll just make a trip to the ladies' and I'll meet you outside.'

Because it was still relatively early in the evening, the Uber was only four minutes away, so Emily and Amy made their way outside to the busy pavement. With the car coming, and Betsy about to return, there wasn't long enough to talk about anything important. Emily wanted to tell Amy how anxious she was about her second scan. But she didn't.

Keeping an eye on the road for Emily's Uber, Amy sighed. 'Look, sorry if I'm in a funny mood. I got my period this morning. Then we had a tough day with our new client.'

Emily reached out and stroked her arm. 'I'm sorry, Amy. I really am. Look, if you want me to come to the fertility clinic with you, I can—'

Amy shrugged her off, then tried to cover it with a smile. 'I'm fine. Just need a good night out tonight and then I'll be ready to go again.'

Betsy appeared beside her and linked her arm with Amy's. 'Good plan. Nice to meet you, Emily. Hope to see you again soon.'

'Yes. You too,' Emily lied.

Even though she wasn't far from home, it took a while to get through the traffic at that time on a Friday night. The rest of the world was moving from pub to club or the other way around. It was unfair of her to blame Amy for preferring to spend her night with someone who could drink cocktails and stand up for more than half an hour without getting a backache, but she'd really wanted to talk to her. Really wanted someone to reassure her that she wasn't going crazy.

Of course, she should really talk to Pete about it, but it wasn't a good time. Jamie's birthday tomorrow was already weighing on him. He was going to have to spend pretty much the whole day with his ex-wife, and she knew how difficult that was for him. No, she was just going to have to keep these feelings under control herself and hope that they would subside soon.

CHAPTER SEVEN

CAROLINE

Even though it was a Saturday, there were plenty of students milling around the modern Colchester campus in the unexpected March sunshine: coffee cups in hand, the sound of laughter in the air. It was the village feel of the connected quads and the large lake in Wivenhoe Park itself which had attracted Jamie to the University of Essex. On their first visit, a student guide had drawn him in with tales of the students hanging out around the lake in the summer, as well as showing him around the campus bars and the continually moving paternoster lift serving the many floors of the Albert Sloman Library. Pete had thought he should go further afield, be more independent. Caroline had been secretly pleased that he would be less than two hours' drive from their home near Crystal Palace in south London.

The three of them had always been together for Jamie's birthdays. Even at eighteen, when his chosen celebration had been a pub crawl with the friends who had already reached the heady height of legal public drinking, they had had a dinner together before he left. Pete had sold it to him on the basis that it would line his stomach for the night ahead.

Today should have been his twenty-first birthday. If things had been different, they would have been arranging a party or buying

him a car or taking him away for the weekend. Not visiting a
bench with his name on a brass plaque.

Pete had collected her in his flashy sports car this morning. It
was unfair how good he still looked. Not a strand of grey in his
thick dark hair. Not an ounce of extra weight on his well-toned
body. When you split up from your husband, it would be the
decent thing for him to go downhill in deference to the fact that
he is nothing without you. In many ways, Pete looked better. His
clothes, for a start, were more stylish than the shapeless jeans she
used to nag him about. Clearly a younger girlfriend was suiting
him. Although she was hoping that the novelty of someone over
a decade his junior had begun to wear off.

Caroline carried the flowers she'd ordered from the good florist
on Gipsy Hill a couple of weeks ago. The young girl who'd served
her looked as if she'd just left school, but she had been so kind. It
was difficult to choose flowers for a boy. In the end, she'd settled
on white gladioli. Good strong stems. Clutching them to her
body, she was grateful for Pete's hand in the small of her back,
keeping her upright and moving towards the bench.

The bench had been Faith's idea. Jamie had always been
surrounded by friends, she'd said; it would be somewhere they
could go and hang out and think about him. Plus, it would give
Caroline and Pete a place to visit rather than the crematorium.
As they approached the bench, Caroline could see that there was
a bunch of flowers already there. Beth.

Beth had been Jamie's girlfriend pretty much since Fresh-
ers' Week. He'd had a couple of girlfriends during sixth form,
but nothing serious as far as Caroline knew. She'd been a little
concerned about him getting a girlfriend so soon after starting
university. That it might stop him making other friends. Until
she'd met Beth in person.

'Shall we sit?' Pete's smile wavered. She could see that he was
trying to be strong, but being here was hard. Students walked

past them in a million different styles of jeans, hurrying to meet friends, laughing into mobiles, holding hands. There was so much life here. Were they already looking towards a bright future? Careers? Families? Travel? What would Jamie be planning if he were here among them?

They must have looked odd, her and Pete, sitting on the bench. Sideways glances from some of the young people. Did they know Jamie? Had they read the inscription on the bench?

Beth had come to Jamie's funeral, but – apart from the inquest – they hadn't heard much from her since. It was understandable; they'd only been together for six months. She had come on the day they'd dedicated the bench though. And Caroline had texted her to say they were coming today and would love to see her. The flowers suggested she had been and gone.

Pete stood and moved from one foot to the other. He never could sit still with his emotion. After Jamie's death, it had felt as if he was constantly moving around. Cooking or tidying or going to the shops. It had been a relief when he'd gone back to work and left her in peace. 'Shall I go and find us some coffee?'

Now, though, she was grateful for his company. Hopeful, even. She nodded. 'A mint tea would be great, thanks.'

The bench was solid oak. 'Made to last,' the carpenter had said. 'That bench'll outlive the both of us.' His face had frozen as he realised what he'd said. 'I'm so sorry.'

She'd waved his apologies away. 'It's fine. I'm glad. I want it to be there forever.'

Now she spread her palm flat on its arm. There was a warmth to wood. As if the life of the tree was still there. There had been a bench just like this in the park she'd taken Jamie to as a boy. She'd hardly noticed it at first – too busy hovering over his every step. When he'd grown bigger and more independent, she'd sat on it and watched him swinging on the monkey bars or clambering to the top of the climbing wall.

She bit down on her lip; her vision blurred. Though she was getting better at riding these emotional waves, it didn't make them any less powerful. Nowadays, she kept a packet of tissues in her bag, in amongst the mints and hand cream and her two purses: the practical one and the small embroidered one with a stuck zip that Jamie had made at secondary school. When she found a tissue and looked up, she realised that there was a third bunch of flowers in front of her. This time, Beth was holding them.

'Hi, Caroline. I hope it was okay to come?' She stood with one leg bent, her hand in the crook of her other elbow. Her outward awkwardness reflected the lack of confidence she carried around like a weight. If only these young women could see how beautiful they were, how precious in their youth.

'Hello, love. Of course, I'm so glad you came. More flowers? I thought these ones were from you?' She pointed at the bunch already there.

Beth looked confused. She moved her weight to the other foot. 'No. They're not from me.'

Who were they from, then? 'Oh, well, it doesn't matter. It's lovely that you're here. How have you been? Are your studies going well?'

Beth rubbed at her arm, tucked her floppy fringe behind her ear. 'Yes, they're fine. I'm...' She looked up at Caroline with tears in her eyes. 'I'm seeing someone else. It's serious.'

Of course, she was seeing someone else. It hurt because Caroline wished it was Jamie, but she wouldn't have wanted this young girl to put her life on hold. It had been almost two years since Jamie's accident. 'I'm pleased for you, Beth, I really am. I hope he treats you well?'

The relief on her face was palpable. 'Yes. He does. He's a nice guy.' She gave Caroline a watery smile. 'I only ever go out with nice guys.'

She really was a sweet girl. It must have been awful for her losing her boyfriend like that. After the call from the university, she'd had a call from Beth, almost hysterical. 'It's Jamie. He's at the hospital. It's bad. It's really bad.' Caroline slammed the door on the memory. Today was about remembering the good times.

She patted the bench beside her. 'Do you want to sit for a while?'

Beth shook her head. 'I wanted to talk to you about something—'

She jumped at the sound of Pete's voice behind her. 'Hi, Beth. We saw the flowers and thought that you'd already been and gone.'

Beth looked startled at the sight of him. 'Oh. I didn't realise you were here, too.' She looked back at Caroline. 'Together.'

Last time they'd seen Beth, when the bench had been installed last year, they had already separated. Caroline opened her mouth to explain that they hadn't reunited but Pete was busy doing his social bit. 'And you brought more flowers. That's kind.'

'These ones weren't from Beth, actually.' Caroline glanced down at the anonymous bunch. Maybe there was a card?

When she looked back up, Beth had taken a step back. 'I should leave you both to it. I need to get to a netball match soon anyway.'

'Really?' Caroline was disappointed. It had been awkward between them at the inquest, and then when the bench had been installed, they'd both been too upset to talk. She had been hoping to share some memories of Jamie with her today. 'But you hadn't finished what you were saying.'

Beth shook her head. 'It wasn't important. Thanks for including me today. I really appreciate it.' Almost as an afterthought, she propelled herself forward and kissed Caroline on the cheek. For a second, their tears mingled and she dropped her voice to a trembling whisper. 'He really loved you, you know.'

Caroline wrapped her arms around Beth's birdlike frame and squeezed. 'He loved you too. Very much.'

They watched as she hurried away. A boy about the same age was waiting for her with his arms outstretched. What had she been about to tell her? Surely everything that Beth knew had been included in her tearful testimony at the inquest. The poor girl. Caroline couldn't pull her eyes away as Beth fell into the boy's arms and they walked away. She wished happiness for Beth, but it was painful to think she would be starting the next chapter in her life when Jamie's part in it had ended so abruptly.

She and Pete sat in silence for the next ten minutes, lost in their own memories. At some point, Pete moved his coffee cup to the arm of the bench and took her hand in his. It felt nice. It felt like home.

The more she had seen of him in recent weeks, the more she had begun to think that maybe, just maybe, they had a chance at making another go of it. If everything was going so well with Emily, he wouldn't be visiting Caroline so often, would he? One of them had to make the first move towards something else and it might as well be her. She took a deep breath. 'How is Emily?'

Pete scratched his head. 'She's, er, she's okay, I guess.'

There was something in the way he wasn't looking at her that made Caroline suspicious. Being married to someone for over twenty years meant you knew their tells. Had she been right about them? Was everything not perfect in paradise? It felt important to keep her voice light, jokey. It was too soon to show her hand. 'Only okay? I thought you two were living your best lives. Aren't you out every night at fancy bars and restaurants?'

Still, he wasn't looking at her. 'Er, no. Not exactly.'

Was he about to say that they were splitting up? Was that why he had been coming to see Caroline so often, because he couldn't face going home? 'Stop being so cryptic, Pete. What's going on?'

Finally, he looked at her. Took a deep breath. 'The thing is…' He paused, scratched behind his ear like he always did when he was embarrassed. 'The thing is, that Emily and I got married a couple of months ago.'

Though she heard the words, Caroline wasn't sure she completely understood. If he'd got married, surely he would have mentioned it before now? Was this some kind of joke? '*Married?*'

'Yes. Married. I didn't really know how to tell you, so I—'

'Didn't? You just *didn't* tell me?' Was this real? Was he actually married to someone else? She knew he tried to avoid anything emotionally difficult but this was on a whole other level. It was utterly unbelievable.

'And…' he coughed, 'and she's pregnant.'

CHAPTER EIGHT

EMILY

In the clinic there were four rows of plastic chairs and a small reception hatch, where Emily had handed over her appointment card twenty minutes ago. Pete had already walked the length of the far wall, reading the thank you cards from a thousand grateful parents, hands clasped behind his back. Usually, she teased him for his inability to stay in one place for more than five minutes. Today it was just irritating her. 'Can't you just sit down? You're making me nervous.'

She'd offered several times to go with Pete to the memorial bench on Jamie's birthday last Saturday, but he had told her it wasn't necessary, that she should stay home and get some rest. What he'd actually meant was Caroline wouldn't like it. Considering how horrible his ex-wife had been to him, it still amazed Emily how conscientious he was about keeping her happy.

On some level, he must have realised that she was upset at being excluded from Jamie's birthday because he couldn't have been nicer to her this week. He hadn't been late home once and he had waited on her hand and foot when he was there. Even that hadn't made her feel any better. She wanted to be held tightly, passionately, not treated like a small child or a fragile vase. Something had shifted between them and she had no idea how to get it back.

Today was a big deal and she was supposed to be excited. The second scan. In the end, they'd agreed that they would find out the sex of the baby. Everyone in the office had wished her well when she'd left at ten. The MD's secretary had started a sweepstake about the sex of the baby, the weight of the baby and the date and time of arrival. Emily had played along, but all she wanted to know was that the baby was okay.

Even sitting down, Pete couldn't keep still in the rigid plastic chair of the waiting room. 'I wonder how much we'll be able to see. Did I tell you about Jamie's scan? He was facing forwards and the picture we got looked like a ghoul from a horror show.' When his smile got no reaction, he rearranged his face. It was painful watching him tiptoe around her, but she didn't have the energy to make him feel better about it. He tried again. 'What I mean is, do you think we will be able to see for ourselves if it's a boy or a girl? Or just the sonographer?'

Why *wasn't* she more excited? Surely finding out the sex of the baby would make it feel more real? More like an actual person? They could start to get serious about name choices too. But she wasn't. If anything, he was making her anxious with his constant conversation. 'No idea. We'll find out in a minute.'

Over the last couple of weeks, she'd felt lower and lower. The books she'd read explained about the roller-coaster hormones, but she only seemed to have the downs, not the ups. She'd started waking up early too. Before five this morning. Lying there in bed, her head going around and around. It was like her brain had got hold of something and then refused to let go. Chewing on it like a bone. This morning it had been the scan and what they might find out. Stupidly she had googled the list of things they were going to check for: anencephaly, open spina bifida, cleft lip, diaphragmatic hernia, gastroschisis, exomphalos… The list went on and on, and round and round in her head. These were conditions she'd never heard of. Hadn't even known to worry about.

Sitting here, she couldn't push away a feeling of impending doom. There was a couple up the row from them with their heads close together, whispering; a man behind had his hand on his partner's bump, feeling the baby kick. Around her, the air was heavy with happiness and expectancy. Inside was just dread and fear. What if something had gone wrong? Her bump looked so much smaller than everyone else's in the waiting room. What if there wasn't a baby anymore? Was that even possible?

Pete had that look on his face. If he asked her again if she wanted a hot chocolate, she might actually scream. He picked up her hand, which had been lying limply on her lap. 'Are you okay, Em? What are you thinking about?'

As if she was going to tell him that she was imagining the worst. Knowing that Pete had already experienced the pain of losing a child, she wasn't about to make him worry about one that wasn't even here yet. But this scan was also for looking in detail at the baby's bones, heart, brain, spinal cord, face, kidneys and abdomen. So many things. So many possibilities that something was wrong. 'Nothing. Just thinking about something that happened at work.'

He didn't look as if he believed her. 'Something bad?'

Judging by the concern on his face, she must be looking miserable. When they'd first got together, he had told her over and over how he loved her optimism, her desire to grab life with both hands. As their relationship deepened, he'd called her the best therapy he could have ever had. When dark moments threatened him, she was there to bring the sunshine, to make him smile. He must have been rethinking that now. Wondering where that woman had gone and why she had left this absolute misery guts in her place.

So, she pulled on a smile for his sake. 'Not really. Just something I forgot to do before I left. I can sort it when I go back.'

Pete scratched his head. 'You're going back today? I assumed you had the rest of the day off? We could go out and get something to eat after. You know, celebrate.'

As long as we have something to celebrate. Emily didn't mean to start tapping her foot, but she saw him notice it. 'I can't. I need to—'

'Emily Simmons?' A robust nurse in sensible black shoes called her name into the waiting room.

They stood together and followed the direction she indicated into Examination Room B. This was it.

'Second scan, so you know the drill.' The sonographer smiled and pointed to the bed with a fresh layer of disposable blue towel laid on it. As soon as Emily lay down, she lowered the elasticated waist of her black leggings. One of the women at work had recommended a website for what she called the most comfortable maternity trousers in the world, adding, 'I'd still be wearing them now if I could get away with it,' but Emily hadn't wanted to tempt fate by ordering them this week.

'I know that my bump is quite small for twenty-one weeks.'

The sonographer snapped on a pair of rubber gloves and turned back towards her with a large tube in her hands. 'We get all shapes and sizes of bumps in here. It's not necessarily an indication of anything.'

Not necessarily. Which meant it might be? Her heart started to thump at her ribcage. *Just get this over with.*

Pete took hold of her hand again. Squeaky with sweat, it must have felt sticky and unpleasant: the heat in this room was unbearable. The tube of gel spread its oily contents onto her stomach.

For the next few moments, she held her breath, trying to still the beating of the blood in her head. Thankfully, the sonographer put her out of her misery quite quickly. 'Everything looks good. Heartbeat is lovely and strong. I just need to take a few measurements.' The monitor creaked as she turned it around to face their direction. 'Here's your baby.'

She tilted the screen down slightly, and there it was. In black and white. A head, a body, two arms, two legs. A real baby. Pete squeezed her hand tightly. There were tears in his eyes. Were they tears for the baby inside her or the baby he had lost?

Her own face was dry. Everything in front of her could have been a scene from a paint-by-numbers Hollywood movie. Doting father, smiling sonographer, grainy image of a longed-for child. Except that the mother-to-be, who should have been crying happy tears and kissing her husband, felt as if she wasn't even here.

The room was quiet except for the click of the computer mouse as the nurse took measurements. Emily focused on her finger, scared to look too long at Pete's eager face. If he saw her eyes, he'd know for sure that something was up. That she wasn't normal.

The sonographer smiled again. 'Everything is progressing well. No concerns at all.'

Pete rubbed at her arm, then coughed. 'That's great, thank you so much. Is it possible to find out the sex of the baby?'

'Would you like to know?' She looked at Emily for confirmation.

Although they had agreed to find out, she suddenly wondered if they should. But when Pete stroked her hand with his thumb, she nodded. 'Yes, please. We would.'

The sonographer turned to her screen. 'We can't say with one hundred per cent certainty. But it looks to me as if you have a very healthy-looking baby boy.'

Pete grinned. 'Another boy. That's brilliant.' He leaned in and kissed Emily on the top of her head. 'That's great, isn't it, Em?'

A boy. A little boy. Pete had already had a little boy. Was that what they were doing? Were they just filling the void that Jamie had left?

Was this all a terrible mistake?

CHAPTER NINE

CAROLINE

It had been a month since Pete's revelation and Caroline had successfully managed to avoid his calls and texts since. Her head told her that nothing had changed – they were divorced, after all. But her heart felt as if her marriage had ended all over again.

On Saturday afternoon, he caught her at a weak moment. With the receptionist on holiday yesterday, she'd had a day of welcoming mothers and babies to the children's centre. It had been a double whammy of keeping her emotions in check at work and then the house feeling more painfully quiet than usual once she got home.

When she'd been a young mum and Jamie had needed her all the time, she'd sometimes fantasised about having time alone to just *be*. Much as she'd adored him, the eternal cycle of feeding and nappy-changing and entertaining and rocking to sleep could sometimes feel endless. Maybe she would have looked at someone like her, with only herself to please, with envy. Certainly, she could go where she wanted right now, whenever she wanted. There was no one relying on her, no one expecting her to do something or be somewhere.

But being alone every night quickly lost its novelty. Her friends were fantastic, always on the end of a phone if she needed them, but they had their own lives, their own families. Coming home from work with hours to fill, the night would stretch out in front of her. She would make preparing dinner take as long as she could, not wanting to sit down in front of the television yet because that would be all she would do for the rest of the night. She used to be a real bookworm, but since Jamie's death, she hadn't been able to get through more than a few pages before her mind started wandering.

Sometimes, when the anaesthesia of a Netflix series wasn't working, she would take out photo albums, watch home movies of Jamie, pulling the memories over herself like a blanket. When the pain was particularly bad, she would spritz his favourite Lynx body spray onto a pillow and hold it tight, letting it absorb her tears. She'd replaced the can four times.

Today, she'd been for a walk, eaten lunch and was looking down the barrel of just such an afternoon and evening ahead when there was a knock on the door. It wouldn't be Faith or Gabby because they always called first. Had Robbie from next door forgotten his key again?

But when she opened the door, Pete was standing on the doorstep, bearing a bottle of wine and a hopeful expression. 'I think there's something wrong with your phone. I can't seem to get through.'

Really? He thought humour was going to get him off the hook? 'There's nothing wrong with my phone. And I am just about to watch a film. It's not convenient right now.'

His face was taut. 'Please, Caroline. I need to talk to you. I can't bear to leave it like this. I've made a mess of everything. Things aren't great at home and I don't know what to do.'

She pictured Faith's face telling her to get rid of him, but it was easier said than done when he was standing here on her doorstep, arms folded against an April breeze, pleading with eyes which would always look like their son's. 'Come in.'

While Pete found wine glasses and poured their drinks, she waited on the sofa, still undecided about whether she was being completely mad to let him in. He, meanwhile, seemed to think he'd been given the green light to revert to their new normal. 'How was your week?'

He had never been this attentive when they'd been married. In fact, after Jamie had left for university, she'd wondered if there would be any conversation in the house at all. She pushed a coaster along the coffee table for her glass of wine. 'It was okay.'

Pete lifted the glass he had already placed directly on the table. 'Sorry. I'm out of the habit of coasters.'

Was that supposed to be some kind of dig? 'Well, the young don't see the need for it, I suppose.'

Pete's face fell. 'No, I didn't mean… Sorry. It's good. That you keep everything so nice.'

She did like a tidy house and it was easy these days when she was the only one living here. Even the sofa cushions were rarely disturbed by anything other than her rearranging them for something to do. She missed falling over that pile of trainers by the front door. She had no idea what Pete and Emily's flat looked like, nor did she care. 'Oh, well, I'm sure she makes up for the lack of coasters in other ways.'

He winced. 'Caroline, I didn't come here to fight.'

This was classic Pete. Poke at you and then stand back and ask why you were upset. What planet had she been on when she'd thought they could make a go of it again? 'What did you come here for?'

Although it wasn't unheard of for them to have one glass at the weekend with their lunch, Caroline was surprised to see Pete take such a large gulp of his wine. 'There's something I need to ask… Actually, before I get on to that, I know that it is completely tactless to talk to you about this, but I really don't know what to do. Emily isn't right.'

Had she missed the turning point in their relationship when she'd become his confidant? Much as she wanted to tell him that, yes, it was completely tactless – even cruel – her irritation wasn't strong enough to override her curiosity. 'What does that mean?'

He began to pace the floor, waving his glass around. She had the feeling he had already been turning this over in his mind before he'd knocked on the door. 'In herself. She's not right. I can't explain it, but I expected her to be more… happy about having a baby. You know. Like you were.'

His casual reference to her pregnancy hit her like a slap. It had been the best moment of her life to that point when they'd discovered that the food poisoning she'd thought was the fallout from a prawn korma was actually morning sickness. She'd never been so happy to have her head over the toilet.

'Well, maybe that's what happens when you shack up with someone a decade younger, Pete. They don't behave as you'd expect.'

Pete's face when he turned to her was hurt and confused. Was he really so used to her solving his problems? 'Please, Caro. Don't be like that.'

Much as she wanted to keep Pete at arm's length, it was impossible to let him suffer in front of her. That was the trouble with loving someone for a long time; you couldn't just turn it off like a tap. 'Maybe she's just getting her head around it all. Maybe it's just the logistics of fitting everything in.'

Pete shook his head. 'No. It's more than that. She just seems sad, and tired all the time too. Barely able to get up in the morning. Falling asleep on the sofa by about eight o'clock. It's even worse now than it was in the first trimester. And she's really emotional all the time.'

Years of social work training kicked in. Many women experienced exhaustion at the start, but that usually improved during the middle of a pregnancy. Hormones made you emotional, of course. But the combination of the two might be a cause for concern. 'Have you spoken to her about it? Asked if she's okay?'

He looked hurt. 'Of course, I have. I'm not a Neanderthal, you know.'

Caroline raised an eyebrow. So now he was a modern man? He hadn't been that in touch with his emotional side when she was married to him. Maybe that had come with the designer jeans and Converse trainers. 'If it's really bad, you should ask her to speak to her midwife. Or the doctor. Do you think it could be depression?'

Pete shot her a glance. It wasn't as if he didn't know what a woman with depression looked like. Hadn't he watched her in the early weeks after Jamie's death when it was all she could do to peel herself out of bed? 'I suppose it could be that. But she hasn't even had the baby yet.'

That didn't mean anything; depression didn't work to a calendar. 'Well, was she ever happy about the baby? At the beginning, I mean.'

'Yes. Well, she seemed to be. She was more worried that I wouldn't be happy about it, she said. But now…' He leaned back on the sofa and raked his fingers through his suspiciously grey-free hair. 'God, it's all such a complete mess.'

Caroline picked up her wine glass. If Faith and Gabby could see her right now, they would be furious. She should wrap this up. Tell him to sort his own life out. But it was much harder to do that than they'd think. 'It does sound like you need to get her to a doctor. Have you spoken to the midwife even?'

He shook his head. 'She goes to those appointments on her own. I tried to get her to speak to someone last month, when we went for the second scan.'

'You've had a twenty-week scan already?' When he'd told her about the pregnancy, she'd assumed he'd just found out about it.

He wasn't meeting her eyes. 'Yeah. A few weeks ago. All fine. Baby is healthy.'

Caroline's face was hot and it wasn't the Rioja. She pressed her lips together, tried to keep the sarcasm from her voice. 'Well. That's good then, isn't it?'

He stared into his wine glass. What wasn't he telling her? 'Yep. All good.'

Like pressing a bruise, she had to ask the next question. 'Did you find out what you're having? Did you ask about the sex?'

Still, he didn't look at her. 'Yes. Emily wanted to know. Well, so did I.'

'And?'

Now he looked at her, his eyes deep wells that she might drown in. 'It's a boy. He's a boy. We're having a boy.'

There'd been a fifty per cent chance that the baby would be a boy. She knew that. So why did it hit her so hard knowing that Pete was going to have another son? Her face flushed a deeper red and she could feel her throat tightening. She bit down on her lip to stop it from trembling.

Pete put down his wine and reached out to take her hand. 'I'm sorry, Caroline. I really am. I know I've screwed everything up.'

She pulled her hand away and wiped the tears before they fell. 'It's fine. What does it matter to me that he's a boy? It makes no difference at all.'

'It does, though. I know it does.'

Caroline's head buzzed with thoughts, each one with a sting in its tail. Would he look like Jamie? Sound like Jamie? Would there be a little boy growing up who looked exactly like her son had looked? She wasn't sure she could bear the thought of it. 'Look, Pete. You cannot come here again. You're married. You're expecting a baby. The situation has changed.'

He groaned and put his head in his hands. 'I know, I know. It's all just a horrible, horrible mess.' He let out another groan and then sat up. 'I was in love with Emily. I *am* in love with Emily. But when I look at you, when I think about… I know it's an awful thing to say, Caro, but I worry that it was all a big mistake.'

A big mistake? He'd torn apart the last shreds of her when she'd found out he'd met someone else. He hadn't even had the decency to come clean himself. When she and Gabby had seen them together in that coffee shop, smiling and holding hands, it had felt like a knife in her back. And now he was sitting here saying that it might have been a *mistake*?

There was worse to come. 'I know that I probably shouldn't say this, but I had begun to think that you and I… that we might be able to have… *something* together again.'

That was the final push. She felt the roar coming from somewhere deep inside. 'And you thought that I'd just say, "Okay, Pete, I know you moved in with a woman over a decade younger than me when the ink was barely dry on our divorce papers, but now that you're bored of her, just come on back home?"'

Pete looked startled. 'No. No. I didn't mean it like that. And to be fair, it was *you* who threw *me* out.'

'To be fair? To be bloody *fair*? There is nothing fair in this, Pete. Nothing! I was grieving. Our son had just died, for God's sake. And you… you were… on at me all the time to move on and go out and I just needed time.' All this had happened two years ago but it hurt like it was yesterday.

Pete leaned forwards, his elbows on his thighs, his face in his hands. 'I'm sorry, Caroline. I was so weak. After the divorce went through, I was lonely and…'

'Take some responsibility! You *chose* to do that. You *chose* to sleep with someone else.'

'Just listen to me for a minute! I didn't expect to fall in love again. That's the truth. I didn't know that she would be so… good for me, I suppose. I was in pain, Caroline. You didn't want to see that. I was in pain, too.'

Anger, sympathy and grief were battling to get to the surface. What the hell was he expecting her to say?

Pete softened his voice. 'I need to see you, Caroline. Now this baby is coming, I can't leave Emily, you must know that. But I can't imagine my life without you in it, either. I can't talk to Emily like I can talk to you.'

She was openly crying now, but Caroline couldn't believe what he was saying. Was he honestly telling his ex-wife that his new wife didn't understand him? Was he asking *her* to be the other woman now?

'I feel like we've got so much closer since I moved out. We didn't used to talk like this. After Jamie, it was so difficult to talk about anything. You didn't seem to want me. You didn't even sleep in the same bed as me.'

Sharp memories cut in of the nights she'd fallen asleep, fully clothed, on Jamie's bed. 'Sex? Is that what you want to make this about? Sex?'

'No. But you barely let me touch you and I didn't know what to do and I was broken too. I was broken too, Caroline.'

'Well, lucky for you, there was Emily to put you back together, eh?' She didn't want to be nasty but the pain of his words was giving her anger a poisonous edge.

'That's what I'm trying to say. It did help, it did. But now, oh God, everything has gone to hell, hasn't it? And it's all my fault. And now there's a new baby, which is wonderful but terrifying. And I have to come here and offer to buy you out of the house so that I can move us out of the flat, but I don't know if I can do any of this and now Emily seems depressed and...'

Buy her out of this house? Her home? When the divorce was finalised, Pete had readily agreed to let her stay in the house and pay him out his share when she sold it. At the time she'd seen it as a generous gesture. Now it felt like another punch she had not seen coming. Had he not hurt her enough? She squeezed her fingernails into her palms. Caroline had never hit anyone in her life but right now she wanted to pull back her fist and ram it full force into his pained expression. 'Get out.'

Pete frowned. 'What?'

'Get out of this house and don't come here again. You made your choice. And now you get to have a son. Be bloody grateful that you get a second chance, Pete. I don't want to know about it. I don't want to hear about it. When you leave this house, I am going to do everything I can to pretend that you and your new little family do not exist. Get. Out.'

As she left the room, she heard him get up as if to stop her and then change his mind. She meant it this time. She was lonely but she wasn't going to be a mug anymore.

CHAPTER TEN

EMILY

Close to Emily's childhood home in Ipswich, standing in the corner of the park, was a huge oak tree. Growing up, whenever she'd had something big on her mind, something too vast and consuming to contain in her small bedroom at home, she would take herself off to the park and sit under this tree. There was something about its wide solid trunk, the whisper of its leaves, that soothed her and helped get everything into perspective. Even when her so-called close pal Nicola Brady kissed Emily's date at the Year 11 leavers' disco, the tree had worked its magic – as did hot chocolate and a day in her mum's bed watching TV.

Real friends don't do that, had been her mother's sage advice. She was right. Along with all the other mantras that Emily had grown up with about the value of good friends and the importance of loyalty. Her mum had finally left her dad just before Emily started secondary school, and it was her mum's best friend Julia who had been the one to put them up, run interference when he turned up at the door drunk, then helped them to find a house of their own. *Close friends are more precious than gold, Em. Don't ever forget that.*

Which was one of the reasons she was so upset about falling out with Amy.

Last night, Pete had had a client dinner and the flat had felt so empty. Trying to escape the weight which had settled on her, she'd gone to bed early. For almost an hour, she'd lain awake, eyes wide open. Her mind wouldn't quiet, the walls were closing in on her and the cherubs in the vintage yellow wallpaper she'd bought for the bedroom seemed to be mocking her insomnia.

Her mobile was close to the bed and calling Amy was a much better idea than laying there, stewing in her own thoughts. It only rang twice before Amy picked up. 'Hello.'

'Hi, Amy. It's me, Emily.' That had been a stupid thing to say. The caller display would have told her that much.

'Hi. How are you doing?'

'Erm, I'm okay. I just… Pete's out and I thought we could catch up.'

Amy had made a noise at the other end. Was that a little laugh? 'I'm just on my way out with Betsy, but I've got a few minutes. What did you want to talk about?'

Emily's stomach had prickled. A few minutes? She'd need that just to get started. Amy used to spend every Friday night watching a film with Stuart. When had she started going out on a Friday? 'Oh, don't worry. I'll call another time.'

'It's fine. I'm all ready to go and Betsy is usually late anyway. We can talk for a bit.'

Usually late. That knowledge suggested that they were together a lot of the time. She had no right to be jealous. She was the one who had got pregnant and stopped going out. 'I just, you know, wanted to see how you are.'

'I'm fine. How are you?'

It had been like having a conversation with a stranger. She'd wanted to talk to Amy. *Really* talk to her. The way she'd talk to her girlfriends in her youth when they'd lie on one of their beds and open their hearts like a display cabinet. 'I'm not so good actually.'

There had been a pause at the other end. 'Really? What's up?'

She'd wanted to say it. Wanted to cry and tell Amy that she wasn't sure she was capable of doing this. Having a child, being a mother. But the words had twisted like a ball of steel wool in her throat. 'I'm just feeling a bit down.'

If she hadn't been so close to tears, she could have laughed at the level of understatement.

Amy had coughed at the other end. Hadn't spoken immediately. 'Oh, well, that's probably hormones or something.'

Was she right? Was that all this was? Like a really bad prolonged bout of PMS? She'd closed her eyes, taken a deep breath. *Just say it.* 'I'm not sure I can be a mother, Amy. I'm not sure I can do this.'

Another pause. When Amy had spoken, there'd been an edge to her voice. 'Well, it's a bit late for that, eh? You'll be fine, Emily. You always are.'

What does that mean? 'The thing is—'

Amy had cut her off. 'The thing is, Emily, life just falls into place for you. You wanted a job here in London; you got the job at the news agency. Then you met Pete and you wanted him to move in, so he moved in. Now you have a baby on the way. You've got everything and you just need to realise how bloody lucky you are. You could be going out to drown your sorrows because, yet again, your period has arrived with bells on to confirm that, once again, you are not going to be a mother in nine months.'

She'd felt as if she'd been slapped. Amy was always a straight talker, but she was usually less brutal than this. Emily shouldn't have called. Should have realised that speaking to Amy about this was a bad idea. 'Amy, I'm sorry I—'

Again, she'd cut her off. 'Emily, I've got to go. Betsy is here. I hope you feel better, but, you know, count your blessings or something.'

She'd rung off without even saying goodbye. Emily had dropped the mobile on the bed and lay there until Pete got home, tears pooling at the back of her neck. When she'd heard his key in the door, she'd closed her eyes and pretended to be asleep.

Now, sitting with her back against a different tree, fifteen minutes' walk from their flat, she closed her eyes again. How was it possible to feel this tired and yet keep going? It was incredible that she was still working and not making a terrible mistake somewhere.

This tree had become a replacement for 'her' tree back home. The first week in the flat in Sydenham Hill, when she was still wondering if she'd done the right thing in leaving her home town, she'd come to Crystal Palace Park and just sat against this tree for an hour, thinking about her mum and how proud she would have been to know that Emily had been offered a job at the agency. It didn't matter how difficult it was; she was going to work hard and make something of herself.

She'd never found it difficult to make friends before, so she hadn't been concerned that the news agency she worked for was small: a handful of journalists who were rarely in the building for two consecutive days and a couple of older PAs who always went straight home to see their kids. She'd known it was just a matter of time before she got chatting to someone who worked for another of the companies in the building and started to unpick who were the people to get to know if she wanted to be invited out to the pub on a Friday. Sure enough, she and Amy had got chatting when the whole building had been evacuated for a fire drill and Amy had invited Emily out to celebrate someone's birthday the same night. They were a good crowd, but Amy was the only one she would count as the kind of friend she could rely on, be honest with. At least, she had.

She opened her eyes at the sound of snuffling: a small white dog, wondering who the strange woman sitting at the bottom of the tree might be.

'Bertie, come away!' A woman around her age jogged over and grabbed him by his collar. 'Sorry. He's my mum's dog and he's very nosy.' She nodded in the direction of a woman twenty or so years older who was stood with her hands on her hips, waiting for her dog and daughter to return.

'No problem, I was about to go anyway.' It was later than she'd realised. Pete would be at home, wondering where she was. She stood and brushed the grass from the back of her legs, watched as the woman put the dog on his lead and took him back to her mother. They linked arms and continued on their walk. It tore something inside of Emily. If only her mum was here right now. What would she give to just jump on a train and go home? Her real home. Have her mum open her front door and then her arms. *Just tell me the truth and I will be able to help.* That's what she used to say. *There's nothing you can say that would stop me loving you.* Is it possible for anyone to love you like your mother does?

Walking towards the exit, she wrapped her arms around herself, placing her right palm on her bump. 'I'm going to try, little boy. I'm really going to try.'

She didn't have her mum and she didn't have Amy. But she had Pete. Could she be totally honest with him about her feelings? Would he recoil in horror, think there was something wrong with her? Or would he understand? Would he... *could he*, help? There was only one way to find out.

When she opened the door to the flat, she was expecting to hear the sound of a rugby match from some corner of the globe, but there was only silence. They'd had words before she'd left for the park. He'd made a comment about the living room being untidy and she had taken it personally and snapped at him. They'd barely spoken for an hour, so when she announced that she was going out for a while, he'd looked relieved.

'Pete?'

Silence. Where was he? She really needed him. She needed to be held by someone who loved her, who was real. To tell him everything before she lost her nerve.

'Pete? Are you there?'

Still nothing. She slipped off her shoes and headed for the bedroom. Not there either.

There wasn't a text on her phone, but when she wandered into the kitchen she spotted a note scribbled on the back of an envelope, its corner tucked under the kettle: *Back soon.*

Where had he gone? Emily pressed his name on her mobile and listened to it ring and ring. At the same time as his voicemail kicked in, there was the shrill ringing of the doorbell. He must have forgotten his key. Maybe he'd just popped out for milk or something.

But when she opened the door, there was no Pete. In the communal hallway stood two police officers.

CHAPTER ELEVEN

CAROLINE

Caroline slammed the cupboard door shut so hard that that cutlery jangled in the drawer above. Then she opened it purely so that she could slam it shut again.

After his devastating request, she'd told Pete to get the hell out of her house. She wouldn't be able to say that much longer. Pretty soon, the house, this kitchen, this bloody cupboard door would be theirs: his and Emily's. She opened the fridge to get the milk and then kicked it closed with her foot. Who gave a damn if she dented the bloody thing?

After he'd left this afternoon, she'd lain face down on the bed and cried. Angry tears. Tears of disappointment. Of loss. Then she'd got up, washed her face and had spent the next two hours cleaning the bathroom, vacuuming the bedrooms, even changing all the bedclothes: determined not to think about him. But it was impossible. As she scrubbed tiles, tore off sheets and banged the vacuum into the bottom of the beds, she had fought with an anger she didn't know what to do with. Without him here to shout at, it had nowhere to go.

On the wall next to the fridge were the measurements of Jamie's height. Children don't grow in steady increments. There are bursts of growth. Hardly any change for three months and then, bang, three centimetres in a month. It's a surprise that you don't see them actually growing as you watch. He used to cost them a fortune in trousers. No sooner had they kitted him out with new jeans or school trousers than they were flapping an inch above his ankles like a flag at half-mast. Caroline ran her finger down the line: 15 1/2, 13y 2m, 11, 9, 7 right down to 13 months, which was when he could stand unaided long enough for Pete to be able to balance a book on his head and draw the line on the wall.

These feelings were too big to deal with alone. Leaving the teabag in the mug, she grabbed her mobile from the coffee table. Gabby answered on the second ring. 'Hey, lovely, how are you doing?'

With her best pals, there was no need for the opening niceties. 'You were right. Pete is an utter bastard.' She coughed out the sob which she'd been pushing down her throat for the last hour.

Gabby didn't even take a breath. 'Give me thirty minutes and I'll be there.'

Gabby was actually on the doorstep in twenty-five minutes, accompanied by Faith and what looked like the contents of an entire bakery. 'I've brought reinforcements.'

Faith held out her arms and pulled Caroline in for a tight hug. 'I'd like to think she means me, but I think she's actually referring to the cake.'

It didn't take long to update them on Pete's news and they were so shocked that she managed to draw a veil over the fact he'd delivered it in person rather than over the phone. Having cried on separate calls to each of them about Pete's marriage and the baby as soon as she'd got back from the university on Jamie's birthday, she knew how angry they would be, but this time she got to see their physical reaction to the new development, their faces moving from open-mouthed shock to red-faced fury.

Recounting their conversation brought home to Caroline the enormity of what Pete had said. He wanted to live here, raise his new family in the home they'd built together. It would be as if she and Jamie had never existed.

'I cannot believe the barefaced front of that man.' Faith pulled apart a pastry as if it was to blame. 'Are you seriously going to let them have the house?'

Despite her best efforts to push Pete from her mind, Caroline had spent the last few hours turning the problem over in her head. She couldn't decide what was worse: letting Pete and Emily move in here or giving the house up to total strangers. 'I don't see that I have a huge amount of choice. I know that we could sell it, but that would mean showing around an endless stream of people who might pick holes in the choice of wallpaper or the amount of storage.'

It wasn't just the criticism of her decor choices that was preying on her mind. How could she let other families into Jamie's bedroom? How would she explain that, yes, it did look like a teenage boy's bedroom but, no, there was no teenage boy living here with her? Worse still, what if another little boy came to claim it as his own. She squeezed the sodden tissue in her hand.

Faith was shaking her head, her lips pressed together tightly. When she took in a deep breath, she wobbled slightly in fury. 'If he was here right now, I would tell him exactly what I think of him. Of all the cruel things he could have done. Turfing you out of your home!'

Caroline picked up the coffee that Gabby had made for her and blew on it. Her outward breath still trembled, but she felt calmer than she had before they came. Either the cake or the support of her friends had been cathartic. Probably both. She could at least look the situation in the eye now. 'Well, I suppose it was his home too and he could have asked me to sell it when we got divorced. Problem is, much as I am grateful to you for my job at the children's centre, it won't enable me to remortgage a four-bedroom house so I can pay him out his share.'

On a purely practical level, it was probably ridiculous for her to still be living here on her own. She had no idea how big the flat was that Pete and Emily had, but he'd made it sound like a bedsit. There was no way she could let them bring up a baby there while she was floating around in all this space. It was unconscionable.

Gabby looked as if she was measuring the weight of her words before sharing them. 'What about if you went back to your old job? Could you afford to remortgage then?'

'Maybe.' She'd thought about that this afternoon, too. 'But I don't think I can do it. I mean, there may not be a job for me to walk into – even if there was, I'm not sure that I'm up to it.'

Gabby glanced at Faith. Was this a tag team? Had they hatched a plan before arriving here? Faith took up the baton. 'Well, if not that, what else could you see yourself doing?'

Butterflies started up in the pit of Caroline's stomach. 'Are you trying to tell me that I'm getting fired?'

'No. No, of course not. You're great at your job and everyone loves having you there. It's just that I'll be advertising the outreach worker role soon and you really would be perfect for it. It pays more than you're getting at the moment. I don't know if it would be enough to cover your remortgage, but...'

Caroline stared into her mug. She had enjoyed her job in social work and the outreach job really did sound like something she could do well. But the mere thought of the emotional toll that a job like that might take on her wasn't something she could handle right now. If ever. 'No. I'm not ready.'

Faith sat back. Caroline knew that they wouldn't push her more than a gentle nudge. 'Okay. So, no job change. What about if we try and fix you up with a millionaire with a penchant for rescuing middle-aged women who have a fetish for antique door knobs?'

The warmth of her smile almost made Caroline cry again. She knew they only wanted the best for her. 'Only if he is tall enough to reach the pans in the cupboard above the extractor fan. I haven't seen inside there since Pete left.'

'Hmmm.' Gabby was nodding. 'Height is useful. Other than that, most men can be replaced by a contraption for opening jars and a buzzing you-know-what.'

'Gabby!' Caroline laughed. The first time she had all day. It felt good.

Faith picked up her mug. 'So, what is the plan, then? If you do move out, you know you're welcome to move into my spare room while you find somewhere.'

'Thanks. I have no idea how much a small house would cost, to be honest. Or how much this place would fetch.' She held her hands up to her face and pressed her eyes until a kaleidoscope started behind her lids. 'I just can't face any of it.'

After Pete had left, and she'd pushed herself back up from the bed where she'd gone to have a good cry, she'd gone from room to room. The bathroom mirror where she'd watched a gap-toothed Jamie brush his teeth. The hole in his door where he'd hung a 'Parent-Free Zone' sign in his early teens and then taken it down again a couple of years later because he was far too cool to find it funny anymore.

Then her bedroom, the one she used to share with Pete. Where a bright-eyed Jamie would drag his sack of presents at some unacceptably early hour of Christmas morning. *He's been, Mum! Father Christmas has been!*

How was she going to give this place up? It was impossible to even think about living anywhere else. Because anywhere else that she lived, *he* would never have lived. Would never have existed in.

A tear dripped from the end of her nose into her coffee. She hadn't even realised she was crying again. 'I just feel like I'm going to have to leave him behind.'

Gabby moved up the sofa so that she was close enough to put an arm around her. 'Jamie isn't in this house, my love. He's with you. He's always with you.'

'I know. I know that you're right. It's just… when I'm here I can see him. He's everywhere I look. And if I'm not here, I'm scared that I'll forget things.'

Just the thought of taking down his football posters from the wall, or selling the desk where he sat to – *sometimes* – study for his A-levels. It felt disloyal. Just wrong.

Faith put down her drink, sat on the arm of the sofa on the other side from Gabby and took hold of Caroline's hand. 'We've got you, honey. Wherever you are, we've got you.'

The three of them sat in silence for a few moments. The air too heavy with emotion for any of them to speak. Until a beep from Caroline's phone interrupted their thoughts.

Since that awful day when the call had come to tell them about Jamie, Caroline never let a call go to voicemail or left a message unread. Her phone was in the kitchen, so she was alone when she read the message for the first time. She wandered back into the lounge as she read it again. 'It's from Emily.'

Faith folded her arms. 'What the hell does she want? The dimensions of the hallway for a new carpet?'

Caroline shook her head slowly as she read the message a third time, trying to make sense of it. 'She's at the hospital. It's Pete. There's been an accident.'

CHAPTER TWELVE

EMILY

The journey to the hospital in the back of the police car had been surreal. Emily had seen it so many times on those detective shows that Pete loved. A man or woman at home, having a perfectly normal time washing up or watching TV, and then that knock on the door. Two policemen – why were there always two? – kind smiles, soft voices. *Mrs Simmons? Can we come in?* Pete always made the same joke about the fact there was always someone at home when the police came bearing bad news.

She had hoped that arriving with a police escort would mean she could get straight through all the reception desks and security doors and into wherever Pete was. She'd been upset with him earlier but something like this put everything in perspective. Once he recovered, she'd be honest with him about how she was feeling. Even go to the doctor if need be. Get some help.

But they hadn't taken her to Pete. Instead, she was in a small room with fake leather sofas and a bookcase of romance novels. Posters on the wall explaining *The Importance of Handwashing* and *The Signs of a Stroke* next to a Monet print in a silver frame.

A nurse had explained that Pete was in the operating theatre and offered Emily a tea or coffee. What did people offer you in a crisis if you didn't drink either of those? She'd shaken her head. 'I'm fine, thanks.'

And now she sat and waited.

The last time she had been in a waiting room at this hospital, she'd been here for her second scan. Pete had been beside her, holding her hand. She looked down at her hands now. Her wedding ring, still so shiny and new.

Everyone was talking quietly, even the two police officers who had brought her in. Why were they still here? Did they need to talk to Pete about what had happened? All they'd told her was that there had been a car accident. That Pete had been involved and that he'd been brought here in an ambulance.

'Is he going to be okay?' she'd asked the nurse who had offered her a drink.

'They are doing everything they can.' Emily had watched enough episodes of *Grey's Anatomy* to know what that meant. *Never promise the family anything.* Wasn't that what the interns were taught? And why couldn't she stop thinking about TV shows right now?

There was a gentle knock on the door and the kindly nurse reappeared with a clipboard. 'Sorry, we've had quite a busy night tonight. Is there anyone coming in to be with you?'

Emily shook her head. 'Can I go and see Pete now?'

'He's still on the surgical floor at the moment, I'm afraid. I just need to get a few details from you if that's okay?'

'Of course.'

The nurse pulled a plastic chair away from the wall. Its legs scraped across the floor and made Emily's back teeth hurt.

'The questions are all pretty straightforward. You are Pete's wife?'

Images of their wedding day, her knee-length, fifties-style dress, Pete's huge smile, the flashy dinner afterwards. 'Yes. Yes, I am. His second wife.'

She wasn't sure why she'd added that. Surely it made no difference.

The nurse's expression didn't change. 'Okay. Then I just need to get a few details from you and then we're done. What is your husband's date of birth?'

The back of Emily's neck started to sweat. It was so hot in here. She knew Pete's birthday, of course she did. But what year was he born? She knew his age, why couldn't she work it out? 'I don't know. I mean, I can't remember. Can we not wait and ask him when he wakes up?'

This time the nurse reached out and took her hand. 'It's a lot easier if we get it done now. A doctor will come and speak to you shortly, but Pete's injuries are pretty extensive. They are doing everything they can but you might have to prepare yourself for difficult news. I'm so sorry. Are you sure there is no one I can call for you? You shouldn't be here alone.'

She could hear the nurse's words but they weren't quite making sense. It was as if she was in a goldfish bowl and they weren't getting through to her. These were TV conversations, not ones that happened in real life. To her.

The nurse was looking at her, waiting for her to speak. What would Emily give to be able to call her mother right now? She pulled her mind back to the present. What was the point of thinking about that? Her mother was gone. 'No, I don't have anyone who lives close by.'

'Not even a friend who might come?'

The closest friend she had nearby was Amy. But after the tone of their last conversation, she didn't feel she could ask for her support. What must the nurse think of her that she had no one to call in an emergency? As well as not knowing her own husband's date of birth? 'No, I'm fine on my own. Honestly. I just want to see Pete. I just want to check he's okay.'

The nurse frowned and opened her mouth to say something. Then closed it again before finally saying, 'Let's leave the forms for now. I'll see if I can find one of the surgical team to come and have a chat with you.'

The room was silent again after the door clicked shut. As if the words the nurse had spoken were still floating in the air, they settled in her brain until Emily realised what she'd said. This was serious. Pete was in trouble. The room was so hot, she could barely work out what she should do. What if she didn't have the information they needed? She didn't even know Pete's blood type. Was that important? But who *would* know that?

Her mind flashed to Caroline. Whatever had happened between her and Pete, surely his first wife would want to know if he'd been in an accident? And maybe she would know something vital that could help them to save Pete's life.

When she took her mobile phone out of her bag, she realised that her hands were trembling. Pete didn't know, but she had Caroline's number in her phone. Last Christmas, he'd called round to see Caroline to check she was okay, but he'd left his phone at the office, so he'd called Emily from Caroline's phone to tell her he'd be late. She'd saved the number for some reason. Maybe she'd known she might need it someday.

She typed out the message with her thumb.

Hi Caroline. This is Emily. There's been an accident. Pete's in hospital. Can you come?

Ten minutes later, the door to the room opened and a tall man in a white coat walked in, nodded at the police officers who then stepped outside. The nurse followed and closed the door, resting her back against it as if she was standing guard.

The man held out his hand. When she shook it, it was cool and dry. 'Hi. I'm Dr Philips. Sorry to keep you waiting in here. Do you mind if I sit down?'

Why did they all keep asking her permission for everything? 'Please do.'

'The accident that your husband was involved in was very serious. By the time he came in, the paramedics had been working on him for some time. We have done our best but I'm afraid we were unable to save him.'

Again, it was as if he were speaking through glass. 'I don't understand.'

The doctor looked her in the eye. 'He died on the operating table a few moments ago. My colleagues are in the process of bringing him down to a room where you can go to see him if you would like to.'

Emily's body was paralysed. It took her a moment to realise that the pain in her chest was a lack of oxygen and she took in a breath. Her body felt as if it was swaying and her vision blurred at the edges. She felt sick.

'She's going to go—'

She heard the nurse's voice and then the flash of her uniform before everything disappeared.

CHAPTER THIRTEEN

CAROLINE

It wasn't until she was standing at the reception desk that Caroline realised she was wearing odd shoes. She tried to explain to the receptionist who she was. 'My husband – I mean, my ex-husband – has been brought in. A car accident. Pete Simmons. I'm Caroline Simmons.'

It was strange to think that she still shared his name. She'd considered changing it after the divorce, but Simmons was also Jamie's name. Was Emily a Simmons too, now? Or had she kept her own surname?

Her phone rang and she pressed the green icon before it could ring again. 'I'm here, Emily. Where are you?'

Gabby had driven her to the hospital; Caroline was in no fit state to drive herself. Trying to reassure her, Gabby had kept a steady stream of conversation going for the fourteen minutes it had taken to get there. *Try to stay calm. I'm sure he's fine.* Caroline had barely been aware of the words. All she could hear was her own inner voice. *Not again. Not again. Not again.*

Gabby had also offered to park the car and come in with her, but Caroline had insisted she go home. Accident and Emergency wasn't the place for lots of people, and Emily would be there anyway – plus whoever else was with her. Gabby had dropped her off near the entrance, making her promise to call if she needed her.

Caroline followed the directions Emily gave her until she saw her face, her foot halfway out the door of a small room. She looked small, pale, fragile. Caroline tried to remember what Emily had looked like the time she'd seen her and Pete together. Found she couldn't. 'How is he? How's Pete. Can I see him?'

Emily just stared at her, mute and lifeless. And then Caroline knew. She just knew.

The police thought it was likely to have been a drunk driver or joyrider. Either way, it had been a hit-and-run. Pete's car had overturned and had spun over into oncoming traffic.

'I don't even know where he was.' Pulling at the tissue in her hand, Emily had repeated this three times over. Caroline knew exactly where he'd been. Less than six hours ago, he had been sitting in her lounge. Guilt crept at the edges of her grief, but how would it help to tell Emily that he'd been with her?

Even though they were divorced, it had hit her like a brick when she'd found out Pete was moving in with someone else. It had seemed more final than the papers they'd signed: he was moving on and she was stood still. Had she fantasised about destroying his car, or pushing him down the stairs, or humiliating him in some way? Of course, she had. But never, even in the darkest, deepest depths of her vitriol, had she wished him dead. He was the man she had loved for many years. The father of her son. And now they were both gone.

She sniffed at the paper cup of ghastly grey tea from the machine. It was foul, but there was nothing else to do but drink it. They'd been advised to wait until the medical team had had a chance to prepare Pete for them to see. Caroline shuddered at what that meant. What state his poor body might be in.

No mother should have to see the dead body of her child. From the moment Jamie was born, Caroline's every instinct had been to protect him, to keep him safe. Locks on the cupboard doors when he started to crawl, encouraging friendships with children who were kind when he was at school, collecting him at midnight when he couldn't get a cab home from a night out. He was her only child. Everything she had, she'd invested in him.

That terrible day, it was five hours before they'd got to the hospital. She'd been on her own when the call came from the university, but she'd only needed to make out the words *Jamie* and *accident* to be already pulling on her coat and trying to get hold of Pete. He'd been away on a work conference but had left to collect her as soon as she told him what had happened. She'd been in no fit state to drive there alone. The kind nurse she'd spoken to on the telephone had reminded her gently that there was no need to rush. It wouldn't change anything. But she couldn't bear the thought of him lying there alone for a moment longer than was necessary.

In the early hours of the morning, the hospital had been quiet apart from a couple of patched-up drunks shuffling from A & E. They'd been taken straight to Jamie and were able to sit with him for a few hours. It was him, and yet it wasn't. His vitality, his laugh, the silly faces he made – they'd all gone. Still, he was her beautiful boy and she hadn't wanted to leave him. Eventually, Pete had had to put his arm around her and gently lead her outside. She had collapsed onto him then, her face buried in the dip between his shoulder and his chest. 'I can't leave him, Pete. I can't leave him there.'

He had rocked her. Kissed the top of her head. 'Shh. He's gone, Caro. We're not leaving him. He's gone.'

Her memory of the following few weeks was a blur. She did remember that Pete had been so strong. It was him who had organised everything: bringing Jamie back home, making the funeral arrangements, telling their friends. All the while, he'd kept checking on her, reassuring her that they would get through this. If he could have picked her up and carried her, she thought he would have.

The day of the funeral was patchy, too. She recalled that the crematorium had been packed. It had brought them a little comfort, seeing how much he was loved by so many people. At least thirty people were there from Colchester, including his girlfriend, Beth. Beth's mother had come too and had kept her propped up during the service. She had been inconsolable. Blamed herself for the horrible accident, for letting him go back to his room on his own when he'd been drunk. It wasn't her fault, Pete had told her at the wake. No one could tell Jamie what to do when he had his stubborn head on. Caroline had agreed – she hadn't wanted the poor girl to feel any worse. But all the while, the same thoughts swam around her head. *If only I'd been there. I would have looked out for him. I would have kept him safe.*

People liked to tell her that time was a great healer and, in many ways, that was probably true. But losing a child is different. It's not in the natural order of things, so there's no way to make sense of it. There wasn't a day that went by that she didn't think of him. Remembering events from the past or imagining a future that he would never have.

A nurse appeared at the door to the small room. 'Oh, good. I'm glad you've got someone with you. Pete is in a room further down the corridor. You can come and see him now if you're ready?'

They both stood up and Emily wavered like a reed in the breeze. Caroline caught her elbow. 'Are you okay? Do you want to wait a minute?'

The nurse looked concerned. 'Are you feeling light-headed again? This is a lot for you to be dealing with in your condition. Do you want to wait a while?'

'No. I want to go now.'

Caroline understood Emily completely. She wanted to see Pete too.

Still, the nurse didn't look confident about her going. 'Would you like me to bring a wheelchair for you so that you don't have to walk?'

Emily shook her head. 'I'll be okay.' She looked at Caroline. 'I know this is a lot to ask, but can I take your arm?'

This was a time to put aside any animosity or reproach. 'Of course.'

It was getting late and, as they followed the nurse up a white corridor, the squeak of her shoes on the shiny floor were the only sound. When they got to the door of Pete's room, Emily looked at Caroline, her eyes wide and round like a rabbit caught in the glare of oncoming headlights.

Caroline's heart was hurting in her chest. The pain of today layering onto the pain she carried every day of her life. She patted Emily's hand. 'It's okay. I'm here with you.'

To an onlooker, it must have seemed like a scene from a Greek tragedy: Pete laid on the bed with his wives past and present sitting beside him, his unborn child in the womb of the second. For the next hour, they sat quietly together in the dimly lit room, barely speaking. What could they say to one another? Emily repeated her confusion about where he'd been that afternoon, worrying at it like a knot in a shoelace. It heaped more guilt onto Caroline. There was no way she could tell Emily that she'd seen Pete only a few hours before. That her last words to him had been angry ones. That her last memory would be the hurt on his face as she told him that she never wanted to see him again. The very thought of it made her want to double over.

How had this come to pass? Three years ago, they had been a family of three. Caroline and Pete's marriage might have dulled but they were together, and Jamie had been all the brightness they needed. Now she was the only one left.

She watched as Emily laid her forehead on the side of the mattress next to Pete's open hand. Her shoulders vibrated with grief, yet she made no sound. For the first time, Caroline wondered about her being here alone. Where were her family, her friends? Pete had told her that Emily wasn't coping with her pregnancy. How was she going to do this alone?

Eventually, Emily was still. Almost as if she was sleeping. Her pregnancy was none of Caroline's business. With Pete gone, she had no connection to this woman at all. She would sit with her as long as she needed tonight; it was the right thing to do. To make sure she was okay. But after she had seen her home safely, they would say goodbye and Emily would have to rely on her own friends and family to get her through.

Then Caroline would go home to her own house and prepare herself for another funeral of a man she'd loved.

CHAPTER FOURTEEN

EMILY

When she was young, Emily used to read her favourite book under her blanket with a torch. The funeral director's office was as quiet and comforting as that. Everyone spoke in soft, smooth voices. Even the teacup that the receptionist brought her didn't dare to rattle in its saucer.

The funeral director wore a black suit and tie and a crisp white shirt. He stood to shake her hand across a large antique desk with a dark green leather inlay. 'I'm so sorry for your loss, Mrs Simmons.'

Emily acknowledged this with a nod. She knew the routine. Hadn't she been in a similar office only a handful of years before, planning the funeral of her mother? These platitudes existed for a reason. If she just stayed on script, she could get through this. 'Thank you.'

'Are we waiting for anyone else, or would you like me to talk you through your options?'

The night of Pete's accident, after Caroline had travelled back to the flat with her in a cab and made sure she was home safely, Emily had lain awake on the bed, still wearing her coat and shoes. Caroline had offered to come in and make her something to eat, or at least a hot drink, but she had politely declined. Having her in their home would just feel too weird, too uncomfortable.

For a long time, she'd stared at the ceiling, unable to sleep or even to close her eyes. Had she been hot or cold? She barely knew. It was as if the universe had shifted and she was waiting to regain her balance, find her place.

It wasn't until the next morning that the reality of Pete's death had knocked her over like a rolling wave. The sun came through the blinds she had neglected to close and she reached for him in bed, to shake his arm, ask him to shut out the light so that she could sleep. For a second, she was confused, then the memory of his pale stillness the night before caught up with her and made her roll onto her side with a groan. 'Pete. Pete. Pete.' Her cries came from somewhere deep inside her guts. 'I can't do this without you.'

The funeral director was quietly waiting for her response, obviously used to dealing with people who needed time to process what was being asked. His face was a professional version of comfort and empathy.

'Please start. It's just me.' She placed a hand on her stomach. That wasn't strictly true.

She'd spent the last three days alone in the flat, eating small amounts of whatever was in the fridge. A few olives. Some dark chocolate. A couple of crackers. She knew she had to keep her strength up because of the baby, but she couldn't physically eat more than that. Her throat was so tight and sore that she could only manage morsels of food, eating slowly enough that she could force them down.

Caroline had kindly offered to inform Pete's mother and anyone else who needed to be told. The only contact Emily had made had been a text message to Amy. In response, Amy had left a barrage of voicemails and a long text full of well-meant promises of support that Emily hadn't even got to the end of. Every message ended with an offer to come over, but Emily had asked for time alone, unable to face the prospect of talking about Pete's death out loud. His absence from her life had opened a chasm that she was afraid to look inside. She inched around it, holding onto the furniture, the TV controller, the cuffs of his bathrobe which she had worn for the last three days. This morning she had showered for the first time in order to keep the appointment here.

The funeral director slid a leather folder in her direction. 'Shall we start by choosing a coffin?'

Was she actually going to be sick or was this just nausea? She breathed in slowly through her nose, counted to four, then breathed out again. 'I don't need to look at those. I'll have a mahogany one with brass handles.'

He didn't make any comment about her familiarity with coffin types, merely nodded and made a note in his book. Even upside down, she could see that his handwriting was neat, precise.

'Do you have a date in mind for the funeral? Are there any family members you need to consult for availability?'

Her mind went blank. More deep breaths. 'His mother lives in Norfolk. I should check with her, I suppose. She might be able to contact Pete's close family members to ask them.'

She'd been relieved when Caroline offered to call Pete's mother to let her know what had happened. Emily had never actually spoken to her before. Pete had told her that they weren't close. He barely spoke to her himself. It had always seemed very strange to Emily. Having been so close to her own mother, she couldn't understand it. She'd wondered if something awful had happened to Pete in childhood. But he'd said no, it had been fine. They just had different lives.

More neat notes in the book. 'Anyone else?'

In a previous life, it would have been comical to see the briefest hint of surprise cross his face when she said, 'His ex-wife. She'll have to be there.'

He composed himself pretty quickly, though. Probably cross with himself for allowing the lapse. 'Do you have a rough idea of the number of people who will want to attend? The crematorium has three rooms although one of them is quite small. We'll book the one which is most appropriate.'

Again, her mind was blank. This was even harder than she'd thought it would be. Who should she even invite? What friends should she ask?

In the time they'd been together, they hadn't socialised with many of Pete's friends. Once, he'd joked that Caroline had been awarded all their friends in the divorce. It hadn't seemed to bother him much. He had one mate that he'd occasionally go for a pint with: Steve, who'd been a witness at their wedding. She'd invite him. But who else? Her head ached. 'Can you give me a couple of days to come up with a list?'

The director's voice was calm and reassuring, but there were more questions to come. 'Of course. What about music? Have you thought about what you might like?'

Why was there so much to decide on? All of these questions had been so straightforward when she'd had to organise her mum's funeral. It was easy when you knew someone that well – their tastes, their likes, the things that were important to them. Did she not know Pete at all? Had he really never mentioned any favourite songs? Did he like any hymns?

Her face was getting hotter. She needed to get some air. 'Actually, can you make me a list of the things I need to think about that I can take home? It all feels too much today, I…'

The funeral director was the picture of consideration. 'Of course. Of course. Take as long as you need.' He tore a page from the notepad on his desk and started to make a list.

Watching the neat list of bullet points grow longer down the page, Emily felt increasingly overwhelmed. And this was just the funeral. After that, she had bank accounts to manage, bills to change the name on, shopping to do. Hospital appointments to attend… All she wanted to do was roll up in a ball and ignore the world.

She could almost hear her mother's sage advice: *Concentrate on the job in hand.*

The funeral. She just needed to organise the funeral right now. And if she couldn't do this on her own, there was only one person she could ask.

CHAPTER FIFTEEN

CAROLINE

When Caroline told Gabby that she'd agreed to help Emily with the funeral, she could have predicted her reaction. 'Are you spinning me?'

Gabby's creativity with replacement swear words never failed to make Caroline smile. 'What could I say, Gab? When she called, she was so sad. She sounded like she was at the end of her rope.'

After making sure she got home from the hospital safely, she really hadn't expected to hear from Emily again. From her halting speech on the phone, it had clearly cost her a lot to ask for Caroline's help. If she was honest, Caroline was glad to do it.

'At the end of her rope? Really?' Gabby's tone was uncharacteristically sarcastic. 'You mean like *you* were when Pete – God rest his soul – moved in with this same Emily only a couple of months after your divorce was finalised? That level of sad? Because – and you know I don't begrudge it and I'd do it again in a heartbeat – it took us days to get you out of your own front door after that.'

Caroline didn't want to think about that right now. For now, it was easier to keep that memory separate from the grieving woman she'd sat with at the hospital. 'I know. And I'll be eternally grateful to you for threatening to pull me out of the bedroom by my knicker elastic, but I don't think she has a Gabby in her life to do that.'

'Even so. This is her problem now, not yours. You're too nice sometimes, Caro.'

Gabby might not be so keen to applaud her kindness if she knew that Pete had been with her the night he'd died. She wasn't ready to say that out loud yet. Not even to her closest friend. 'Just the funeral and then that's it. I want to do it, anyway. He was my husband. And Jamie's dad.'

No one could argue against the Jamie card. 'Okay. You win. But make sure that you take care of yourself. I mean it, Caroline. This is going to bring up a lot of things for you. I don't want you getting hurt again.'

If anything, Gabby's words had made her more certain that she was doing the right thing. Last night, she'd poured herself a glass of wine to take the edge off the pain of flicking through old photographs on the home computer. Pete had always fancied himself an amateur photographer and would take several shots of the same thing, intending to choose the best one later. That's why there were so many of the same smiling face missing a tooth, or the first school day, or a flag waving at the top of Snowdon.

Organising the photographs was a job they never quite got around to. *We'll do it when we're retired*, Pete would say. Caroline realised now that it's a job you should do immediately. Deleting photographs of your nine-year-old is easy to do when he is still nine and you can take many more. It's not so easy when you'll never be able to take that photograph again.

Eventually, she'd selected some of Pete and Jamie to print and take to Emily's this morning, plus some of Pete on his own in the early days when she'd first known him. Maybe one of them would be suitable for the Order of Service. Caroline hadn't had to do much of this for Jamie's funeral. Between Pete and her girlfriends, the most she'd had to do was point a finger at one of a selection of photos, choose between a couple of song options. All the admin had been done somewhere else outside her consciousness.

Pete and Emily's flat was a short drive from her house, near to Sydenham Hill station. The parking spaces in the courtyard were numbered and Emily had given her the number for Pete's old space. His car had been towed to a breaker's yard after the police had taken the photographs they needed at the scene.

Although she'd seen Emily to her door the night of the accident, this was the first time she'd been inside their flat and she wasn't sure what to expect. Pete had made a passing reference to the fact they didn't use coasters, but that still didn't prepare her for what she found.

When Emily opened the door, she looked exhausted. Her hair was scraped back into a ponytail and it seemed to have pulled any colour from her face. She was wearing a man's shirt over a white T-shirt and a pair of dark blue leggings. Her bump pushed the shirt open. 'Thanks so much for coming.'

She turned and led the way back down a narrow hallway into a living room which overflowed with mugs and pieces of paper and what looked like half of Pete's wardrobe. Emily picked up a mug and a folder and then didn't seem to know what to do with them. 'Sorry. I was trying to sort things out. I haven't...' Her shoulders sagged and she sighed. 'I'm struggling to get on top of things.'

Because of what Pete had said in his last visit, Caroline knew that Emily hadn't been coping for a while, but as Emily didn't know that Caroline had been speaking to him, she couldn't lead with that. She took the plate from her hands. 'You've got a lot on. Let me do that. Why don't you have a look through these photographs and I'll clear this away and make us a drink.'

Their kitchen was small but modern. It only took a couple of attempts to find the dishwasher and Caroline loaded it with the crockery from the front room and other items that lined the kitchen worktop. Mostly it was mugs and bowls. There didn't seem to be anything that indicated dinner. She washed up two mugs at the sink and made tea, which she brought through to the lounge. 'Have you eaten today?'

Emily didn't look up from the photos in her hand. 'I just had some cereal. I'm not feeling very hungry at the moment.'

That sounded familiar. 'Grief can do that. You need to eat though. Especially because of the baby.'

Emily looked up with a frown. 'Shall we just get on with the planning? I need to make a list of people to invite. I don't even know Pete's mother's address. When I called to give her the date and time of the funeral, I got the impression that he hadn't even told her about the baby. She never seemed interested in hearing about me when he told her we were together. I assume that she must have been a pretty big fan of yours?'

Caroline snorted. 'I don't know what could have possibly given you that idea. His mother hated me. To be honest, I don't think she was that keen on Pete, either. Did he tell you that he came to London to do his degree at LSE and never went back to Norfolk to live? She blamed me for that, I think. For luring her boy away to the carnal desires of the Big Smoke.'

'Is she very religious, then?'

'Only if Marks and Spencer have started a twin-set-wearing cult. No church-going as far as I know, but she has a very long moral yardstick which she liked to beat us with. Did he tell you how appalled she was that we moved in together before we got married?'

Emily looked surprised. 'No. He didn't.'

Caroline nodded. 'Iris almost refused to come to the wedding. Mind you, Pete used to enjoy baiting her. He didn't tell her we were getting married until the actual invitations went out. And, when he announced that we were having a baby, he let her think we were going to join a commune and call him Pluto.' She smiled at the memory. Pete had been so much fun when they were first together. When had that stopped?

Emily returned to flicking through the photographs. 'That actually makes me feel a little better about it. I'd begun to wonder whether Pete was ashamed of me. Of the baby.'

She looked so fragile, so sad. Caroline had a surprising urge to comfort her. 'No. I would take it that he was actually trying to protect you. Believe me, she would have brought nothing to your life except judgement and stale fruitcake.'

Emily's smile was weak. 'Speaking of cake – Pete's office sent over a hamper for me, and there's cake in it. Would you like some? I can't face it and it would be ungrateful to let it just go bad.'

She looked like she could do with a lot more than cake to bring some flesh and colour to her face. And why was she alone in all this? 'Isn't there anyone you could stay with for a while? A friend? Family?'

She shook her head. 'I lost my mum before I met Pete. She'd been ill. Breast cancer. But it was still a shock. You're never old enough to lose your mum, are you?'

Caroline still had her mother, although in recent months dementia had gradually been taking parts of her away. She lived two hours away, on Caroline's sister's farm. When Jamie died, it had been awful to hear her anguish. *It should have been me. It should have been me who went first.* 'No. You're never old enough for that.'

Emily pulled her knees up underneath her. With no make-up, she looked like a young girl. 'When I first found out I was pregnant, I kind of forgot for a second that she'd gone. I know that sounds nuts, but it's true. For a moment, I thought, "I can't wait to call Mum." I got like a… I don't know how to describe it. It was like a surge of excitement. Then I remembered that she wasn't here anymore and it was like tripping up at the top of a hill and then tumbling down. It was horrible.'

Caroline stopped shuffling paper into piles and looked at Emily. She looked as if the life was being sucked out of her. 'I can imagine.'

'It's like I'm losing her all over again. The first time, I grieved for myself. As a daughter losing a mother. Now it's even worse. All I can think about is that she won't ever know her grandson. And that she won't know me as a mother. She would have been such a brilliant grandmother.' Emily made a face. 'I don't do a particularly good job of holding onto people, do I? Maybe I need to book myself in to get my aura cleansed or something?'

That was a dangerous road to go down. 'It's just bad luck.'

Caroline had taken a long time to learn that. When there's a tragedy, it's almost instinctive to try and make sense of it. Try to understand what has happened and why. But there is no rhyme or reason. It's just bloody awful luck if you get a bad roll of the dice.

Emily nodded. 'I wish she was here. She wouldn't be impressed with me sitting in all this mess. I can just imagine what she'd say. "How can you expect to feel better with yesterday's make-up on your face?"' She glanced around the room. 'It's not normally like this, you know. I'm not normally like this. I don't expect you to care either way, but I'm normally pretty tidy.'

It was on the tip of Caroline's tongue to say that she'd heard differently from Pete. Thankfully, she stopped it just in time. 'Have you been feeling this way for long? Before Pete's accident, I mean. Were you feeling down before that happened?'

Emily dropped her chin onto her chest. She didn't speak for a while. Caroline gave her time. She'd learned that from years in social work. You couldn't put words in someone's mouth. You had to give them time to say things in their own way.

'I was okay at the beginning, I think. I mean, I was happy to be pregnant. I thought…' She glanced up at Caroline before continuing, 'I thought it would be a good thing for us. But nothing seems to be as I expected. I don't feel *natural*.'

'What do you mean by natural?'

'Pregnant women are supposed to be happy and content. I just feel restless and like I don't own my body. And I can't shake a feeling of dread. Like something really bad is going to happen. Pete kept telling me that it was my hormones, but now…' She put her hands over her face and her shoulders started to shake.

There was no way Caroline could leave her like this. She needed to see a doctor. If she had already been struggling, Pete's death might be enough to make her seriously ill. Caroline knew from her training that stress was not good at all for Emily's baby. It was all very well the girls telling her that she shouldn't get herself involved, but surely she didn't have a choice. 'Emily, I really think you should speak to someone about getting some help. Your midwife, maybe? Or your doctor?'

Emily shook her head. 'I can't yet. Let me get this funeral organised and then I'll see about it.'

Even the way she spoke about Pete's funeral didn't feel right. She was clearly upset but it was as if she was experiencing it through a window. Maybe the best help Caroline could be to her now was to organise the funeral. As soon as it was over, she'd insist Emily make an appointment with her doctor. With any luck, they'd assign someone to keep an eye on her. Then Caroline could walk away with a clear conscience.

CHAPTER SIXTEEN

EMILY

A week later, the bright May morning had disappeared into a grey drizzle by the time of the one o'clock funeral. The service itself had been mercifully brief. Emily had sat in the front row with Pete's friend Steve on one side of her and Pete's mother on the other. She'd invited Caroline to sit there, too, but she hadn't wanted to. Said it wouldn't seem appropriate.

It didn't matter though. At the wake, Caroline may as well have still been married to Pete; she was the one who everyone wanted to talk to. It was a relief, if she was honest. It had been all Emily could do to drag herself out of bed and get dressed. Making conversation with people she barely knew felt impossible right now.

The church hall was across the road from the crematorium. Its walls were bare apart from a couple of framed prints of landscapes and a noticeboard of curled, faded announcements. Emily had found a quiet corner to sit away from the general melee in the centre. The flat was far too small for people to come back to, so Caroline had helped her to organise tea and coffee here. She seemed to have an army of friends willing to pass around sandwiches and lay out tablecloths. They hadn't spoken to Emily other than a nod and a standard 'sorry for your loss'.

Funerals were very strange things. Before the ceremony, everyone had spoken in hushed voices. After, the drink flowed and people laughed and chatted. The first funeral she'd attended had been her grandmother's when she was only fifteen. She hadn't been able to understand the change in mood once the funeral-goers had made it back to her mum's house. 'Why are they laughing?' she'd asked her mum. 'My gran is dead.'

Pete's mother, Iris, sat across from her on a blue plastic chair, a paper plate on her lap with a sausage roll, a triangular egg and cress sandwich and two crisps. She looked a lot older than Emily had expected. Dressed in a short-sleeved black dress, her sensible black shoes pressed together, she sat very straight in her chair. 'When's the baby coming?'

Emily had answered this question so many times today that she wished she'd had it printed on the Order of Service. 'He's due in July.'

'He? You know the sex?' Her face showed her disapproval. 'Takes all the surprise out of it.'

Iris had sat next to her all through the service as rigid as a mannequin. Not once had she said anything that gave comfort or betrayed emotion. And now she was passing comment on the baby. Emily wanted to tell the sour-faced old bat that she'd had enough surprises lately, but she held her tongue. 'Pete was pleased. About him being a boy. We'd been talking about names and stuff.'

Taking the smallest of bites out of her sausage roll, Iris chewed several times before speaking again. 'Well, I'm not going to be able to help you out moneywise, I'm afraid. I've only got my pension.'

Emily's face burned. She'd had no intention of asking for money. They'd already bought most of the things she would need, anyway. Only a handful of weeks ago, Pete had tried to cheer her up by showing her baby clothes websites and taking her shopping for the bigger items. Test-driving prams while providing his own Formula One sound effects. She'd tried to be interested for his sake, but she hadn't done a very good job of it. If only she could go back in time, she would tell him how grateful she was for everything he was doing.

Across the room, she could see Marie, who had briefly introduced herself as the Human Resources manager of the company Pete worked for. She was holding Caroline's hands in hers and speaking earnestly to her. Caroline glanced over in Emily's direction then snapped her eyes back again. What was the woman saying to her?

Iris was watching too while still taking tiny bites from the sausage roll. She seemed to look at Caroline with active dislike. 'Madam over there seems to be taking control of everything. Who's that she's talking to?'

Emily couldn't keep the suspicion from her voice. 'Marie. She worked with Pete. Pete mentioned her once. Said she loves a gossip.'

Iris nodded. 'She looks the type. Well, I'll give Caroline her due, she can work a room. I remember her at Jamie's christening. It was like a royal event. Of course, she must have had it harder with Pete than you did. First wives always do. By the time the second wife gets hold of them, they've already been broken in. Still, I'm not sure I'd be letting her take over like this if I were you.'

Her cruel words stung. Emily didn't want to remind Pete's mother that she hadn't been his wife for very long. It might also remind her that she hadn't been invited to the wedding. 'Caroline knows everyone better than I do. They were married a long time.'

At that, Iris coughed out a dry, derisive laugh. 'I'm not sure I'd be so magnanimous. Anyway, is there no one here that *you've* invited? What about your parents? Have you not invited them?'

All day long, Emily had forced herself not to think about her mother. 'I'm not in contact with my father and I lost my mum a few years ago.'

Iris looked more interested in her than she had all day. 'Cancer?'

God, she's blunt. 'Yes.'

She seemed pleased to be right. 'We lost Pete's father to lung cancer ten years ago. Did he tell you?' She didn't wait for a response. 'He had a terrible time of it. I don't know what's worse: to have to go through a long illness like that but have time to say your goodbyes, or to go suddenly, in an accident.'

Inside her head, Emily was screaming. Why wouldn't Pete's mother just shut up? She was beginning to understand Pete's reluctance to introduce them now. It wasn't that he'd been ashamed of his younger girlfriend; it was that he'd wanted to protect her from this woman's cruel cynicism.

A wave at the door caught her eye. Amy. She had come. Emily's grateful heart rose at the sight of her friend. She smiled at Iris. 'Can you excuse me for a moment.' And she walked to meet her friend halfway.

Amy held out her arms as soon as she saw her. 'I hope it was okay for me to come.'

'Of course. It's great to see you.'

'I'm so sorry, Emily.'

Emily nodded. 'I know. Thanks. It's been really tough.'

Amy released her from the tight hug she'd held her in but took one of Emily's hands in hers and squeezed it. 'Not just about Pete. I'm sorry for the way I spoke to you. On the phone. I was a total bitch and I'm so sorry.'

Emily didn't care about any of that now. She was just grateful to have Amy here. 'It's okay.'

'No. It's really not. I'm supposed to be your friend. I think it was just... jealousy. It felt like you had everything I wanted. Well, the baby mainly. I was totally jealous and I wasn't in a very good place emotionally.'

The relief of having Amy here with her, her friend, washed over Emily. In a sea of unfriendly faces, Amy's smile was a lifeboat. She could tell Amy how she was feeling, explain that, actually, she shouldn't be jealous of Emily at all. She was miserable, lost and unhappy. But now she had a friend who she could talk to about that.

Amy was smiling at her. 'I think the reason that I was so emotional was my hormones. They were all over the place. But now... well... the thing is... now I'm pregnant too.'

Emily's heart almost stopped. She was glad for her friend, of course she was. Amy had wanted this for so long.

How could she tell her about the darkness in her head while she was so happy? How could she burst her bubble of joy by telling her that not all pregnant women celebrated the idea of growing another life inside them?

Amy could obviously see the shock on her face. 'Sorry. I shouldn't be talking about this at Pete's funeral. I'm being totally insensitive. I wasn't even going to say anything today, but it just kind of fell out of my mouth.'

Emily pressed out a smile. 'Of course, it did. Don't apologise. I'm so pleased for you, really, I am. You deserve this, Amy.'

Amy pulled her into another awkward hug, so she wouldn't have seen the pain that crossed Emily's face over her shoulder. 'You'll get through this, Em, I know you will. I'll be there to help you. We should even be on maternity leave for a bit together.'

Emily knew that she meant it. But the question was: did she want her there? Could she bear to see Amy enjoying every moment of her longed-for pregnancy while she felt more and more like this was the worst possible thing that could be happening right now?

CHAPTER SEVENTEEN

CAROLINE

Faith's house was always meticulously tidy, so it was amusing to see the bedroom looking like a Boy Scout jumble sale.

'So, you're saying that some of Pete's money will come to you because you're still named on the paperwork?' Faith was flicking through her wardrobe. Caroline had come to hers for the evening to help her pack for her weekend away with the new man.

Caroline shook her head at the maxi dress that Faith was holding up. 'It's nice, but you'll trip over the hem and fall head first into the canal. And yes, that's what Marie, the woman from his human resources department, said.'

She'd actually made Caroline quite uncomfortable at the funeral with her exhortations to call her on Monday at the office so they could go through it all.

'She seemed to almost relish the idea that Pete's pension might automatically come to me rather than Emily. It was as if she hated her.'

Faith tilted her head and raised an eyebrow. 'Whereas we obviously love the woman who is having your ex-husband's baby?'

It had been a week since the funeral and Caroline still couldn't get her head around Pete being gone. When you didn't see someone every day, it was easy to pretend that nothing had changed. When she thought about it, there was a dull ache of loss that she couldn't shift. But it wasn't the same as her grief for Jamie: it was more complex than that. She started to refold some of the discarded items of clothing on the bed. 'Do you miss yours?'

Faith frowned. 'My what?'

'Your ex-husband, Richard. Do you miss him?'

Faith snorted. 'Other than when I need a jar opened or a spider caught, you mean?'

'Seriously.'

Faith sat down on the bed. 'I don't know. Maybe sometimes. When it's just me at home and the kids are out and something comes on the TV that we used to watch together. But that's memories of what it used to be like. Not what it was like in those last couple of years when the armchair was practically moulded to the shape of his backside. I was so bored of him. So fed up of being the one who had to suggest doing anything. Laying out options of where to go for dinner or who we could visit like a menu for him to peruse.'

'Was he shocked? When you left?'

'He said he was, but I don't know why. It wasn't as if I hadn't been saying for years that I wanted to do more together. He got old before his time and I couldn't think about another thirty years of me begging him for attention.'

Caroline wondered if that was where she and Pete would have got to, even if Jamie hadn't died. When Jamie went to university, their life became so quiet. Pete worked such long hours. She hadn't noticed it so much when Jamie was there. But with him gone, she'd ended up having dinner alone most evenings. They'd still loved each other, didn't argue, but it had been dull. Then Jamie had died and she would have sold her soul to go back to dull.

Faith was watching her face. 'How are you feeling about Pete? It must be very strange.'

'Yes, it is. I mean, we weren't together obviously, but he was my husband for a long time.' She'd never told her friends how she'd been feeling just before Pete's death. It wasn't as if they'd judge her – they'd all been pals far too long for that. It was more that she judged herself. 'I did sometimes wonder if I'd done the right thing in asking him to leave.'

Faith nodded slowly. 'It was a terrible thing to go through and he was making it harder for you. You did what you needed to do at the time.'

Her grief had been so big, it was impossible to see anything else. From the minute she would wake in the morning, it would be there: pushing into her, surrounding, suffocating. And, yes, Pete had just made it worse and it was too much. He had been too much.

Staring down at a short-sleeved cardigan on the bed, she started to fasten the row of tiny buttons. 'I saw him that day – the day of his accident. He'd come to the house and I was so angry. I lost my temper with him. Told him to get out.' It was a relief to say this out loud. Ever since that night in the hospital, it had been going around and around her head like a loop. She couldn't tell Emily because then she would have to explain what her husband had been doing at his ex-wife's house. And why she had been so upset with him.

Faith frowned. 'I thought he'd asked you about the house on the phone?'

Caroline chewed at her lip. 'That's what I said because I felt a fool for letting him in again. I didn't want you and Gabby to think I was an idiot.'

Faith reached for her arm. 'Hey. You know we wouldn't judge you. We might tell you off, but we don't judge.' She narrowed her eyes. 'Please don't tell me that you're feeling guilty? None of this is your fault, Caroline.'

'I wonder if… if he was upset and wasn't paying attention to the road. He was such a good driver usually. I can't understand how it could have happened.'

'It was an accident. The police have confirmed that. There were witnesses to that other car driving erratically. They found it burned out. Kids. Joyriders. It's their fault, no one else's. And definitely not yours.'

She nodded. Faith was right, but she still felt uneasy. And Marie's words at the funeral had only compounded her feelings of responsibility. 'It's not right though, is it? If they try and give me money from Pete's pension? I mean, we weren't still married. He just hadn't got around to changing the names. Surely there are laws about that?'

Faith shrugged. 'You were together a long time, though. You should get the house outright, for a start.'

Maybe Faith wasn't the right person to speak to about this. Her divorce from Richard had turned pretty acrimonious. 'I don't know, Faith. It's not sitting right with me. She's having a baby.'

Faith got up and continued rummaging in her wardrobe. 'I'm not suggesting you see the woman out on the street. But this may mean you can keep the house. You won't have to move.'

It would be a huge relief if she could stay in their family home. 'I think we have insurances for that, anyway. We both had life assurance policies that would pay off the mortgage. But with Emily having Pete's child, I'm sure she or the baby will qualify as next of kin over me?' It was strange thinking of Emily's baby in this way. As a real person rather than a concept.

'Probably. I mean, if they try and give his money to you, she'll probably contest it anyway.'

The way Emily had looked at the funeral, Caroline didn't think she'd have the strength to contest the wrong price on a shopping receipt. Since then, Caroline hadn't been able to stop thinking about her. How tired she'd looked. How lonely. If Marie had been right and all the pensions and benefits would come to her, she had a duty to make sure that provisions were made for his son. Once she had all the information, she'd arrange to visit Emily and discuss a fair share for both of them. She owed that to Pete.

At the end of the funeral, she had insisted that Emily go home and leave the clearing up to her. It had been a relief that a friend of hers had turned up and offered to drive Emily home, although where had this Amy person been hiding all this time when Emily had needed her? When Amy had popped to the toilet, Caroline had taken the opportunity to speak to Emily alone.

'Are you going to be okay? Tonight, I mean.'

'Yes. Amy will take me home. Thanks for everything today. I couldn't have done all this.'

She'd waved an arm to encompass the hall, empty apart from Faith and Gabby ambling around filling large black bags with used paper plates and cups. If Emily's friend Amy was anything like Caroline's pals, she'd get her through.

Emily wasn't Caroline's responsibility, but the image of her at her flat, surrounded by mess, had played on her mind. 'And you'll talk to your midwife? About getting some support?'

Emily had looked irritated, glancing towards the toilets where her friend was. Maybe she had been thinking the same, that she wanted Caroline to keep her nose out of her business. 'Yes. If I need to, I will.'

Amy had reappeared then, said a brief goodbye and the two of them had left.

Faith was holding a swimsuit at arm's length and looking at it as if it had done something terrible to her in the past. 'Do you think I need to take one of these? I mean, you don't swim in the canal or anything when you're on a narrowboat, do you?'

Caroline laughed. 'Not unless you're a duck, no. I think you can safely put that back in the drawer.'

'Thank goodness.' Faith threw it on the bed. 'So, when will you go to see Emily about the money? Do you want me to come with you?'

'No. I'll be fine. I think it'll take a couple of weeks or so before the information comes through, anyway. It's not urgent, so I'll leave it a while for the dust to settle before calling her. Then I can just pop round to the flat again to go through everything.'

Hopefully, by then, Emily might feel a little bit more like herself. Now the funeral was out of the way, she could take some time to process everything that had happened, and her friend, or the midwife, or whoever she had spoken to would have started the support she clearly needed. Caroline knew better than anyone that Emily's real grieving would only just be beginning.

CHAPTER EIGHTEEN

EMILY

Caroline's call about Pete's money had come out of the blue yesterday. Emily hadn't even considered that there would be life insurance and pensions to sort through: it had been traumatic enough thinking about taking Pete's name off the joint bank account they used for their mortgage and household bills.

In the six weeks since the funeral, she'd just become more and more tired. No one at work had given her a deadline to return. When one of the PAs had called a couple of weeks ago to see how she was, she got the feeling that they were tentatively asking when she would be ready to come back. When she'd said she wasn't ready, they'd been so kind. Had gently suggested that Emily speak to her doctor, get signed off for a while longer. Even until her maternity leave started if she needed to. At thirty-five weeks, she didn't have long to go anyway. She knew she would have to do one or the other – see the doctor or return to work – but she couldn't work out what would be worse. Amy had continued to call and check on her, too, but Emily didn't have the energy to meet up with her either, so she'd managed to persuade her that she was doing okay.

But she wasn't. She spent her days dragging fatigue around like a heavy coat, only leaving the flat to buy convenience food in individual-sized portions. When she opened the fridge door, the stack of plastic tubs sitting in judgement made her feel even worse: Pete had been such a fanatic about cooking everything from scratch. Often, the only time she wasn't tired was in her actual bed at night. She'd tried reading or watching TV until her eyelids grew heavy. But as soon as she closed her eyes, her brain would reawaken and start running its own filmstrip of misery. Instead, she napped in the day, having hauled her duvet and pillow from the bedroom onto the couch. She was practically nocturnal.

But now Caroline was coming and she needed to hold it together for the hour or so she would be here. She'd taken the bedding back to her room and picked up the empty food wrappers from the floor. As she did so, irritation bubbled at the fact she was tidying up for Pete's ex-wife. Why did she have to come here rather than just tell Emily what she needed to know over the phone? Emily had been grateful to have her with her at the hospital and she had been great at helping to arrange the funeral. But Emily had seen a different side to her at the wake. Pete's mum was a miserable old woman, but she'd been right about Caroline taking over. As far as anyone there was concerned, it was Caroline who deserved their sympathy. The abandoned wife of over twenty years. Not the young replacement who'd managed to get herself knocked up, probably just to keep her man. Didn't they know that it was Caroline who had asked Pete to leave?

In the kitchen, she stuffed the food wrappings into a bin that needed emptying. Did she even have any milk in the house to make Caroline a cup of tea? She couldn't face going out to the nearest shop to get any. Would it be strange to ask her to bring some? She'd get dressed then think about it.

A glance in the bedroom mirror made it clear she had bigger issues than tea to deal with. Caroline would probably take one look at her greasy hair and blotchy face and call social services in. With that thought came another – wasn't Caroline a social worker? Or she once had been? Emily's heart started to race. Caroline was due here in twenty minutes, and going by Pete's description of her uptight attitudes, she was definitely the sort of person to be here right on schedule. Did she have time for a bath? A shower would be faster, but theirs – *hers* – was over the bath and her growing bump made her anxious about losing balance. She'd have to be quick.

After she'd turned both taps to full, Emily sat on the toilet seat and watched the water tumble into the bath. Years ago, this was how women performed backstreet abortions. Hot baths, gin, knitting needles. It wasn't rocket science why so many desperate women lost their lives. Going back further in history, even those who made it the full nine months didn't have a great success rate. Childbirth was a common killer. Emily had none of that to worry about. The National Health Service would take good care of her and her child. So why was she feeling like this?

Caroline would be here in fifteen minutes, so she couldn't wait any longer to get in the bath. She pulled her pyjama top over her head, stepped out of the bottoms, got in carefully. A slip in the bath could have disastrous consequences. Like a film clip on fast-forward, she saw herself slip, thudding onto her back, hitting her head, losing consciousness... *No. No.* She shook the thought away. *Must stop thinking in catastrophes.*

The water level rose as she got in but it still wasn't deep enough to cover her stomach, which poked out of the water like a desert island. She let her head fall back. Eyes closed. Tried to breathe. Concentrated on the sound of the water from the tap. *Focus. Focus.*

But she couldn't. The feelings were dragging her under, whirling around her head. Over and over in her mind. How could she live without Pete? How was she going to raise this baby alone?

She slipped down further into the bath. If it had been deep enough, she would have liked to slip beneath the surface, blocking out everything else.

The doorbell rang. Caroline must be early. Why was she early? Was she trying to catch Emily out? Emily pushed herself back up. She needed to get out of the bath. Not easy in a hurry at thirty-five weeks pregnant. She pushed herself up onto her knees. Maybe that would be easier?

The doorbell rang again.

'Give me a damn minute!' There was no way Caroline could hear her, but the shout made her feel better for a few seconds. All she needed to do was get out of the bath. From her kneeling position, she dragged one leg up so that her foot was flat on the floor of the bath. Then the next one. She could do this.

The doorbell rang a third time.

Emily wanted to scream. *Give me a bloody break!* She stepped out of the bath.

Maybe there was water on the floor. Maybe she hadn't put her foot down at the right angle. It all happened too fast for her to know. Her left leg slid out in front of her, and she couldn't lift the right one out of the bath quick enough to right herself. She fell hard into the wall, her shoulder, her side, then onto the floor.

For a few moments, she just lay there. Was she okay? There was numbness in her hip, but she hadn't knocked her bump, had she? Her chest hurt, but that might have been because her breath was coming in short gasps.

In the lounge, she could hear her mobile begin to ring. Caroline must have been wondering where the hell she was.

Now the initial shock was over, the danger she might have just put the baby in began to dawn on her. She put a hand on her stomach. 'I'm sorry, baby. I'm sorry.' She started to cry.

The phone kept ringing. She pulled herself up, her wet hair dripping down her back. She pulled a towelling robe from the back of the door. It was Pete's. The smell of his aftershave on it was so strong that she felt the ache of missing him and her tears fell faster.

Somehow, she stumbled to the front door. Wiping furiously at her nose with the cuff of Pete's robe, she opened it to Caroline's back, her mobile phone pressed to her ear. Caroline turned in surprise when the door opened and her eyes widened when she saw the wet, bedraggled Emily in front of her.

'Oh! I thought you weren't in. Sorry, I was calling to see if I'd missed you.'

Caroline looked so well put together, so smart and serene. She must have been looking at Emily and thinking, *What the hell did he see in you?*

'I was in the bath.'

'I see. Do you want me to come back later? Another time?'

How would that help? Better to just get whatever it was over with. 'No, come in. I'll go and get dressed.' There was no point now trying to pretend that everything was okay. Caroline could think what the hell she liked. She just wanted to get rid of her so that she could climb into bed and pull the duvet over her head.

'Emily?'

Caroline's voice sounded urgent. When Emily turned back, Caroline was staring at her legs, her face white.

'Emily. You're bleeding.'

CHAPTER NINETEEN

CAROLINE

That familiar hospital smell – disinfectant, reheated food, fear – hit Caroline as she helped Emily through the heavy double doors onto the shiny floor of Accident and Emergency. Her stomach lurched and she squeezed the hand that wasn't around Emily's back into a fist. How were they back here again so soon?

Within seconds of seeing the blood trickling down the inside of Emily's calf, they'd made a decision that Caroline would get her here quicker than if they called an ambulance. Actually, Caroline had decided; Emily had been almost catatonic, her eyes wide in absolute terror. Her voice had been barely audible as Caroline guided her into the car, trying to be both fast and gentle at the same time. The whole way here, Caroline had tried to soothe her, telling her not to panic, it was going to be okay, but Emily had folded in on herself, repeating the same word over and over: 'Please. Please. Please.'

The receptionist was an angel with red hair and a nose ring. As soon as Caroline explained that Emily had fallen, was thirty-five weeks pregnant and bleeding, she rushed them through another set of doors and in front of a doctor. When Caroline tried to take a step back, Emily gripped her arm like a drowning woman. 'Please. Please stay with me. I'm sorry. But please. Please don't go.'

The doctor spoke directly to Emily in soothing tones. 'It's fine for your friend to stay. But you are going to have to let go, Emily. I need to examine you and check how your baby is doing.'

Caroline almost laughed. Friend? If he only knew. Although, it *was* the second time she'd been to this very same hospital with Emily in the last couple of months. She shivered.

Slowly, Emily unclenched her hand and released Caroline's fingers. Her eyes were still wide and terrified as they held Caroline in their beam. 'Don't leave, please don't leave.'

Caroline swallowed. 'It's okay, I'll be right here. I won't go anywhere, I promise.'

Whatever their history, she would have to be a monster to walk out and leave Emily here alone. And that was without the nagging thought chewing at the back of her brain that Emily had fallen because she was rushing to answer the door to her. Emily wasn't her favourite person by far, but she didn't deserve this. And the baby definitely didn't. Hadn't they suffered enough?

Please let her be okay.

The doctor squeezed gel onto Emily's stomach and used a doppler to locate the baby's heartbeat. He'd already asked the nurse to fetch the portable scanner. It felt like just a moment – and a thousand years – ago that Caroline had been the one on the table, waiting to give birth.

She'd fallen pregnant quickly with Jamie and he had been such an easy baby. She and Pete had still been able to eat out, go away for weekends, even take luxury holidays: Jamie just came along with them. She'd loved every minute of being his mum, but they'd decided to wait a few years before trying for a brother or sister, reasoning that two young children might not be such an easy proposition.

However, nothing had happened. She had only been in her early thirties and there was no reason why she shouldn't fall pregnant again. But it just didn't happen.

It became a bit of an obsession. She used an ovulation predictor kit, they had sex to a timetable, then she was devastated every month when the second blue line refused to appear on the pregnancy test. They started to discuss fertility treatment, but the waiting lists where they lived were desperately long. The fact she already had a child counted against her. After a heartbreaking discussion, they decided to be grateful for the son they had and enjoy being a family of three. She had been sad about it, of course she had. But it was also a relief to make the decision. She could focus on Jamie and enjoy her son.

After what felt like a lifetime, the doctor smiled at Emily. 'I can hear the baby's heartbeat. That's great news, Mrs Simmons.'

Emily's breath was ragged. 'Does that mean he's going to be okay?'

They were interrupted by the arrival of the mobile scanner. 'Let's have a look at him, shall we?'

He turned the screen so that neither Emily nor Caroline could see it, and pressed the scanner onto Emily's stomach. No one spoke a word. Eventually, he nodded as he watched the screen. 'Okay. The good news is that the baby is wriggling around, but his heart rate is a little erratic. I can also see a large placental abruption which must be what's causing the bleeding.'

Caroline stepped forwards to ask what that meant and then stopped herself: it wasn't her place to ask.

'Is that dangerous?' Emily's voice trembled. This time Caroline did step forwards. She took Emily's hand in hers and faced the doctor.

'Normally, we would keep you in, just observe for a while, then send you home to rest. But the baby's heart rate is a concern. Hopefully, it will settle back down, but if it doesn't, my advice is that we deliver your baby today.' He glanced at Caroline and then back to Emily. 'Is there anyone you need to call?'

Caroline squeezed Emily's hand for what she knew was coming. Emily shook her head. 'No. My husband passed away recently.'

The doctor's face turned a shade lighter, but he kept his professional composure. 'I'm very sorry for your loss. We'll leave this portable monitor on you for now until we can get you onto a ward. Please call someone or hit the alarm if you feel any pain or anything that worries you.' He looked at Caroline. 'Anything at all.'

The curtain swished closed and Emily started to cry. 'It's all my fault. I slipped getting out of the bath. I should have been more careful. It's all my fault.'

'It was an accident, Emily. It's not your fault.' Again, the idea that it had actually been *her* fault for getting there early twittered in Caroline's ear. 'The doctor said that the baby is okay.'

'He said he *seemed* okay. But if he wants to observe me, he must be thinking something is going to go wrong. What is going to happen? What's going wrong?'

Caroline recognised this spiral of anxiety and it wasn't going to do the baby any good. She scraped a plastic chair across the floor so that she could sit close to Emily. 'Listen. Thirty-five weeks is practically a full-term pregnancy. Even if they have to deliver the baby now, he'll be okay.'

Emily chewed at her lip. 'Dylan. We hadn't decided, but Pete wanted to call him Dylan.'

A sharp shard sliced across Caroline's heart. That was one of the names Pete had touted for Jamie twenty-one years ago. His love of Bob Dylan had clearly been one of the things that had never changed. She pushed the jealousy aside and focused on the frightened woman in front of her. 'Dylan is going to be fine. Just try and focus on that. You are going to be a mum.'

After Jamie died, Caroline's counsellor had suggested she attend a group for bereaved parents. It had helped to talk and listen to other mothers and fathers. To realise that the feelings of guilt and anger and helplessness were normal. But everyone there had had other children. Other sons or daughters to cling to. Over and again, she heard people confess that it was only their other kids who had kept them putting one foot in front of the other each day. The only people in their life that gave them something to smile about. These people were still mothers and fathers. But she and Pete had lost their only child. They weren't parents anymore. How does someone get over that?

'Ouch.' Emily winced; her hand flew to her right side. 'Something hurts.'

Caroline hit the call button in the cubicle, then pulled open the curtain and called to the nurse in a pale blue uniform who was updating something on a computer screen. 'Nurse? Can you help, please? She's in pain. Can you come?'

The nurse was there in three long strides.

Now Emily was doubled over on the bed. 'What's going on? Am I in labour? Something really hurts.'

The nurse was calm and controlled. 'It seems as if you might be, my love. Let's check you over.'

The doctor appeared at the other side of her bed, checking the heart rate monitor with a concerned look on his face. 'Okay, Emily, we are going to take you upstairs now. The baby's heart rate has dropped and we need to get him out as quickly as we can, which means a C-section. I'd like to get you up to theatre now. Is that okay, Emily?'

He kept his voice smooth, but Caroline could see the concern on his face.

'Can Caroline come?' They were pushing the sides up on her bed and wheeling her away.

'I'm afraid not.' The doctor continued his explanation, but they pushed Emily away too quickly for Caroline to hear what he said.

The nurse in the blue uniform was still beside her. 'You can't be with her because they are likely going to need to do a general anaesthetic. It'll be the quickest way to get the baby out safely. I'll show you where you can wait.'

CHAPTER TWENTY

EMILY

The wheels of the trolley rattled as they hurtled out of A & E and down a corridor. People turned, stood back, watched as the doctor and a different nurse and possibly some other people pushed Emily past. Hot and sharp, the pain in her side was getting worse. Alongside the tearing, a cramping had started, low down. She gripped the sides of the bed which the nurse had flipped up before they'd moved, the metal cold and solid in her hand. Tried to breathe. To will her body to behave.

This wasn't going to end well. She just knew it.

The nurse patted the top of her knuckles, her voice strident and bright. 'We'll be there soon, Emily. Everything is going to be okay.'

She was doing her best to reassure her, but even from below, Emily could see the expressions on their faces. The tone of their mutual glances. Onwards, click-clacking over the seams in the floor, she watched the strip lights on the ceiling travel past like white lines on a motorway. She pressed down with her elbows, tried to push her head off the bed, but the pain made her gasp. 'Is he okay? Is the baby going to be okay?'

She didn't care about herself, didn't care about the pain. Maybe she had this coming. Maybe they'd both had it coming, her and Pete. But none of this was the baby's fault. He needed to be okay. They had to make him safe. *A mother will sacrifice anything for her child.*

The doctor tipped his face downwards for a brief moment while still looking in a forward direction. 'We can still hear his heartbeat. It's nice and strong. He's going to be with you really shortly.'

A metallic ring sounded – a lift door had appeared and they wheeled her into it. The nurse was checking something; the doctor was speaking quietly to her. Another ring and the lift doors rattled open. She was on the move again.

Another searing pain. She started to cry. 'Please, please save my baby.'

'We're nearly there, Emily. Nearly there.'

People were talking above her, now she was in a small room, another doctor was talking to her. Everything was happening in slow motion. As if the air were thick like water. And she was drowning.

'Help us, please. Please, help my baby.'

Could they hear her?

'It's okay, Emily. We've got you. Just relax now.' This was another voice. Where had the nurse gone?

In the middle of all the pain and uncertainty, one thought was crystal-clear. She grabbed someone's arm. 'Give him to Caroline. If anything happens to me, give him to Caroline.'

Were they even listening to her? Could she be heard? The voice just kept speaking. 'You need to let go of me, now. Everything is going to be okay. You're going to feel a sharp scratch and then I'd like you to count down from ten.'

Like sand through an hourglass, she felt herself slipping away. Her tongue could barely form the words. 'The baby's name is Dylan. Please tell Caroline not to forget. His name is Dylan.'

Then everything went dark.

CHAPTER TWENTY-ONE

CAROLINE

As they'd wheeled Emily away, her face had been terrified, haunted even. What else could Caroline do except promise to stay until she came round?

The kind young nurse showed her to a room where she could wait. Fear, guilt and shock sat on her shoulders as she perched on one of the square armchairs with her face in the palms of her hands and wept. When there was nothing left to cry, she wiped at her face with a tissue from a box on the small coffee table and watched the clock on the wall: its hands moved painfully slowly. How could this be happening? *Please God, let this baby be okay.*

Years ago, expectant fathers would sit in a room like this, waiting for news of their child's birth. When Jamie had been born, Pete hadn't stopped moving around: holding her hand and kissing her head one minute; darting down to the 'business' end the next and giving her excited updates. 'I can see a head. There's a head, Caro!'

She could remember the midwife's sardonic response: 'Well, that's a bonus.'

Pete should be here. He should be in that room seeing his son being born. What was wrong with the world? Why the hell had the universe taken this baby's father before he'd even taken his first breath? There were thousands of fathers out there who didn't even deserve the name. Fathers who beat their kids, or worse. Why take one of the good ones? Pete – for all his apparent faults as a husband – had been a good dad. And Dylan would never, ever know that. Never get to have his dad teach him to swim or ride a bike or…

She'd thought she'd cried herself dry, but she was wrong.

After what seemed like days, a nurse appeared at the door, holding a white bundle. 'Well, here he is. Mum made me promise to bring him out to you as soon as I could.'

Caroline stood up and tried to read the nurse's face. 'Is Emily okay?'

The nurse nodded. 'She's absolutely fine. They'll be taking her into recovery shortly and then you can go and see her.' She smiled down at the baby in her arms. 'And you can meet your mummy, little man.'

All that Caroline could see of him was the hospital blanket. She took a step towards them and then stopped. 'Is *he* okay?'

The nurse laughed and tilted the bundle towards her. 'Come and see for yourself. Do you have a sleepsuit for him?'

Caroline remembered spending hours deliberating Jamie's first outfit. Pete had laughed at her. *I don't think the baby will care.* But it had felt terribly important. 'No, I… we… It was all a bit of a rush.'

'Not a problem. We have some emergency ones here.' The nurse opened a cupboard on the wall and nodded to the changing table in the corner. 'Would you like to dress him?'

Caroline was surprised to be asked. It felt momentous and intimate somehow. Maybe they thought she and Emily were partners. 'No. Can you do it?'

The nurse laid him on the table and deftly swept him out of the blanket and into the sleepsuit in about three moves. Caroline caught sight of his body, so fragile and vulnerable. Had Jamie ever been that small? He'd been a hefty ten-pound baby, moving into three-month-sized clothes in a matter of days. 'How much does he weigh?'

'Five pounds, two ounces. Which is very respectable considering he was five weeks early. We've checked him over and he's absolutely fine, no need to go to the special care baby unit. There you go, little boy. Does he have a name yet?'

'Dylan. She wants to call him Dylan.'

'Well, then, Dylan. Why don't I hand you over to...' She looked up at Caroline.

It took Caroline a couple of beats to realise that the nurse expected her to insert her name. And also to take the baby. 'Caroline. Maybe you should take him straight back to Emily.'

'She's not awake yet. But before we put her under anaesthetic, she was pretty insistent that I bring him straight to you when he was born. She nearly had the anaesthetist by the throat.' She laughed.

Caroline wasn't surprised that Emily had been so insistent, having lost someone in this hospital already. She looked at the bundle in the nurse's arms. Leaning but not taking a step forwards. Was this what she had become? Scared to even hold a newborn baby?

Expertly, the nurse cradled his head in one hand and his bottom in the other so that she could transfer him to Caroline's arms with ease. As his head touched the inside of her elbow, Caroline sighed involuntarily. There was something in the weight and warmth of him, resting on her inner arm, that took her back twenty-one years. She couldn't take her eyes from him. This tiny, red, crumpled human being who had no idea about the pain he had just caused his mother.

'Hello, Dylan. Nice to meet you.'

The nurse seemed satisfied that she had completed her mission. 'I'll just go and see how his mum is doing and come back to you shortly.'

Caroline was barely aware of her leaving. She raised her arm so that she could see Dylan more clearly. Did she want to see Jamie in him or not? Was it possible to want it and hate the idea at the same time? He frowned in his sleep and the recognition almost made her gasp. The crease at the top of his nose was exactly like Pete's. It was so sad that this boy wouldn't know his father.

That newborn-baby smell. If you could bottle it, you'd make a fortune. She stroked his cheek with her finger, his skin softer than tissue. His mouth moved as if he were imagining suckling in his sleep. Wasn't it amazing how babies knew how to do everything from the moment they were born? She remembered watching Jamie for hours when he was a baby. Just staring at him in his cot.

It felt like only moments later that the nurse reappeared. 'Mum is awake. Would you like to come through with him?'

That was a step too far. It was bad enough that Caroline had met Emily's son before she had. 'No. I think you should just take him. I'll go down to the shop and pick up some things that she'll need.'

An hour later, Caroline, Emily and Dylan were back on the maternity ward. Dylan looked so tiny in the plastic crib, his face a screwed-up raspberry, lost in his sleepsuit and the white cap and tiny yellow scratch mittens which Caroline had picked up in the hospital shop. Even with his head halfway down the mattress, his feet didn't reach the end. His knees tucked into his stomach as if he were still inside his mother.

After a brief, awkward conversation, Caroline disappeared to the toilet, just for something to do. Before she'd got back, Emily had fallen asleep and it was the perfect opportunity for Caroline to slip out and leave her to it. The baby was fine, Emily was fine, and it wasn't as if Caroline was responsible for either of them. And yet, she couldn't leave. The tiny human being in the clear plastic cot seemed to be exerting a force over her: she couldn't stop looking at him.

She'd forgotten how much newborns slept in the first few days. When Jamie had been born, she'd been so smug about how easy he was. Her own mother had laughed and told her to wait and see. She hadn't been wrong. Once he'd shrugged off the exhaustion – or hormones – of being born, he more than made up for it with a vociferous objection to any kind of suggestion of sleep. At least she'd had Pete, or her mother, in whose arms she could thrust him so that she could get a few hours' uninterrupted rest.

Beneath the edge of the cap, Dylan's eyelashes fluttered. Jamie used to do that too. She and Pete would watch him as he slept, wondering what he was dreaming about. Could Dylan remember being in the womb where he was safe? Did he miss it?

A rattle of a tea trolley appeared around the corner. 'Hello. Can I get either of you a cup of tea?'

Caroline glanced at Emily. She was still sound asleep. 'I think we're okay, thanks.'

'Are you sure? I've got Hobnobs.' The tea lady leaned in to look at Dylan. 'He's a handsome lad. Does he have a name yet?'

It didn't feel right speaking on Emily's behalf. Telling the nurse was one thing, but what could she say without seeming rude? 'Dylan. His mum is going to call him Dylan.'

'Lovely. Has she had anything to eat yet?'

'She's had some toast and some water.'

'And what about you?'

'Me? I need to make a move soon, anyway.'

'Well, why don't I make you a drink before you go?'

Trying to argue with this woman was like trying to get out of her mother's house without a cardigan on. 'A black coffee would be great, thanks.'

The tea lady left a cup and saucer on the table which had been pushed to the end of Emily's bed. The rattle of the tea cups as she bumped her trolley out of the ward must have woken the baby and he started to mew like a kitten, pushing his legs and waving his tiny fists.

Caroline leaned over the crib and gently rubbed his tummy. 'Hey, little man. Everything is all right.'

If anything, he started to cry louder and she looked at Emily to see if she was going to wake up and tend to her son. When she didn't move, she glanced around for a nurse, but there was no one about. Should she just pick him up?

Loud and insistent, the poor little thing was really working himself up into an angry fit now. If he was hungry, there'd be nothing she could do, but maybe he just needed a cuddle. She reached out to Emily's shoulder and pulled on it. 'Emily. The baby needs you.'

She must have been exhausted because she didn't even stir. Caroline had barely slept for the first six months of Jamie's life. He only had to breathe differently and she was out of bed and by his side.

Emily had had a tough time of it though and she'd also had a general anaesthetic. Maybe it was better to let her sleep. She reached into the cot and picked up Dylan. She could feel the vibrations of his cries start to slow and soften as she laid him on her chest and rubbed his back. *It all comes back so quickly.*

One of the midwives on the ward stuck her head round the corner. 'Everything okay?' She smiled at Dylan. 'He's gorgeous. And I don't say that about all of them, believe me.'

She wouldn't get any argument from Caroline. He was a very handsome little boy. 'I'm just glad they are both all right.'

The midwife smiled. 'It's great that you were there for her. Have you been friends a long time?'

Friends? How did she even begin to answer that question? Sticking to the facts was probably best. 'We've actually only known each other for a short while.'

The midwife looked surprised but clearly knew better than to pry. Midwives must see all manner of situations coming through the ward. Although being the birthing partner of her dead ex-husband's second wife must surely rank pretty highly. If she wasn't so tired, she might laugh. Or cry.

Dylan did start to cry again. Stronger and throatier this time.

'Poor mite, he might want feeding again,' the midwife reached out and stroked his cheek. 'We'll wake up Mum and get some more skin-to-skin contact going too. It's even more important to get that after a C-section. For Mum as much as Baby.' She hesitated. There was clearly something else she wanted to say. 'If she's on her own, she'll need some help at home for the first week at least.'

Caroline nodded. Emily had seemed to be struggling before today. How was she going to be now he was here? Especially as she wouldn't be as mobile for a few days at least. How would she cope?

Caroline looked at Dylan. Whatever history she had with his mother and father wasn't his fault. 'Looks like I might have to hang around for a while, if that's okay with you?'

While the midwife gently woke Emily, Caroline lay Dylan back in the crook of her arm, his head on her elbow, ready to hand him over to be fed. Even with his face screwed up like that, he looked like Pete. Like Jamie. His thick dark hair and the width of his nose. From nowhere, she felt a rush of love so strong it almost took her breath away. Whatever Emily needed for this little one, she would do her best to provide. She would look after them both.

CHAPTER TWENTY-TWO

EMILY

This end of the maternity ward had only four beds and one was empty. At visiting time, according to the red and white sign on the wall, there were only supposed to be two visitors to each bed, but the rules seemed to be relaxed as long as people kept their voices down. Emily was the only person on her own.

It was difficult to keep her gaze away from the bed opposite. The mother was younger than her, maybe late twenties, and this must have been her second baby because her visitors were a man and a small boy. She'd watched as 'the baby' had given the boy a gift and he'd been more interested in the toy train than in the new sibling they were waving under his nose. The man and woman kept smiling at each other; he couldn't stop touching her, making her comfortable, pressing his lips to the top of her head. Her face radiated joy as she watched her small son and the new baby together. Complete.

What would Pete be doing now if he were here? Would he have arrived with a huge bunch of flowers? Scooped up Dylan and kissed her on the cheek? It wouldn't have been his first time as a father either. How had he been when Jamie was born?

A large brown bag appeared around the corner. From behind it, Caroline's face peeked out. 'Hi. How are you feeling?'

Emily pulled the bedsheet to cover her bare legs. 'Oh, hi. Yeah, I'm okay. I didn't know you were coming in.'

After yesterday, the dash to the hospital, clutching Caroline's arm in A & E, then seeing her straight after the birth: it had all been so intimate. And now she was back to being just Caroline again. Pete's first wife. A virtual stranger. Emily had never actually had a drunken one-night stand, but she could imagine that this weirdness might be what the morning after would feel like.

'Well, I hadn't actually planned to come back so soon, to be honest. But I was in Waitrose and I thought I could pick you up some fruit and other bits. I smelled the food on the trolley when I left yesterday and I wouldn't feed that to a dog.'

Caroline's unexpected kindness made the tears come. Emily had done nothing to deserve this. How could she find the words to say all that she wanted to? 'Thanks so much for being with me yesterday. I don't think I'd have coped otherwise.'

Caroline started to unpack the bag onto the side table. 'I didn't have much choice. They had to peel your fingers off me to get you into bed.'

Emily felt her cheeks burn at the memory. 'I'm sorry. I was just...'

Caroline smiled. 'I'm teasing. There was no way I would have left you on your own. Have you been out of bed?'

'Yes. They like you to move around as much as possible. It helps the healing. I've got a leaflet somewhere about what I can and can't do. No ironing, apparently, so that's not a huge loss.' The ward sister had almost bullied her into the shower this morning. *You'll feel so much better once you're clean.* Shuffling along the ward like an old woman, holding onto her stomach, she hadn't relished the idea of trying to get undressed and redressed. Much as she didn't want to admit it, though, she had felt a little better.

Caroline had her fingers on the corner of Dylan's cot. 'And Dylan is doing well?'

It was a huge relief that Dylan was okay. At one point yesterday, she couldn't believe that they were both going to get through the experience unscathed. According to the nurse he was doing great. But once the initial relief had worn off, the fear had crept back. How was she going to look after him?

Despite the nurses encouraging her to get out of bed as often as she could, she had drawn the line at holding Dylan while she was standing up. When he cried to be fed, they would come and get him and hand him to her, but the last time they did it, they warned her that she'd have to start getting him herself. She felt like she was being punished.

Feeding had been absolutely awful. Wasn't breastfeeding supposed to be natural? Why was it so difficult and painful, and how was his mouth so sharp when he didn't have teeth? One nurse had been kind and shown her what to do but the one on the ward now seemed to just be leaving her to it. Was he even getting anything to eat from her? Was that why he was waking up so often?

As if on cue, he started to cry and she closed her eyes. *Please don't let him need feeding again.* When she opened them, Caroline was looking at her for permission to hold him. 'Yes, please do.'

Caroline was clearly a natural mother. As soon as she picked Dylan up and rocked him from side to side, he stopped crying. She looked mesmerised, as if he were a miracle. 'You and Pete have made a very beautiful boy.'

As if someone was kneeling on Emily's chest, a feeling of helplessness overwhelmed her. Hard as she tried to hold it together, it was impossible to stop the tears from filling her lower lids. The family opposite were pretending not to watch them. What were they thinking about her? She took a deep breath and stared at the window opposite. She couldn't cry in front of Caroline. She couldn't. 'I can't do this.'

'Hey, it's natural to feel overwhelmed. Wait a minute.' Caroline pulled the curtain around, still managing to rock Dylan at the same time. Once they were privately enclosed, she came to sit down on the red plastic chair by the side of Emily's bed. 'Let's take one thing at a time. What specifically are you thinking about right at this moment?'

What wasn't she thinking about? That Pete wasn't here to meet his son. That she didn't know what the hell she was doing with a baby. That her stomach hurt and she couldn't walk without wincing. That she didn't even have a clue how she was going to get home or look after Dylan. That she just felt so, so sad. 'They won't let me go home unless I have someone to help me. I tried to tell them that my husband… that Pete…'

She couldn't finish. Couldn't get the words out.

Caroline reached out and took her hand. 'You can come home with me.'

For a moment, Emily thought she'd misheard her. 'What?'

'The nurse told me yesterday that they wouldn't let you home if you were living on your own. I've thought about it and you should come home with me for at least a week or two. I can't let you struggle on your own.'

This was unbelievable. Lying in bed this morning, she had berated herself for dragging Caroline into this at all. And now she was offering to take her home and look after her? This was quite possibly the most unexpected proposition she could have imagined. But what other options did she have? 'Are you sure?'

Caroline lifted her shoulders into a shrug. 'Honestly? No, I'm not. But I also can't see what else you're going to do and I won't have it on my conscience if anything happens to you or to Dylan.' The whole time she spoke, she looked at him rather than at Emily.

What was she seeing? After the scan had revealed that he was going to be a boy, Emily had wondered whether their baby would look like Jamie and how that might make Pete feel. Neither of them had mentioned it. He probably hadn't wanted her to think that he would compare their baby to his first son. She hadn't wanted to stir up memories for him: he had been well and truly broken by Jamie's death.

But this was Caroline. Did she look at Dylan and see any whispers of the son she'd lost? She knew that Caroline had the boxes of Jamie's baby photographs. It would be easy to compare the two. Especially if Emily and Dylan were staying in her house.

Should she accept Caroline's offer? Surely, she'd taken enough from her. But what else could she do? There was no one else. If her mum had still been here, she'd have gone there in a heartbeat. But she was gone too. There was no one else. It wasn't for her; it was for Dylan.

'Thank you, Caroline. I mean it. Thank you so much.'

CHAPTER TWENTY-THREE

CAROLINE

The July afternoon had been sticky, but now the upstairs hall was cooling in the coming dark of the evening. Two days ago, Emily had moved into Caroline's spare bedroom and she had been up there for the last hour, feeding Dylan and settling him down for a sleep. The last couple of evenings, she had made her excuses and gone to bed herself shortly afterwards, but tonight, when Caroline got to the top of the stairs, she found Emily standing at the doorway to Jamie's bedroom, just looking inside. She started when she heard Caroline's footsteps on the landing. 'Sorry, I didn't mean to pry, I just...'

Caroline put down the basket of laundry that she'd been bringing upstairs. 'It's okay. I leave the door open because I like to walk past it and see his things.'

Emily looked back into the room. 'Like he's still here?'

That made Caroline sound strange and unhinged somehow. 'Not exactly. But it brings me comfort. Not that it was ever as tidy as that when Jamie was in residence. It used to be a dumping ground of plates, glasses and sports kit.'

Caroline wondered whether she should shut the door; it felt like an invasion of privacy the way Emily continued to stare at the room, as if she was committing it to memory. There was clearly something on her mind.

'What was he like?'

Caroline was surprised at the question. 'Jamie? Did Pete never speak about him?'

'Yes, he did. But he talked more about how much he missed him. How much he'd been a brilliant son. I began to think Jamie must have floated a couple of inches above the ground.'

She glanced at Caroline, as if checking that she hadn't made her angry. Caroline knew how proud Pete had been of his son. She could well imagine him making him sound like a cross between Einstein and Bobby Moore. 'Did he?'

'Yes, I mean, don't get me wrong, I know how that happens. When I lost my mum, all I could think about was how lovely she was, how supportive. It was easy to forget the times she'd driven me crackers with her nagging about what I wore or where I was going.'

Caroline smiled. 'Well, Jamie *was* a pretty good kid to be honest. He didn't give us too much trouble. No sex or drugs or orgies.'

Emily seemed too preoccupied to laugh at Caroline's pathetic attempt at lightening the mood. 'But what was he like as a person? Was he outgoing? Shy? Friendly?'

Caroline stopped and considered. It had been a long time since anyone had asked her about Jamie. When she thought of him, he was always laughing. At the TV, at her, at life. 'He loved a joke. He would tease me mercilessly and play pranks. Like, once, because I used to moan about him shoving all the cutlery in the drawer rather than sorting it out, he put a funny "SOS" message on a fork and mixed it in with the spoons. Waited two days before I got to it. But he wasn't unkind with it. He knew not to take any jokes too far; he was sensitive too.'

Another time, on her birthday, she'd been upset because Pete hadn't made much of an effort. The next morning, Jamie had woken her up with a glass of milk and a homemade card and told her that they were going to do a birthday rerun. He had been nine.

Emily was watching her face. 'He sounds like a great kid.'

Caroline swallowed over the tightness in her throat. 'He was. Don't get me wrong, he wasn't perfect. He didn't float above the ground.' She smiled to show Emily she hadn't taken any offence. 'His trainers smelled like a sewer and trying to get him out of bed in the morning was like getting a bear out of hibernation.'

Emily rubbed at the bottom of her stomach; maybe her C-section scar was sore. 'I was thinking just now about Jamie being Dylan's half-brother. Quite possibly the only brother he will ever have. And, with Pete gone, I'm the only one who'll be able to tell him anything about him.'

Caroline's chest tightened. Of course, she knew that Dylan was Jamie's brother, but she hadn't fully thought out what it meant that Dylan shared Jamie's DNA. As he grew, he might look like him. Sound like him. That was too huge to think about right now. Instead, Caroline nodded towards the bedroom. 'Come in.'

She'd tidied the room after Jamie had left for university for the last time. She always did. *Either clean it yourself or don't leave anything under the bed that you don't want me to find*, she used to warn him. Now all she did was give it a light dust and run the vacuum over.

It wasn't a shrine. She hadn't kept it this way on purpose. But what was she supposed to do with all his things? She'd given away a lot of his clothes to a family she knew with a teenage son. Gabby and Faith had come over and helped her with that. But what about the things that no one else would want? The Spurs calendar they gave him every Christmas which was hanging on the wall, trainers that were grubby and worn, a sculpture he'd made for his GCSE art project. What would be junk to other people was her treasure.

Emily followed her into the bedroom. Caroline sat herself on the edge of Jamie's bed and pointed to the chair by his desk for Emily. 'So, what do you want to know?'

Emily shrugged. She perched on the edge of the office chair like a hesitant intruder. She picked at the skin on her thumb. 'I don't know. What were his hobbies?'

'He was in a drama club. Did Pete tell you that? Just an amateur group. He used to go with some of his friends from sixth form. The girls were taking drama and they were pretty serious about it – one of them got into RADA – but he just went for fun. He was pretty good though, especially in the comic roles.'

As she spoke, a smile spread over her face. She hadn't allowed herself to think about Jamie onstage. Playing to the audience, his cheeky grin perfect for the Cheshire Cat or the Artful Dodger.

Emily leaned forwards. 'Really? Do you have any of his performances on film?'

The theatre had had a strict no-filming policy, but there was a recording of a dress rehearsal which the director had authorised for 'improvement purposes'. Jamie had emailed it to her, but only after she and Pete had seen the final performance. It was on her laptop. She wasn't ready to share that yet. 'Yes. I'll find it sometime and show you.'

'What else was he into?'

'Well, he was a big maths geek. That's what he was studying at university. He loved numbers and science. He and Pete would watch documentaries about scientific discoveries that sent me off to bed early with my book.'

Emily nodded. 'Pete watches those at home too. I mean... he *did*. He used to.' She dropped her gaze down to her hands, twisting her wedding ring around her finger.

Talking about someone in the past tense took a lot of getting your head around. Caroline dipped her head to catch Emily's eye. 'Boring as hell, aren't they?'

Emily looked up with a watery smile. 'Completely.' She nodded in the direction of the back bedroom where Dylan was sleeping. 'I wonder if I will have to watch those with this one?'

Caroline's throat tightened so fast, it was as if she was being strangled. That was the big difference between them: she was referring to the past whereas Emily's concern was for the future. She *had* a future to think about. All the precious moments with Jamie that Caroline would unwrap from her memory like chocolates from a box – Emily had all that to come.

To hide her tears, she got up and opened the door to the wardrobe. With the door between them for safety, she caught her breath again. 'I'm pretty sure there's some medals in here that Jamie won at a county Mathletics competition.'

It had been in his first year of secondary school. She'd been worried about him starting there. He'd been the only one from his primary school and he wouldn't have the buffer of his small but close group of friends. For the first couple of weeks, he had really struggled with the early mornings and the organisation. There had been tears of tiredness. But he had found his tribe, a wonderful group of boys and girls who had pretty much stayed the same until he left at the end of sixth form seven years later.

She pulled a box out from the wardrobe. These were proper packing boxes that Pete had bought to transfer Jamie's belongings to and from university. It was strange to see Pete's familiar handwriting across the top: *Jamie Uni Stuff.*

As she pushed it further into the room, Emily spoke. 'We've got one of those at the flat.'

Caroline peered round the wardrobe door. 'One of what?'

Emily pointed at the packing cases. 'Those boxes. With "Jamie's Uni Stuff" written on it.'

That didn't make sense. Why would Pete have taken a box of Jamie's things to the flat with him? 'Do you mean an empty box? One like this that Pete used to bring his clothes and things to yours?'

Emily shook her head. 'No. It has Jamie's belongings in it. I don't know what exactly because Pete didn't ever show me. I saw a university scarf once that he was holding. He used to sit in the bedroom with it sometimes. With a glass of wine. He didn't want my company.'

Tears came to Caroline's eyes. How many evenings had Pete sat in his bedroom at the flat remembering their son while she was here doing exactly the same? They should have been comforting one another. 'And you never asked to see what was inside it?'

Emily looked uncomfortable. 'I didn't feel I should. Pete talked about Jamie often, but there were times… well, it was as if a shadow came over him. That's when he would sit in the bedroom with the box of Jamie's things. On his own.' She looked off to the side, as if she was picturing him, then shook herself back to the present, back to Caroline. 'Would you like me to bring the box here? It obviously belongs to you now more than anyone.'

Caroline was intrigued to see what was inside it. As far as she'd known, everything from Jamie's room at university was here. What had Pete taken with him? What were the items that reminded him most of his son? 'Yes. I would like to have it. But you need to rest. I can always pick it up if you need me to collect any more of your things from the flat.'

'That would be great. I can tell you exactly where it is.'

Dylan's cry warbled from the bedroom. With a sigh, Emily got up to go to him.

CHAPTER TWENTY-FOUR

EMILY

Dark clouds loomed on the horizon and the park was empty, but Emily didn't care. The witching hour was coming and this was her only hope of getting through it. As the evening approached, she could feel herself tightening with expectation. At five o'clock every night, it was like a switch went off in Dylan's head and he'd start to scream. Relentlessly.

The first two nights after he was born, he just slept. Maybe he'd been exhausted from the traumatic birth – she definitely was – but she allowed herself to relax a little, to hope that things weren't going to be as difficult as she'd feared they would. On day three, everything changed.

She'd been embarrassed to bring it up with the health visitor. All babies cried, didn't they? She'd probably think Emily was an idiot. But Caroline had encouraged her, even sat with Emily as she tried to explain it. The health visitor hadn't made her feel stupid, but she hadn't been able to offer much advice, either. She'd said it was 'just colic' and would pass. There was no *just* about the level of his screams. They got higher and louder until it felt like a screwdriver through her brain. The health visitor had also said it happened a bit more often when babies were premature. *Something else to feel guilty about.*

Now, two weeks after her C-section, Emily could at least take him out for a walk in the pram to try and settle him; sometimes it would work, sometimes it wouldn't. When it didn't, she would have to endure the judgement which emanated from passers-by who clearly thought she didn't care about her baby's screams. *It doesn't make any difference*, she wanted to say. *I could pick him up or put him down and it doesn't stop. The crying just won't stop.*

Though the July day was warm, the wind was getting up, and leaves gathered around the frame of the swings in front of her. They were the type with a cradle to keep smaller children safe. Twenty minutes ago, she'd watched a mother extricate her kicking toddler from inside, carrying her screaming under her arm back to the buggy. She'd nodded at Dylan's pram. 'Make the most of them at that age. It just gets harder.' Emily had returned her well-meaning laugh with a smile she didn't feel.

Even when Dylan's crying was piercing, Caroline was amazing with him. For almost an hour, she would walk up and down the hallway, between the front door and the lounge, singing and rocking and shushing him until he gave in. When Emily tried the same thing, it just seemed to make it worse. Maybe it was her anxiety that he was picking up on. Or maybe she just wasn't any good at this.

She hadn't been able to feed him herself, either. Even though she had tried so hard. After his scary birth she felt like she owed it to him. But he wasn't interested at all and it wasn't helped by the fact that her milk had taken so long to come in. In the hospital, the midwife had suggested expressing the milk and then feeding it to him in a tiny cup but it had been so hard. Hooked up to a machine by the suction caps on her breasts, she felt like a cow being milked and it left her so sore that even wrapping a towel around herself after a shower felt as if her nipples were being grated. In the end, she had asked Caroline through tears to pick her up some formula milk from the shops. Her head told her that it really didn't matter how he got his milk as long as he was fed. The rest of her felt the ache of something else she couldn't do properly.

She was pretty much failing at all of it.

Another gust of wind made the leaves at her feet lift and swirl, and the clouds in the sky began to look more threatening. She reached over to tuck in Dylan's blanket, trying not to touch him, scared he might wake up. In his sleep, his tiny mouth made sucking movements; he would need feeding soon. She didn't want to leave yet. Didn't want to go back to the house. Caroline's house.

Staying with Caroline had been a godsend in the first few days. Although she was recovering pretty quickly from the C-section, she wasn't able to push the pram too far yet, so she would have been trapped in the flat alone. Well, not alone, obviously. But Dylan wasn't much in the way of company yet.

It had been almost two weeks now, though, and Caroline must have been wondering when she was going to move back home. It had been such a relief to let Caroline change Dylan, feed Dylan, comfort Dylan when she was too exhausted to do it. Some mornings, Caroline would take him and let her go back to bed to catch up on sleep. When she woke up again, she would lie there for a while longer, wondering how long she could give it before getting up and taking responsibility for him again.

In the last couple of days, though, she'd noticed Caroline looking at her strangely. Encouraging her to take Dylan more. She'd gone back to work after having a week off with them both and she would be wondering when they were going to go. She must want her house, and her life, back.

Emily wanted her life back, too. She wanted to be back in her flat with Pete. To be spending her maternity leave meeting other mothers, going to baby groups, waiting for her partner to come home from work so that she could tell him something cute that their baby had done. She wanted to watch Pete hold Dylan, wanted him to kiss her and tell her how much he loved them both.

A sob erupted from her chest and she wiped the tears from her eyes with the back of a gloved hand. It was a good job the park was empty otherwise she'd look like a crazy woman.

Her mum used to take her to a park just like this one when she was small. Their back garden was the size of a handkerchief, so summer weekends they would spend at the park. Looking back through adult eyes, her mother must have had an endless supply of patience. How many hours had she spent pushing Emily on a swing, waiting for her at the bottom of a slide?

Dylan sighed and fidgeted in the pram. Emily held her breath. *Please don't wake up.*

It wasn't that she didn't love him. She did. She loved him deeply. But everything just seemed so hard. She closed her eyes. If her mum was here now, she would have been able to help. She and Dylan could have moved in with her mum and she would have helped Emily, taught her how to be a better mother. Caroline had been great, but they weren't *friends*. She couldn't open up to her entirely and tell her how absolutely terrified she felt. She'd tried it once. Started with asking her about Jamie as a baby. Had he had colic too, maybe? But Caroline had merely smiled and said that Jamie had been a perfect baby. They'd not had any problems with sleep or food or crying. Was that true? Or just the way that she remembered it?

No Pete, no Mum and not Caroline: there was no one she could talk to about these feelings. Even mentioning it to Amy wasn't an option. Amy had come to visit her yesterday. Emily had suggested that she come after lunch. Dylan was always sleepy around then. It wouldn't do to terrify Amy about what was to come.

Amy had radiated joy from every pore. She'd sat on Caroline's sofa with her hands encircling an almost bump, looking every inch the happy mother-to-be. Emily wanted more than anything to talk to her friend about how hard it was for her. But how could she? Amy had waited so long to be pregnant; how could Emily tell her that this was the hardest thing she'd done in her whole life?

However much anyone – Caroline, the health visitor, the Internet – tried to tell her that Dylan's relentless crying in the evenings was normal for a lot of babies, she couldn't escape the feeling that she had caused this somehow. Her mood when she'd been pregnant, the shock of Pete's death and then her fall from the bath. How could those things not have affected Dylan? Even now, she was struggling to complete the most basic of parenting tasks properly. Only yesterday, she had burst into tears because he had gone to the toilet everywhere mid-nappy change and she couldn't work out how to hold him safely on the changing table while clearing up the urine and getting another nappy on him. If that made her cry, how the hell was she going to cope when he was older and things got harder?

She thought of the mother and the struggling toddler. *Make the most of it while they're small.*

The first spots of rain appeared just as Dylan woke up and started to cry.

CHAPTER TWENTY-FIVE

CAROLINE

'So, she has moved into your house?'

The two of them looked at Caroline with varying levels of incredulity. Gabby had actually paused with her fork halfway to her mouth while she waited for Caroline to answer Faith's question.

Normally, they would be the first people she would have told about something as big as this, but her excuse was that she hadn't seen the two of them together for the last two weeks. If she was honest, Caroline knew what their reaction would be and she'd been putting off telling them. 'Emily and Dylan are staying with me. Just till she properly recovers from her C-section. They wouldn't let her go home unless there was someone to look after her and I wasn't about to move into her flat.'

'Of course not.' Faith raised an eyebrow. 'Because *that* would be crazy.'

She'd fully anticipated this response, which was why she'd waited to see them in person to let them know about Emily and Dylan moving in. Foolishly, she'd thought it would be easier to explain it to both of them at once. 'If you could have seen her in the hospital, you would understand. And she's not in a good way. I'm worried about her.'

The first few weeks with a new baby were hard for any mother, and it was always going to be more difficult for Emily after losing Pete. But it was more than that. Caroline was no expert in postnatal depression but she knew that Emily needed to see a doctor if she didn't start to feel a little better soon.

'Worried about her how?' Faith frowned.

'She doesn't seem well. Mentally, I mean.'

Gabby sighed. 'Well, she must still be grieving for Pete. And it must be really hard to come to terms with bringing up a baby on her own when she wasn't expecting it. I mean, every time she looks at him, every time he does something for the first time, she must be thinking that Pete isn't there to share it with her.'

Faith put down her fork. 'Crikey, Gab, you need to stop or we'll all start feeling sorry for her.'

Something had shifted in Caroline in the last few days. When she looked at Emily, she didn't see the woman who had married her ex-husband. The woman she'd seen in the coffee shop that day with Gabby had looked healthy, smiling, confident. This woman was fragile and needed her help. And it wasn't just about her. 'Dylan is Jamie's half-brother. I feel a responsibility to him.'

That stumped them. What could they say against a small baby who was related to the son she'd lost? She looked at the two of them, her best friends. They would arm up and go to war for her. They were good women. Kind women.

Faith was the first to speak. 'Well, we can understand that, obviously.'

She took her acquiescence as an opportunity. 'You should see him. He's a gorgeous baby. Dark hair and dark blue eyes – just like Jamie when he was born.'

Just thinking about him made her smile. He was so tiny, so vulnerable, so easy to love. Evenings were tough going with his colic but she was getting to know what worked, what songs seemed to soothe him. Funnily enough, Jamie's old favourite, 'You Are My Sunshine', seemed to do the trick. Walking him up and down that hallway, she could close her eyes and be back twenty years when she'd rocked Jamie in the same way and Pete would tease that she was making a groove in the floor tiles.

'I guess it's the Pete in the two of them that looks similar. Never mind, there's still a hope that he'll grow out of that, like Jamie did.' Faith winked at her.

'Maybe. He lies in his cot exactly like Jamie, too. It's really strange.' She could see them glancing at each other over her head. Knew what they were thinking. 'I'm not stupid. I know he's not Jamie.'

Gabby reached out for her hand. 'We just don't want to see you getting hurt, honey. It was very kind to ask her to stay with you, but it's been two weeks since she had the baby. We just don't want to see her take advantage of you.'

Faith folded her arms. She had her no-nonsense expression. 'I'm just going to come out and say this. What if you get really attached to him and then she goes home and you don't see him again?'

There was no point thinking about that. She knew that they were protecting her, but she wasn't a child. 'I'll be okay. I'm not getting attached.'

Neither of them looked convinced, but they'd known her long enough to understand when to back off. Faith topped up everyone's wine as she spoke. 'What's happening with all the financial stuff you need to sort out? Did you want me to ask David about it?'

Faith had offered the advice of her new accountant boyfriend when they'd last spoken. 'I think I'm okay at the moment. Pete's company are sending someone round to speak to Emily and me.'

Faith frowned. 'Both of you together? Do you not want to hear what they say before speaking to her about it?'

Caroline shook her head. She'd thought about this a lot since the funeral. 'No. I can't in good conscience take money that should morally be hers. Especially now that Dylan is here. Apparently, I automatically get the house because we were joint owners and I won't even have a mortgage to pay because the life assurance we took out pays it off. That'll be enough for me.' She twirled the glass around by its stem. 'Actually, I was thinking that it might be time to look for a new job.'

That had their attention. Faith got there first. 'New as in return to your old job?'

Caroline shook her head. 'I don't think so. I want something different. A fresh start.'

Faith sat up straight. 'This might be perfect timing. I've finally got the go-ahead to advertise the outreach worker role. The initial funding fell through, but we've managed to find another source, so I want to get moving before it disappears again. Can't I persuade you to apply? Meeting with families, seeing what they need, giving them advice. I know I said it before, but you'd be perfect with your social work experience.'

She'd had a feeling Faith might suggest this, but she still didn't know if it was a good idea. 'That sounds a big role. I'm not sure that I'm ready for that.'

Faith held out her hands. 'It's brand new, so it can be whatever you want it to be. You can grow it in whatever direction you think is needed.'

That did sound appealing. Though she'd loved her job as a social worker, the caseload had got heavier and heavier. She was always bringing work home, much to Pete's annoyance. She'd climbed the mountain of paperwork every night with about as much success as Sisyphus.

Faith took her silence as a possible sign of interest. 'Look, I'll email you the job spec and then we can have a chat about it.'

It wouldn't hurt to look. 'Okay.'

Faith was satisfied with that. She picked up her fork and went back to her spaghetti. 'So how has it been, having Emily in the house? What do you two talk about all evening?'

Caroline was careful not to be too effusive. She'd actually loved having them both there. Even though Emily was quiet and withdrawn some of the time, Caroline had really enjoyed having someone to look after. In the mornings, when Emily needed more rest, she had Dylan to herself. Even if she was just washing up or folding laundry, being able to chat to him as he kicked in his bouncy chair brought light to her mornings. Telling Gabby and Faith that would just make them worry that she was going to get too attached, too hurt when they moved out again. Maybe that was true, but some things are worth a little pain.

'Actually, we've talked about Jamie a bit, which is nice. It sounds as if Pete sometimes found it difficult to talk about him to her.' This had surprised Caroline, actually. When Pete had visited her, he was always keen to talk about Jamie. It was one of the reasons she'd let him keep coming: he'd been the only other person who had loved their son as much as she did. Missed him as much as she did.

Faith picked up the wine bottle and checked how much was left. 'Maybe he thought it would make her jealous. Does she seem the jealous type?'

Caroline had to smile at her eagerness to find another negative character trait. Neither of them was predisposed to think anything good of Emily. 'Maybe it was that. There was one thing she mentioned which was strange. Apparently, Pete had a box of Jamie's things at the flat. He never said anything to me about it.'

Gabby had her hand over her glass to prevent Faith refilling it. 'What kind of things?'

'I don't know. She wasn't sure. I'm going to pick it up from the flat, so I'll let you know when I've seen it.'

With Faith's anecdotes about her recent introduction to David's grown-up kids, they easily managed to stretch out a late lunch into early evening. Caroline wanted to be home to help Emily with bedtime. Dylan's colic was always worse at night; his little legs would bend into his stomach. She'd researched lots of different ways to help with his wind but nothing seemed to work, poor little thing.

The rain was so heavy by the time she got out of the taxi that the dash from the street to the front door left her dripping wet and she ran straight upstairs to get a towel from the bathroom for her hair. It took a few moments to realise that the house was quiet. That was strange. Emily hadn't mentioned that she was going out anywhere, and she wouldn't be walking in this awful weather. She couldn't exactly call her and ask where she was: that would be overstepping.

She felt uneasy. Before Caroline had left for her lunch date, Emily had assured her that they would be fine on their own. She'd seemed almost cross that Caroline was asking.

There was a ring on the doorbell. Caroline was there in two seconds. It was them.

Dylan's screams were louder than she'd ever heard them. Quickly, she grabbed the pram and pushed it into the hall. Emily followed.

'What happened? Where were you?'

Emily made no attempt to attend to Dylan, so Caroline unclipped the pram cover and peeled back his blanket. He was fine. Inside the pram, he'd been cocooned against the weather. Emily, on the other hand, was absolutely soaked through to her skin.

'Emily. Are you okay? What happened?'

She was shivering and sobbing; it was impossible to make out what she was saying.

'Are you hurt? Was there an accident?'

Caroline's heart was racing. This time, she scooped Dylan up into her arms, felt his body for signs of anything unusual.

Emily just stood there, crumpled in on herself, her hair dripping water onto the floor. 'I can't do this, Caroline. I just can't do it.'

CHAPTER TWENTY-SIX

EMILY

Staying in Caroline's guest room was akin to being in a boutique hotel. The bed – and its combination of a thick, down-filled quilt and memory-foam mattress – was like sleeping in a cloud. On the bedside table, a small wicker chest with its lid open offered up toiletries, toothbrushes and tissues. Against the wall, under the window, a small bookcase suggested a range of well-known books from all genres. She really had thought of everything.

After her disastrous walk to the park, Emily had slept so deeply it was as if she was drugged. It was the first time she had slept for eight hours straight since Dylan had been born, and when she turned onto her side, she realised why. Caroline had made up a bed on the floor of her bedroom, next to Dylan's crib. As Emily stepped out of bed, the creak of a floorboard made Caroline stir.

Embarrassed by her breakdown last night, and the memory of Caroline putting her to bed like a poorly child, Emily wasn't sure what to say. 'Hi. Good morning.'

'Good morning.' Caroline sat up and stretched; the floor could not have been comfortable. There was something about seeing her in her floral pyjamas that felt strangely intimate. 'I know this must look weird. I didn't want Dylan to wake you, but I didn't feel right taking him out of your room, either. This seemed like the only solution.'

It *was* weird, but it was also fantastic to get a full night's rest. Emily felt a little wired, as if she'd drunk three cups of strong coffee. 'It's fine. I mean… thanks.' She nodded at the crib. 'While he's sleeping, I'll go and have a shower.'

Caroline's bathroom was also beautiful. Navy-and-white striped towels, three pictures of beach huts on the wall, a wooden sailboat on the windowsill. If Emily tried hard, she could imagine that she was actually staying in a seaside hotel like the one Pete had taken her to in Eastbourne last summer. In the shower, she let her head fall back so that the water could wash over her face. For a few moments, it felt wonderful. Then the anxious thoughts crept up her spine and into her shoulders, her neck, her head. She hadn't actually looked into Dylan's crib. Would Caroline think she was a bad mother for not checking on her son? Was she a bad mother for not even looking at him before leaving the room? What was wrong with her? Why couldn't she remember to just do these things?

Quickly, she washed her hair so that she could get back to the bedroom, prove to Caroline that she hadn't forgotten about him. Before she wrapped a towel around herself, she looked at her body in the full-length mirror on the bathroom door. Her swollen breasts, thick waist, the scar below her abdomen. Even her body was unfamiliar to her now. She covered it over with a large bath sheet, wrapped up her hair and scuttled back to the bedroom. Dylan's crib was empty: Caroline must have taken him downstairs. Relief mixed with guilt fizzed in the pit of Emily's stomach.

When she made it downstairs, she found that Caroline had set the table and was slotting bread into the toaster with her left hand as she held Dylan in her right arm. God, she made everything look so easy.

Over breakfast, which Caroline watched her eat, she started her assault. 'You need to get some professional help. Medical help. You don't need to keep suffering like this.'

Even the thought of saying aloud to a stranger that she couldn't cope with looking after her own son made her terrified. But it was true. 'I know.'

To her credit, Caroline didn't labour the point of her failure. She kept to practicalities. 'You need to make an appointment with Dr Ayoub. Not one of the older doctors – they're useless with anything they can't detect with a stethoscope. Dr Ayoub was wonderful with me after Jamie died.'

When Emily had met Pete, she still hadn't got a GP in London – she'd still been registered at the GP she'd had since childhood, back in Ipswich. When she'd found out she was pregnant, it had made sense to register at Pete's GP which, perhaps obviously, was also Caroline's.

Emily continued to pull small pieces of toast from the triangle on her plate. 'Okay.'

Thinking Caroline had finished, she risked looking at her, but Caroline had obviously been waiting to make eye contact. 'I was in a bad way, Emily. A really bad way. I know what it's like to have my toes over the edge of the abyss.'

Emily blinked hard, bit at her lip. She couldn't trust her voice, but she wanted Caroline to know that she was hearing what she was saying, so she kept looking at her, nodded her understanding.

Caroline kept going. 'I didn't want anyone's help either. I just wanted them to leave me alone. My counsellor helped me to realise that my grief was like a person. If I couldn't have Jamie, then grief was the only companion I wanted. Everyone else, I just pushed away.'

Emily let the tears run down her cheeks. Her grief was less like a person and more like a monster, a ghoul. It loomed behind her, waiting for her to fail. Still, she couldn't speak, but Caroline didn't seem to expect her to.

'Pete tried to help; I can see that now. But I didn't want to get up or go out or do any of the things he suggested. In the end, I asked him to leave. To give me some space.'

She paused. Emily knew that she was being tactful. Pete would never have ended up with Emily if Caroline hadn't kicked him out.

'The thing is, I don't know what might have happened to me if it wasn't for my friends. They didn't give me much of a choice. They came with me to see Dr Ayoub. It was after that day, with the help of antidepressants and counselling, that I started to come back to myself. It didn't happen overnight, and it wasn't a straight road, but it was the first step.'

She reached over and covered Emily's free hand with her own. 'If you'll let me, I'll come with you. You don't have to go alone.'

Two days ago, when they'd had that conversation, it had all made sense. A chink of hope had cracked the darkness that had cast its shadow for what seemed like forever. But the two days it had taken to get an 'emergency' appointment had eroded even that sliver of possibility. Now, Emily wasn't so sure. What was she going to say to the doctor? How would she explain this feeling of being overwhelmed by everything? This doctor didn't know her from Adam. Wouldn't know that normally she was happy, positive, fun. That this – whatever she was at the moment – just wasn't *her*.

Caroline had been right about Dr Ayoub, though. He listened to Emily's description of how she was feeling. That it had started before Dylan was born, before Pete's accident. In fact, Emily couldn't remember when she'd felt like herself in months. Dr Ayoub suggested she start with a low-dosage antidepressant and see how it made her feel. 'One thing you need to bear in mind, though, is that the first day or so of new medication can be rough. Will you have someone with you?'

Caroline spoke before Emily had even looked at her. 'Yes. I'll be there.'

'Good.' The doctor nodded. 'If it's too much, I can prescribe something else alongside it to take the edge off, but that can leave you feeling quite woolly, so it's up to you.'

Emily didn't like the sound of woolly, so she shook her head. 'Just the antidepressants will be fine, thank you.'

The doctor wheeled his chair back to the PC and typed up the prescription. As the printer coughed it out, he turned back. 'Ideally, we'd get you with a counsellor at the same time as starting the medication, but unfortunately the waiting lists are very long. It may even be a few months before I can get you an appointment with someone.'

Medication, counselling. The words spilled over her like rain. Again, she had the feeling that she was watching all of this play out for someone else.

The medical centre had a pharmacy on-site, so she was able to fill the prescription straight away. After discussing it on the way home in the car, they agreed that she wouldn't start taking the medication until Friday night. That way, if there were any adverse side effects, she had until Monday morning when Caroline went back to work.

Caroline clicked the indicator on to pull into her road. 'I can always take a couple of days off if you need me to?'

'No, you've done enough. I really appreciate this.' She still didn't really understand why Caroline was helping her so much. What had she done to deserve her kindness?

On Saturday morning, twelve hours in, she knew why the doctor had insisted that she have someone with her for the first few days.

For a start, she couldn't sit down. At 5 a.m. her eyes flicked open like a switch and she felt hyper-aware of everything around her. Dylan's breathing in the Moses basket beside her bed, the central heating warming the pipes, the tick of her alarm clock.

At 6 a.m. Caroline came downstairs to find her pacing back and forth across the floor of the lounge. 'Hi. What can I do?'

Emily continued to walk; somehow it seemed to help the restless feeling in her arms and legs. 'I don't know. I don't know what to do with myself.'

Caroline perched on the arm of a chair. 'The doctor did say it may take a while for them to even out. This will be what he meant.'

Emily had expected that she might have a headache or upset stomach. Not this. This was intolerable. It was as if every nerve ending in her body needed to be stretched or moved. She needed to walk. And to talk. To get hold of the noise inside and release it somehow. 'I deserve this. I deserve all of it, Caroline.'

She knew she shouldn't be talking like this. Not to Caroline. Obviously, she was just going to be confused.

'What do you mean?'

But there was nothing for it. Now she had opened her mouth, she couldn't stop the flow of thoughts from her brain coming out of her mouth. 'I made this happen. The pregnancy. It wasn't an accident.'

'I don't understand. What are you telling me?'

The words were tumbling out now, one after another. 'Because I thought I was losing him. Pete. I thought it was the only way to get him to stay.'

'Slow down. You're not making sense.'

She might as well tell her now – what pride did she have left after the events of the last few days? She threw her arms in the air, even as she continued to pace up and down. 'Because I don't think he loved me anymore. I think that he was over me.'

When Pete had moved into the flat, they had been so close. So many nights spent talking about his loss and hers. How they loved each other and how they felt that they had been given a second chance at love.

Caroline looked troubled. 'I'm sure that's not true.'

Emily needed to be clearer. Explain what she meant. She stopped pacing. Pressed her fingertips into the roots of her hair. 'I think that he was seeing someone else. He kept coming home late. He said he was working but, for goodness' sake, it went on for weeks. And I called the phone on his desk at work. Over and over. It was easy for me to find out that he wasn't there. Where the hell else would he be that he couldn't tell me?'

Caroline must have thought she was awful, talking about Pete in this way. Clearly so disgusted by her talking about a dead man like this that she couldn't even look at her. 'I don't know, Emily. I don't know what to say.'

Her legs felt restless again; she recommenced the pacing. 'Because it must be true, right? He must have met someone else. Someone his own age. Someone he had more in common with. But I couldn't bear it. I couldn't lose him. So, I got pregnant.'

Now Caroline did look at her. 'Oh, Emily.'

Emily groaned and brought her hands up to cover her eyes so she didn't have to see the shock on Caroline's face. 'I know. I brought this all on myself, right? I wasn't ready to be a mother. I don't even know if Pete wanted another son. It's all my fault.'

CHAPTER TWENTY-SEVEN

CAROLINE

For the next week, apart from going to work, Caroline spent pretty much every waking moment in Emily's company, wanting to reassure herself that Emily was coping. Every time Emily expressed her gratitude, a corkscrew of guilt twisted inside of her. If Emily knew where Pete had been going all those nights that he didn't make it home till late, she might not be so grateful. By the following weekend, Caroline needed a break. Emily had arranged to see Amy for lunch, so Caroline took the opportunity to visit her mother and her sister, Penny.

Caroline's sister lived in a large farmhouse, just outside the M25. Penny had said that George and their two sons would be out in one of the fields with the vet all day, so it would be just the three of them for lunch.

They always left the back door unlocked. Caroline pushed it open and called out to let her sister know she was there. 'Hello! It's the burglars! We're just coming in for the TV.'

Penny's voice carried down the hall. 'We're in the kitchen. If you can carry that ridiculously huge screen, you are welcome to it. It might force my menfolk into some conversation around here.'

Caroline pulled her shoes off in the mudroom. Their shiny black leather was out of place next to the wellington boots and walking shoes. Three working farmers in the house made for a lot of footwear.

When she'd made it up the hall to the kitchen door, Penny was waiting for her, wiping her hands on a tea towel with cows on it.

Penny had married into farming, but anyone who watched her wrestling a calf from a ditch or making lunchtime soup on her Aga would have thought she was born into it. She even looked the part with her Joules fleece and jeans. She pulled Caroline towards her and gave her a squeeze. 'Good to see you, sis.' She lowered her voice and kept her lips close to Caroline's ear. 'I'm so sorry about Pete.'

Caroline kissed her warm cheek. 'Thanks. It was a shock. Have you told…?'

Penny shook her head as she scrutinised her face. 'I didn't know what you wanted to do. How you wanted to play it.'

A thin but well-spoken voice called out to them. 'Is that you, Caroline?'

Their mother had lived with Penny for the last three years. When she was no longer able to live alone, Penny had offered straight away. 'It makes sense. We've got all these rooms and there's someone coming in and out all day.' It was the best option for everyone, but Caroline always felt slightly guilty that her younger sister did so much more for their mum than she did.

She took a deep breath to prepare herself for the inevitable question and stepped into the warm kitchen, where her mum was sat at the large wooden table with a mug of tea.

'Hi, Mum. How are you?'

Her mum frowned and looked behind her before smiling at her face. 'I'm fine, sweetheart. Where's my baby grandson? Where have you left Jamie?'

Maybe every daughter thinks that their mother is beautiful, but it was really true in Caroline's case. Sandra Miller even coordinated her slippers with her pyjamas. Even now, when the dementia kept her living over a decade behind, she would complete a full skincare routine every night just as she had since before Caroline was born. She'd been exasperated with her and Penny growing up. 'Why did God bother to give me daughters if they are going to spend their whole life in jeans?' she used to say after another shopping trip where she'd practically begged them both to let her buy them each a dress. When Penny had met and married George, then spent half her life covered in mud, she had given up altogether. They hadn't even been able to produce a granddaughter between them. Once Jamie, the youngest of the three grandchildren, had been born, Penny had put an arm around her mother in consolation. 'Never mind, Mum. Maybe one of them will become a drag queen?'

Since Jamie had died, Sandra's dementia had got worse. From having lapses in memory, she was now at the stage where lucid moments were rare. Still, they were lucky, Penny believed, because she was happy and content most of the time. Especially since they had given up trying to explain the history that she'd forgotten. Like Jamie's death.

'He's at home with Pete, Mum. I thought it would be nice to be just girls today.'

Sandra held out her arms for Caroline to walk into. Clinique face cream and lemon shampoo: the smells of home. Sandra pressed her lips into her daughter's cheek, sure to leave a trace of the Max Factor lipstick she said she felt naked without. 'Well, it's always lovely to have my girls to myself.' As Caroline stood, Sandra looked from her to Penny. 'Aren't I lucky to have had you both for all these years?'

Penny brought over the teapot, filling a cup for Caroline, topping up her mother's. 'We're the lucky ones, Mum.'

Her mother winked. 'That's true.'

Penny was right: they were lucky that the dementia hadn't robbed their mother of her humour and kindness. The dementia nurse they'd spoken to had also given them good advice; trying to remind their mother of how old they were, or that their father had died twenty years ago and not two, had only served to upset her. But since Jamie had gone, it wasn't so easy to sit with her in a past in which he still existed as a toddler she was desperate to see.

'Have you got some photos for me at least?'

Caroline had asked Penny whether their mum asked her the same thing, but – maybe because she was around them every day – she seemed to have accepted that Penny's boys were now over six foot and had girlfriends. At times she would look confused that a deep-voiced young man was calling her Grandma, but generally she just went with it. Jamie, however, would never grow any older in her imagination. Maybe it was a form of self-preservation? Caroline almost wished she could do the same.

Caroline reached into her handbag and picked out the pocket photo album she'd created a few months ago for this very purpose. 'Of course. Here you go.'

With her arm along the back of the chair, she looked over her mother's shoulder at the photographs of Jamie as a small child. In the bath, asleep in his cot, surrounded by toys. She hadn't noticed at the time how chubby he'd been as a toddler; cheeks she wanted to hold in her palms and kiss.

Her mother's face lit up as she slowly turned the pages, stroked a painted fingernail down his face. 'He's such a handsome boy, Caroline. Has he added any more words to his repertoire?'

After 'Mama' and 'Dada', Jamie's first word had been 'in'. Caroline didn't need the photographs to remember him sitting in front of a cardboard box with his toys, dropping them inside one by one, telling anyone who would listen that they were 'in' each time.

'Actually, yesterday we showed him the picture of you and him in our hall and he said, "Ganma."'

This wasn't a total lie. This had happened. One of the things Jamie had loved to do was point at all the family photos which lined the wall of their hall and ask, 'Who's it?' Eventually he'd started to answer his own question with his version of everyone's name. Only it wasn't yesterday; it was twenty years ago.

It was worth the untruth – her mother's face was delighted. 'Oh, what a clever boy! You must bring him to see me. I haven't seen him in…' Sandra's voice tailed off into uncertainty. These were the moments that needed to be managed.

'It was only a couple of weeks ago, Mum.' Effortlessly, Penny smoothed over the moment. She rested a reassuring hand on her mum's shoulder as she placed a plate of sandwiches on the table. 'Shall we eat?'

Sandra looked relieved. Happy to accept Penny's version of events.

Caroline was also grateful to her sister for changing the subject to the honey roast ham she'd picked up at a farmer's market last week, then if the weather was nice enough for a walk after lunch and lastly whether the boys would make it back in for some cake before Caroline had to leave.

All the time she was listening to her sister, Caroline couldn't help her mind wandering back to those baby photos. Thinking about Jamie made her realise that Dylan would be going through all these same stages in the coming months and years. Talking, walking, learning to feed himself, going to school. She wondered how much he would follow in his brother's footsteps. How much was genetic and how much learned: the age-old debate.

Emily had appeared to be much more in control the last couple of days. Now that the medication was in her system, she looked stronger, more capable. There was a way to go, but she had already started to talk about when she would go home. Caroline should have been relieved, pleased that everything was going to be okay. They'd even spoken about Pete's money and agreed that

Caroline would inherit Pete's share in the house and everything else would go to Emily and Dylan.

She would be sad to see little Dylan go, though. She'd got used to hearing his cries in the morning, hadn't minded watching him so that Emily could go back to bed for an hour.

Thinking about him growing up gave her an odd feeling in the pit of her stomach. Emily had been with her for almost a month and, whatever she had said to Gabby and Faith, she hadn't been able to stop herself getting attached to that beautiful little boy. What would happen when Emily moved back home and restarted her life, maybe one day met someone else and had more children? Would she ever get to see little Dylan again?

CHAPTER TWENTY-EIGHT

EMILY

At the beginning of August, after two weeks of the medication, Emily decided it was time to go home. Caroline had told her more than once that she could stay longer, but Emily knew she must be getting sick of them being there. Dylan's colic seemed to be easing and, gradually, Emily was getting used to looking after him on her own. Everything felt a little more possible, a little less overwhelming. She wouldn't go as far as to say she was enjoying motherhood, but she was doing it. The next step was to do it in her own home. Alone.

Caroline drove her and Dylan back to the flat around ten on a bright Sunday morning, then returned at eleven with the baby bath and Moses basket, which they hadn't been able to fit in the car. Once everything was in its right place, she stood in the small entranceway, holding her car keys.

'I think that's everything.' Caroline looked reluctant to go.

Much as she had wanted to be back home, Emily's stomach twinged at the thought of Caroline going. 'Would you like a cup of tea or something? I have plenty of milk.' She smiled at Caroline, grateful for the box of tea, coffee, milk and biscuits she had thought to pack for their return home.

'No, I'll get off and let you get settled.' She shook her car keys but still she hovered.

Emily felt the same. In a short space of time, it felt as if they had got really close. Caroline had been a life raft in the worst storm of her life, a storm that hadn't quite abated.

The medication was definitely doing its job. Tasks which had seemed insurmountable two weeks ago, she could now face with a deep breath. There had been moments of joy too. Dylan smiling for the first time parted the clouds and let the sunshine in. Still, every moment with him was tinged with the thought that Pete should be there to enjoy it with her.

Caroline reached over and took her hand. 'You can do this. I know you can.'

Emily's chest tightened. She wanted to live up to Caroline's faith in her, she really did. 'I know. We'll be fine.' She looked down at Dylan, still asleep in the car seat, hunched over like a little old man, his knitted hat slipping over one eye. She was putting off getting him out in case it woke him up.

Caroline was looking at him too. 'He's a really gorgeous boy. I know it's hard right now, but it'll get better.'

Do not cry. Do not cry. Why was it so hard to watch Caroline walk out of the door? They weren't even friends. Caroline had helped her a great deal but she was okay now. The medication was working. Dylan had been a little easier to look after and she was going to get the hang of doing this on her own.

'Oh, the box. Let me go and get the box of Jamie's things before you go.'

The bedroom looked just as it had that last night before going into hospital. The bed was unmade, a handful of tissues on the floor, clothes heaped on the foot of the bed. Screwed up in the corner of the room was the towel she'd left there after dressing hurriedly so that Caroline could take her to the hospital. The trace of blood made her look away; she would tidy that later.

Sliding the door of Pete's wardrobe open, she was hit with the smell of his aftershave and it pulled at her from the inside. Rows of trousers, shirts and jackets, shoes neatly paired on the shelves. Everything about Pete was organised, ordered, controlled. If only he were still here, she would have been okay.

There wasn't time to feel this right now. She pulled aside the clothes hangers to where she knew the box would be and shifted it towards her. She tested its weight: it had only been five weeks since her C-section and she didn't want to hurt herself. But it was surprisingly light. Maybe there wasn't as much in there as she'd assumed from the evenings Pete had spent going through it.

Back in the living room, Caroline was sitting on one of the chairs, just gazing at Dylan in his car seat. She really seemed to love the little boy. Maybe it wasn't that; maybe it was just that he reminded her of Jamie. Emily felt a twinge of sadness. Quickly followed by guilt. 'Here you go.'

Caroline turned to her as if she was pulling herself out of a dream. When she saw the box, though, she straightened up in her seat, then stood. 'You shouldn't be carrying that.'

'It's fine.' Emily passed the box over. 'To be honest, it's quite light. I hope I haven't got your hopes up unnecessarily.'

Caroline took the lid off the box. 'There's a university scarf and some cards in here and…' She frowned, put the box down onto the chair and lifted out a hardbacked book. 'A notebook.'

An unpleasant fluttering began in Emily's stomach. 'Lecture notes, maybe?'

Caroline opened the book and flicked through the first couple of pages. Her forehead wrinkled as she looked up at Emily. 'It looks like a diary. I didn't know that Jamie kept a diary.'

The fluttering got worse. 'An appointment diary or, like, a journal?'

Caroline closed the book, held it to her chest. 'A journal, I think. Maybe I shouldn't read it.'

Emily nodded. 'Maybe not. It might be personal stuff.'

Caroline picked up her coat from the arm of the chair and laid it across the top of the box before picking them both up. 'If you're sure you're okay, I think I'd better head home.'

'We're absolutely fine.'

Emily followed Caroline to the door. Emily stepped over the threshold and turned back to her. Was this the last time they would see one another? There was no reason to stay in touch, and yet…

The same thought must have crossed Caroline's mind. 'Will you let me know how you're getting on? How Dylan is getting on?' She nodded her head back in the direction of the lounge.

'Of course. And thank you so much for… everything. Truly.' She looked Caroline in the eye, wanting to convey how much she meant her words.

After she'd closed the front door, she made herself a coffee and sat down in the chair that Caroline had vacated. She was home. They were safe. They were well. All would be okay.

Dylan woke up and started to cry.

CHAPTER TWENTY-NINE

CAROLINE

Early Monday evening, the house was so silent without Emily and Dylan. After dropping them home yesterday, Caroline had considered taking herself off to the shopping centre to kill a few hours, but she didn't want to leave the box of Jamie's things in the car. It wasn't as if anyone would be desperate to steal a box containing a second-hand scarf, some postcards and a diary, but they were precious to her. Clearly, they had been to Pete, too. The thought of him keeping hold of these remnants from Jamie's life filled her with a warmth for him.

Now the diary sat on her dining table, looking at her, tempting her.

She'd been circling around it since yesterday. Had spent last night and this morning before work going backwards and forwards in her mind. Should she read it? Or would she regret it forever? It was an invasion of privacy that she'd never have contemplated if he were still here.

Monday evenings were usually okay. Mondays were busy at the children's centre, and after they'd shut the doors at 3 p.m., she'd come home tired and content to be on her own. Weekends were much harder: Saturday nights were always the lowest point of the week. It was the night that everyone seemed to reserve for family time. She knew that there was an open invitation for her to go to Gabby's or Faith's anytime they were home, but she didn't like to intrude. However good their friendship, to their partners and kids it would be uncomfortable having a guest in the house: they wouldn't be able to relax.

But this Monday afternoon, she couldn't settle to watch TV because she couldn't make up her mind whether to read Jamie's diary. She turned her back on it, made a coffee and then sat back on the sofa and eyed it once more.

Of course, there might be nothing in it. Just the random scribblings of a teenage boy: song lyrics or shopping lists. She hadn't even known that he'd kept a journal of any kind. What else didn't she know about him?

When he'd been small, she had known every single thing about him. What he liked to eat or play with or watch on the TV. The tiny things that made him laugh like a drain. When he'd been around five, he'd told her in all seriousness that he was going to marry her when he grew up.

He'd been about eleven when he'd first started to pull away: figuratively and literally. His hand would slip out of hers as they approached his school, he'd tilt the top of his head to her lips at night rather than kiss her on the cheek. Small changes, but each one took him a little further away.

Having a child is like a one-sided love affair. You are both passionate about one another from the very beginning and for the next few years. Then one of you starts to find outside interests, becomes more independent, doesn't need the other anymore. But the love doesn't change for a mother.

When Jamie left for university, she'd grieved his absence. It hadn't been the same for Pete. He'd missed him, of course he had. But it hadn't been as if he felt the absence as a physical loss like she had. As he'd promised, Jamie had written longish emails a couple of times when he first started and then communication had become only one-way. He had been wrapped up in his new friends and then the girlfriend who was always with him any time Caroline called. Pete had said it was a good thing. He was making friends, enjoying himself. Wasn't that what she wanted?

Of course, it was. It was exactly what she'd wanted. You don't have a child to keep them with you forever, do you? Roots and wings. That's what you're supposed to give them. She just hadn't been ready for him to fly so far and so fast.

What is in that diary?

She considered calling Gabby. Or Faith. Faith would give her an honest opinion. But it was pointless. Whatever advice they gave her wasn't going to change anything. She knew that she was going to read it. So, what was she waiting for?

Putting down her mug, she picked up the diary. The cover didn't reveal anything: a blue striped notebook like the ones he used to take notes in his lectures. Maybe that's why they'd missed what it was when they'd cleared out his room. But Pete must have known that this was a diary, otherwise why had he kept it in this box? And why hadn't he told her about it?

It clearly hadn't been intended as a journal originally. The first several pages were drafts of essays and then some scribbled notes about holiday dates and deadlines. It wasn't until the sixth or seventh page that the entries were dated.

27 January

Beth says I need to talk about this with someone. She says I need to get it out of my head. I suppose that's what you get for dating a psychology student. It was her idea to write it down when I told her that there was no way I could tell Mum. So that's what I'm doing. Even though this feels dead weird.

Caroline pressed the heel of her right hand to her chest to stop it from aching. Just the sight of his handwriting was enough to make her heart hurt. The lazy, half-joined, half-print style that hadn't changed since he was a small boy who was forced to go to handwriting practice every Monday lunchtime. At the 'dead weird' she could actually hear his voice in her ear. *Mum, have you seen this picture of me? It's dead weird.* Oh, God. How was it possible to miss someone this much and still carry on living?

She placed her other hand over the page and gave herself a moment to just breathe. When Jamie was young and had something painful to do, Pete had always told him that he should do it as quickly as possible. Pull out that wobbly tooth, rip off that plaster, tear open those exam results. After, it was Caroline he'd come to. She would soothe any pain, kiss away any tears. Maybe it was because he was her only one, but she was always available for him anytime he needed her.

What was it that he couldn't tell her?

She wiped away her tears with the back of her hand and continued to read.

Dad has been trying to call me but I'm not ready to speak to him yet. I don't know what I'm going to say. I'm so bloody angry that I want to hit him and obviously I can't do that. I've written a couple of texts but I haven't actually sent them. While I'm typing I can feel myself hating him, but then I read them back and I think that this is my dad I'm writing to and I can't do it. I hate him, but I love him.

She paused again. It was too much to take in. He had hated Pete? Why did she have no memory of them falling out? That Christmas he'd been home from university and everything had been wonderful. She'd cooked his favourite food, rolled out all their family traditions, even wrapped him a new set of pyjamas and a book to open the night before like she'd done when he'd been small. He'd been out on Christmas Eve with his old school friends who were also back from university, and she'd been waiting up for him when he'd come home in the early hours of Christmas Day. *Happy Christmas, Mum.* He'd wrapped her in a huge, beery hug and all had been right with the world.

She'd been disappointed when he'd decided to return to Colchester a few days earlier than planned. Beth was going back, apparently, and they'd decided at the last minute to do a Christmas rerun with their friends. He hadn't wanted them to drive him back – even though Pete had tried to persuade him to let them. He'd said he would get the train. She hadn't understood at the time why Pete wouldn't let it go. Kept on and on saying that he would drive him back, that there would be room for all his Christmas gifts in the boot. Now she thought about it, it was strange. According to her husband, it was usually Caroline who tried to mollycoddle him. Jamie had been really irritated by it. That's why he had been so cross when he'd left. Or that's what she'd thought. Surely that wasn't enough for Jamie to hate him though?

The next few entries were about his workload and a lecturer who was on his case about attendance. Then there was another one about Pete.

2 February

Dad turned up at uni today. I was just on my way back to my room so I couldn't avoid him. I was going to tell him to leave me alone, but Beth gave me a look and I knew she was right. I had to talk to him sometime.

First of all, he tried to tell me that I was wrong. That they'd just been messing about. It's like he thinks I'm still a little kid and I'll believe him.

Eventually he gave that up and told me the truth. It was just one night, he said. After his Christmas party. He'd had too much to drink. It wasn't going to happen again. He said he loves Mum and—

She slammed her hand back on the page. If she covered the words, maybe they wouldn't exist. Pete had cheated on her? That Christmas? Their last Christmas as a family? She felt sick. She raised her hand.

—that he doesn't want to hurt her by telling her what happened. Tried to make it out like we were two men talking about it. Tried to get me to understand. I don't know what to do. If I don't tell Mum, I feel like I'm lying to her. But if I do tell her, it will kill her. And I don't want this to split them up, do I?

I made him promise me that he was never going to see this Emily woman again.

Caroline dropped the diary into her lap. Emily? That didn't make sense. He hadn't started seeing Emily until after Jamie had died, until after they'd divorced. Whether she believed his version of when they'd met or her friends' suspicions that it had been going on before the divorce was finalised, it had definitely been after they'd lost Jamie.

Hadn't it?

The next few entries didn't contain anything more about this Emily. There were a couple of mentions of Pete trying to call and Jamie not answering. Then there was another one she didn't understand.

Dad sent me a text saying he'd come up again unless I spoke to him. So I called him. He asked me if I'd said anything to Mum. Wanted to know if I was going to. He said he couldn't cope with not knowing if I was going to say anything. How the hell does he think I feel? I asked him if he'd kept his word. That he hadn't seen her again. He said that she worked in a building near to his, so it was impossible not to bump into her every now and then, but that nothing had happened between them again. He promised me. That's why he wanted me to promise to keep quiet about it.

It *was* Emily. Caroline knew she'd met Pete at the pub after work and it was too much of a coincidence for there to be two of them. Caroline's eyes couldn't move fast enough over the rest of the pages.

Spoke to Mum today. I felt bad but I had to get her off the phone. I can't talk to her when I know I'm lying to her.

She *knew* she hadn't been imagining it. She'd told Pete that something was wrong with him. She thought she'd upset him. Pete had told her that she was being overprotective, oversensitive. Overmothering.

'That's not even a word,' she'd told him.

'It should be,' he'd said. 'Leave the boy alone.'

It all made sense now. Of course, he didn't want her talking to Jamie on her own. Too worried what she might find out.

Like it was yesterday, she was back there. A surge of grief threatened to overwhelm her. To pull her back down into the darkness. Where something else lived; something that she had pushed down deep. So deep that she wouldn't have to ever think about it again.

Anger rose from the depths of her like lava. What could she do with it? Pete wasn't here to answer for what he'd done. The last months she'd had with her son had involved fragmented conversations and brief answers to text messages. She'd told her friends it had felt like a bereavement, not being able to chat to him. That was before she knew what real bereavement felt like.

Clutching the diary tightly, she paced up and down the living room. She wanted to break something, kick something, smash something. She wanted to scream at Pete but he wasn't here to feel the force of the eruption building inside her.

But one person was.

She grabbed her handbag and pulled out her car keys.

CHAPTER THIRTY

EMILY

The row of prams parked outside the clinic confirmed that Emily was in the right place. There was a small space at the end of the row, so Emily picked up Dylan and squeezed the front wheel of her buggy into the slot. She still hadn't got the hang of pushing it by one handle, despite having to regularly hold a fractious Dylan on her hip and steer with the other hand.

At her last visit, the health visitor had urged her to take Dylan to the clinic for the regular weigh-in. 'You can just drop in. Any Monday, three to four in the afternoon. I've got no concerns with his weight, but it might help you to get out and meet some other mums.'

Though she wouldn't actually say it aloud, Emily still didn't feel like a mum. Obviously, she knew that she had a baby – and she loved him – but the concept of being a mum seemed to suggest that she knew what she was doing. Something she did not feel at all.

Even if there hadn't been an A4 notice tacked on its small window, she would have found the door for the clinic by the cacophony of sound echoing from within. Crying babies, rattling toys, a murmur of mothers chatting to one another.

In the past, Emily had never had a problem entering a room full of people. Back home in Ipswich, she used to thrive on it.

Throwing herself into a party or a busy bar, at the centre of her group of friends, organising nights out. Where had that Emily gone? Where was she hiding? She held Dylan close and stepped in.

The room wasn't especially large, but there were two separate sections. To the right, four changing tables containing babies in various stages of undress flanked either side of a desk where a midwife was weighing a chunky-looking baby in front of his proud mother. Clutched in her hand was the red Baby Record.

Emily went cold for a moment. Had she forgotten Dylan's red book, which she was supposed to take to any doctor, nurse or midwife appointment? She unzipped the side of her changing bag, felt warm relief when she spotted it there. Caroline had been the one to suggest she keep it in the bag so she always knew where it was. It had only been twenty-four hours since Caroline had dropped them home, but she was missing her: like having a safety net removed.

To the left, chairs lined three walls facing inwards to a large, soft, plastic playmat which was covered in children from tiny newborns in car seats to chunkier babies on their stomachs or pulling themselves along to reach one of the toys scattered around. Behind them, their mothers were watching, laughing and chatting to one another.

'Do you want me to move up so that you can sit here?'

The woman who had spoken looked around Emily's age, with short dark hair and a wide smile. She picked up the toys on the seat beside her to make room for Emily.

'Thanks.'

'Hi, I'm Gill. Your first time?'

'I'm Emily. Yes. My first time here. I asked if the midwife could come to the house to weigh Dylan but she said she can't do that so…' She stuttered over the end of the sentence. Why was she telling a stranger that? Now she was going to think that there was something wrong, a reason she wanted special treatment.

Thankfully, the woman seemed more wrapped up in her own child to ask. 'I like to bring Amelia every week. She has been on the ninety-fifth percentile since birth. Never wavered from her line.'

Emily wasn't sure how to react to that. Was that a good thing? She looked at the baby kicking her legs happily on the playmat in front of them. 'She has lovely curls.'

That was clearly the right thing to say. 'Yes. She gets those from her daddy. He hates his own, of course, but on her they look adorable.' She rolled her eyes at the mention of her husband. 'Does your little one take after you or his daddy?'

Something sharp twisted inside Emily. 'Er, it's too soon to tell.'

Gill leaned towards Dylan. 'He has very dark hair. And a lot of it.'

Again, from her tone, Emily had no idea whether that was something she approved of or not.

Emily shifted backwards a little. 'When do you know that it's your baby's turn to get weighed? Should I take a ticket or something?'

Gill laughed. 'No. You need to put your red book on the pile over there, then they'll call your name.'

As if on cue, one of the nurses looked in their direction and called out, 'Amelia Harding?'

'That's us. Come on, Millie.' She leaned down and scooped her daughter up in one smooth movement, kissed her on the cheek and picked up a stylish changing bag. 'Give me your book and I'll drop it on the pile for you. See you next time.'

Emily passed over the red book, feeling wrong-footed already. Like she didn't belong here with all these competent women who knew how everything worked. No one else spoke to her, so she laid Dylan down on the mat. He didn't kick his legs as Amelia had done. He just stared at her and she stared at him. He looked so fragile and vulnerable. He deserved to have someone looking after him who knew what they were doing.

She sat like that for the next fifteen minutes until she heard a voice from the other end of the room. 'Dylan Simmons?'

It was their turn. Emily bent over to pick him up, but her stomach was still a little uncomfortable where her trousers rubbed on her C-section wound, so it took her a moment to get him into a position that was easy for her to lift. 'Sorry, we're just coming.'

'There's no rush.' The nurse looked kind. 'You can take Baby over there and get his clothes off and then bring him here.'

Emily laid Dylan on the changing table the midwife had pointed to, and started to take his arms out of the Babygro. They were still so tiny. He had been five weeks premature so he wasn't likely to be one of the bigger babies. The health visitor had reassured her that as long as he was putting on weight, that was fine. One of the reliefs of feeding him from a bottle was that she could at least see how much milk he was having.

As she started to unpeel the tabs of his nappy, the mother next to her leaned in. 'You might want to leave that on till the last minute. They have a habit of going just at the wrong time.'

'Oh. That makes sense. Thanks.' She was grateful. That's what she needed in these situations. Someone to show her the ropes.

She was beginning to feel a bit more in control of the situation when she got to the scales. The same midwife smiled at her. 'Okay, whip the nappy off and we'll see where we are.'

As soon as she took Dylan's nappy off, he began to cry. She passed him over to the midwife, who didn't lose her kind smile. 'Is that a bit cold, little one?'

Despite her soothing noises, he carried on screaming. Other people started to look around. He got louder and louder. And louder. Some of the other babies started to join in. The midwife picked him up and gave him back to Emily. 'There you go. All over. Back to Mummy now.'

As quickly as she could manage, Emily threaded Dylan's flailing limbs back into a nappy and then his sleepsuit. If the midwife assumed that giving him back to her would stop his yelling, she was going to be disappointed. As the pitch rose higher and higher, Emily could feel her shoulders following suit. Once he was dressed, she held him close to her chest and tried to jiggle him up and down the way Caroline had. But it only worked for Caroline.

The nurse beckoned her over to the corner of the room. She had Dylan's red book in her hands. 'Nothing to worry about, but Dylan hasn't gained any weight since his last check-up. It's not necessarily a cause for concern, but because he was premature, we need to keep an extra eye on him. Has he been feeding okay?'

This was Emily's worst nightmare. If Dylan's screams hadn't alerted the whole room, the midwife speaking to her in hushed tones definitely would. 'He… he has been feeding. I switched him to formula a while back because I was having trouble breastfeeding.'

The midwife nodded. 'And how is he getting on with that? Have you had any problems?'

Was she kidding? Dylan screaming in her ear wasn't enough of an indication that she was having problems? Suddenly, the eyes that had seemed so kind were appraising her. Was she being found wanting? 'No. He's fine. Everything is fine.'

The midwife glanced again at the damn red book and then back at Emily. 'Okay. Well, we'll see how he is next week. But if you have any problems at all, you can call your community midwife.'

'Thanks.' Emily grabbed the red book and made for the door. She just wanted to get home.

But even when she got home, the feelings didn't go away. Halfway home, she'd realised that Dylan needed a nappy change but there was nothing to do but keep walking, get home as soon as she could. The front door to the flat bounced on its hinges, she pushed it so hard. 'I'm getting there, Dylan. Just give me a break. Give Mummy a break.'

She pulled the cover off the pram and saw the full extent of the nappy. The poor boy was soaked – and worse. 'Oh, baby, I'm sorry. Mummy is so sorry.'

As quickly as she could, she strode into the bedroom and placed him on the changing table. Her heart was racing: was she getting worse again? Had the medication stopped working? She recalled the doctor's words. *It's not a magic bullet.* The counselling appointment that he'd promised still hadn't come through. Would that actually help? Talking to a stranger about these feelings?

There was someone who wasn't a stranger who she could speak to. But would it be wrong of her to contact Caroline? She had been so thoughtful, so kind and more generous than Emily deserved. Caroline had asked to be kept informed about how things were going. Was it too soon? Even the thought of seeing her made Emily feel a little better. She would call her, invite her over.

Then, as if she had summoned her, she heard Caroline's voice. 'Hello? Emily? Are you there?'

Thank God. Everything was easier when Caroline was here.

CHAPTER THIRTY-ONE

CAROLINE

When she got to the house, the front door was open. She pushed it and called out. 'Hello? Emily? Are you there?'

There was silence. It was 4.15 p.m., which meant Dylan would be due a feed soon and Emily always preferred to be home for that. When she pushed the door open further, she could see the pushchair, loaded up as if for a walk, but there was no child in it. And no Emily.

She called again. Louder this time, directing her voice up the hall. 'Emily? Can I come in? It's Caroline.'

'Caroline? I'm through here. In the bedroom. Come down.'

She didn't want to go any further inside than she had to. Had been hoping that this conversation could take place in the hallway so she could be in and out. Still, she walked the few steps to the bedroom.

Inside, the bedroom was chaos. A coat and a bag flung on the floor. 'We were walking back from the clinic and he decided to fill his nappy. It's everywhere. It's making me feel sick. Up his back, behind his knees, now it's all over me and—'

Caroline wasn't here to make small talk. 'I've read the diary. I know about you and Pete.'

Emily looked up, a crease at the top of her nose, her mind clearly still half on the wriggling child underneath the baby wipe she was wielding. 'What? I don't know what you—'

'I know that you and Pete started seeing each other while we were still married. Before… before Jamie died.'

Now she did look as if she might be physically sick. 'How do you… what do you… look, it's not what you think. Let me just—'

'Don't.' Caroline couldn't help but look at Dylan as he kicked his legs on the changing table. She didn't want to raise her voice in front of him, but she wanted to scream at Emily. Instead, she settled for whispering harshly. 'How could you? How could you have kept this lie for so long?'

Emily's face reddened as if she might cry. 'Please, Caroline. Please just let me get this bloody nappy changed and I can tell you whatever you want to know.' As she finished speaking, a fountain of urine sprayed over her hands. 'Shit. Shit. Shit.'

Caroline automatically reached for the wet wipes and pulled three out. 'Go and get yourself cleaned up. I'll finish this.'

As usual, Emily was more than happy to leave her to it. Maybe Caroline's friends had been spot on about Emily taking advantage. She lifted both his ankles with three fingers and expertly wiped the changing mat underneath him. 'What a messy boy you are.'

None of this was his fault. He kicked his legs again as if there was not a problem in the world. She could see Pete in his eyes, the same blue eyes he had given her son. Now she was left cleaning up his mess and he wasn't even here to shout at.

She kept a hand on Dylan's stomach and opened the second drawer, which contained fresh vests. She thought of how much time she had spent in Emily's company since Dylan had arrived. Helping her. Supporting her. And she had known all along that she had taken Caroline's husband and said nothing.

Emily pushed open the bedroom door. 'I'm clean. All okay in here?'

Caroline picked up Dylan and held him out to her. 'He just needs some clothes. I'll be in the living room.'

*

It was possible that Emily had purposefully chosen to dress Dylan in one of the outfits that Caroline had bought him: a pale blue polo shirt and dark blue dungarees. Using him as some kind of bargaining chip to ward off some of Caroline's anger. But when Emily tried to give him to her, Caroline shook her head. She had to focus on what she wanted to know. Everyone kept telling her that she needed to move on from the past. But how could she move on if she didn't even know the truth about what had happened?

Emily eased Dylan into his bouncy chair. It seemed to take a lot of effort. Her face was tired. Drained of any vitality. A similar face to the one Caroline had seen in the mirror for months after Jamie's death. She hovered next to the sofa. 'Can I get you something to drink? Coffee? Wine?' She smiled nervously at suggesting wine in the middle of the afternoon.

Caroline couldn't have swallowed anything even if she'd wanted to. 'No. I just want to hear it from you. How long was it going on?'

Emily crumpled onto the other end of the sofa. She pulled the long maternity top that she was still wearing over her knees. 'It wasn't like that, Caroline. Honestly.'

'Then what was it like? How can I possibly know what it was like if you're not telling me anything?'

Emily breathed out slowly. 'I didn't know that Pete was married when we met. It started with one stupid kiss. We were both very drunk. I was all over the place emotionally. I hadn't long lost my mum, I was living alone in a new place and I was feeling... lonely, I suppose.'

Lonely? She had no idea what lonely was. Lonely was losing your son and then your husband. Lonely was planning out the whole night's TV so you didn't have to stop and think between switching channels. Lonely was a biting, gnawing belief that everyone else in the world was happy except you. 'And?'

Emily sighed again. 'It was a Christmas party for all the offices in our building. Except it was in November because the party committee had left it too late to get a slot in December. We had to have it at the pub nearby and we weren't the only people there. It was rammed with people from the surrounding offices. My mum had died not long before and I'd not been eating properly since she'd passed. I got drunk. Really drunk.'

Caroline wasn't about to give her an inch. 'And?'

Emily screwed up her eyes. 'The thing is, I'd always been the party girl. All through my twenties. "Emily is up for a laugh. Emily will get the dancing started. Emily will get the drinking going." And it was fine. Until I really needed someone to see me. To support me. To help me. And no one was there.'

Her voice caught in her throat. A week ago, even a day ago, Caroline might have put a hand on her shoulder. Told her not to upset herself. But not today. 'What does this have to do with Pete?'

Emily swallowed. 'I was very drunk. Pete was kind. He was pretty drunk too, I think. Somehow, we got talking outside, and even though he was older than me, there was this... spark between us, I suppose.'

Caroline's chest tightened. Did she really want to hear all this? Was she punishing Emily or herself? 'Then what happened?'

'It's a bit hazy, to be honest. But we kissed. It didn't last long, but it was just what I needed at that moment. Someone's arms around me.'

Caroline pressed her lips together. This was more painful than she thought it would be. 'You're saying that he took advantage of you?'

Emily looked as if she'd hit her. She shook her head. 'No. No, it wasn't like that. We were both drunk. It was just a moment. And he was the one to pull away. He apologised. That he shouldn't have done that. At the time, I didn't know what he meant. I didn't know he was married. I always check for a wedding ring and there wasn't one.'

That one hit her like a punch to the throat. Pete took his wedding ring off when he went out for the night? Months before

Jamie died? If only Pete was here to answer these questions. Was Emily even the first woman he had kissed while he was still married to her? 'But you did do it again?'

'The next week at work, I bumped into him on a run to the sandwich shop on the corner near the office. He asked if I was okay. I know that you won't forgive me, Caroline, but it was so nice to have someone check up on me. When you're a strong person, people just expect you to cope. When they have problems, you're always there to support them. But somehow they don't return the favour when you are the one who is struggling. When you need help or just someone to listen.'

Caroline couldn't help but think about Gabby and Faith. How they had dragged, pushed and carried her through the months after Pete had moved out. Then again when she'd found out he was moving in with Emily. 'And?'

'We went for a coffee. One lunchtime. I told him how lonely I felt since Mum had gone. That life had felt just empty and pointless. Looking back, I realise that I was depressed. It wasn't the first time I'd felt like that. When I was at college, I—'

Caroline waved away her words with a dismissive hand. She wasn't interested in hearing about her mental health history. She'd spent weeks trying to help her with that; support time was over. 'When did the affair start?'

'It wasn't an affair. It was just a friendship. We met for coffee. Then a couple of times at the bar near the office. We just talked. He told me that…' She glanced up at Caroline's face then returned to staring at her own hands. 'He told me that he was divorced. He said that…' She paused. 'Oh, Caroline. Are you sure you want to hear all this?'

'I need to know.'

'He said that the marriage had been over for a long time. That you had drifted apart and that, when Jamie went to university, you'd decided to file for divorce.'

Caroline clenched her fists. Digging her fingernails into her palms. At the same time as Pete was spinning these lies for Emily, he had been joking to Caroline that the two of them were now footloose and fancy-free. All the while, she'd looked at the two of them and thought, is this it? Is this all we're going to be from now on?

'When did you become more than friends?'

Emily chewed at her lip. 'One night just after Christmas, we met up for a drink. I'd had an awful Christmas. My aunt in Basingstoke had insisted I go to hers for Christmas dinner and there was all the forced jollity of board games and Christmas hats and I couldn't stand it. Pete sent me a text the day after Boxing Day to check how I was doing and I told him how bad I felt. He said he was on his own too and we could go for a drink.'

Caroline remembered that day. Jamie had made plans with his old school friends to meet up after they'd been released from family Christmas celebrations. She'd been finding homes for Christmas gifts when Gabby had texted her that Faith was having a bad time of it and she was taking her out for dinner. Pete had said he didn't mind at all if she wanted to go too. Now she knew why.

'The bar was really busy. We ended up outside even though it was freezing cold. Even then, we were pressed up quite close together. I got upset. Pete put his arms around me and... we kissed again.'

'How romantic.'

Emily stuck out her chin, her eyes shining. 'Actually, Caroline, it was. It was really romantic. How was I to know he was married? There were never any times when he said he couldn't see me. Never any weekends when he disappeared. All the things that might have made me suspicious just weren't there. We were besotted with one another. I had *no idea* that you were still married.'

This was a passionate side to Emily that she hadn't seen before. Was this the Emily who existed beneath all the trauma of the last

few months? *There were never any times when he couldn't see me.*
Caroline tried to think back to that period. Had Pete been going
out a lot? Had he been late home? She couldn't even remember.
But she also couldn't remember the two of them going out
together. 'How did Jamie find out?'

Emily's anger seeped out of her with a sigh and her shoulders
drooped. 'He saw us together.'

'How?'

Apparently, he was walking past the bar with his friends. He
didn't come over, but he did take a picture of us. He sent it to
Pete's phone. Didn't even comment. It was awful, Pete didn't
know what to do with himself.'

Poor Jamie. What a shock that must have been for him. 'Did
Pete go after him?'

Emily looked past her, as if she was trying to recall the events.
'At the time, I couldn't understand why Pete was so worried about
it when he was divorced. But he said that Jamie hadn't accepted
that his parents' marriage was over and I believed him. And,
yes, I have asked myself why I was so stupid. I guess it's easy to
delude yourself if you really want to believe something. I didn't
get the full story of what happened next until much later. After
Jamie's accident.'

Right now, Caroline didn't care about Emily's part in this. 'So
what *did* happen next? Did they talk about it?'

Emily nodded. 'That night. You were in bed apparently. Pete
waited up for Jamie to get in and then they had a huge row.
Jamie wanted to wake you up and tell you, but somehow Pete
persuaded him not to. Told him how much it would hurt you.
That it was a one-off. A lapse in judgement. Whatever he said,
it stopped Jamie from telling you. He went back to university
quite soon after that, I think?'

He had gone back earlier than planned, telling Caroline that
Beth had organised that post-Christmas dinner party for their

friends. That he'd missed his girlfriend. He had given her such a huge hug before he'd left and told her that he would call when he got there. He hadn't been able to look her in the face, though. She'd thought at the time it was because he felt guilty for leaving early. But it was a different kind of guilt. His father had turned him into a liar. If Pete was here right now, she would have slapped his lying, cheating face.

'Tell me the rest. Quickly.'

'Once Jamie went back to university, we carried on meeting up. It wasn't serious. Just dinners. Drinks. Until…'

She stopped. Looked at Caroline as if she was gauging whether to continue.

'Until what?'

'Until the night that Jamie died.'

CHAPTER THIRTY-TWO

EMILY

'My wife didn't understand me.' The classic line from a man looking to have an affair. But it wasn't quite what Pete had said. 'My wife didn't want me,' was closer to it.

'She felt lonely without Jamie,' he'd said.

'But that doesn't make sense. You were there.'

He had nodded and stared into his pint. 'I don't think I counted.'

If he'd gone on about it, she would have thought him pathetic, but he'd shaken his head, smiled and asked about her. How she was doing at work, whether she was planning to make London her permanent home. There was something intoxicating about having someone so interested in her. When he'd looked at her – really looked at her – with his dark blue eyes, she hadn't cared that he was ten years older than her.

It wasn't supposed to be a relationship. It was a friendship. Quite quickly, they'd grown to care about one another. If the day at work had been tough, she would much rather spend a night in a quiet pub chatting to Pete than go to the loud bar around the corner with the usual crowd.

Amy had warned her to be careful. 'He's a lot older than you. And divorced.' But Pete didn't seem to think their age difference was an issue, so why should she? On one level she knew where this was heading; on another, she was enjoying his company so much that she'd told herself that it was innocent. The original kiss at the Christmas party had been a drunken mistake. They had forgotten about it, pretended it had never happened.

And then they had kissed again.

That night, she'd been really upset after spending her first Christmas without her mum. Pete had tried to comfort her, put an arm around her. She'd leaned in towards him... It had been so unlucky that Jamie had seen them together. When the picture of the two of them beeped onto Pete's phone, he'd turned ashen.

She should have realised by his reaction that things might not have been as he'd said. But, by then, she'd fallen for him. From that point on, their meetings became less about friendship and more about love. Until Pete suggested they go away and spend the whole weekend together.

It had been the most romantic weekend of her life. He'd booked a room in a manor house hotel in Horsham. There was a four-poster bed and a huge bath in their room. The hotel restaurant was very grand yet intimate, and they had spent a long evening eating a five-course meal with different wines for every course. When they'd slept together for the first time that very night, it had felt so right and so natural. As if they'd been together for years. It had been perfect.

Until the early hours of Sunday morning, when Caroline had called to tell Pete about Jamie's accident.

Pete had shot out the door, buttoning his shirt and apologising for leaving her to pack up and make her own way home. She'd sat at breakfast alone in the dining room watching other couples holding hands over the table, feeling like an abandoned mistress: not knowing then that that's exactly what she was.

At that point, she'd had no idea what had happened to Jamie. Pete had said something about him being drunk, a fall, but she had just woken up and he wasn't making much sense. She checked her phone all day but didn't call him, not wanting to intrude, only allowing herself one text: *I'm here if you need anything.* The longer she didn't hear from him, the more her stomach clenched in fear. What had happened?

When she'd gone to work the next morning, she still hadn't known that Jamie had died. For three days she didn't hear from Pete. When he did get in contact, it was a brief message, telling her what had happened and that he would speak to her soon. For the next few days, she hadn't known what to do with herself. A week later, he'd turned up at her flat and cried. She had taken him into her arms and waited until his body had stopped shaking.

They'd slept together again that night. Slow, gentle, vulnerable, comforting sex. Afterwards, he'd lain his head on her chest and she'd held him close, like a child, stroking his hair. He hadn't stayed the night. Caroline – that was the first time he had ever used his ex-wife's name in their conversations – would need him. Back then, she had wondered what Caroline was like, what she looked like, what kind of person she was. In a thousand years, she couldn't have predicted she would get to know her like this.

'I am sorry, Caroline. I am so very sorry. But I didn't know.'

Caroline's arms were folded, her face thunderous. 'You expect me to believe that? How can you not have suspected something? He told you he was living in the house with me and you didn't wonder if there was something going on?'

Emily felt her cheeks redden. She *had* felt jealous. When Pete told her that he was moving back in with Caroline temporarily so that he could support her, she'd wondered if their son's death might bring the two of them back together. The only person she had confided this to was Amy.

They'd gone for a drink after work and sat opposite each other, two large glasses of Malbec between them. 'It makes me a terrible person, doesn't it? They've just lost their only son and I am worrying whether he's going to leave me and go back to his ex-wife.'

Amy had shaken her head. 'Not terrible at all. I'd be the same. I did warn you about getting involved with a divorced man. Too much history.'

That's what she'd been worried about. He and Caroline would have all their shared history of Jamie. Would that be enough to glue them back together? Pete's reasons for their divorce – *we just drifted apart* – hadn't suggested any huge problems between them. Maybe they would just drift back together again?

'I am a terrible person. I mean, the woman has just lost her son. If they are going to get back together, I shouldn't stand in the way, should I? Shall I tell him to stop coming over? That he should be free to try and make a go of it with... with Caroline?'

It had felt strange even saying her name. Pete had still been visiting her at the flat, but they hadn't been out anywhere since Jamie's death. He just hadn't felt up to it. Aside from his sadness, she hadn't minded staying home together. Quickly, their relationship had deepened. There were no hidden emotions. No secrets. Or so she had thought.

Amy had narrowed her eyes. 'That's very unselfish of you.'

Emily's eyes had filled. She hadn't felt unselfish. She'd wanted to be selfish. She'd wanted Pete back. They'd only been together a short while but the mere thought of losing him had filled her with fear.

Caroline was still waiting for an answer. Emily needed to make her understand. She could hear the pleading in her own voice. 'He told me you were divorced, Caroline. When we first met, he said that he was staying with a friend. He said his friend's wife didn't really want him there, so that's why he couldn't invite me over. He told me that he'd moved back to your house after Jamie's accident, but he said that was just to help you through everything. It wasn't permanent.'

Caroline shook her words away. 'When did you find out the truth?'

Emily closed her eyes for a second. She could still picture Pete's face. His profuse apologies. The begging. 'Not until we were about to get married. I saw the divorce papers. I saw the date of separation. It was the same date as he'd moved in with me. Three months after Jamie's accident.'

According to Pete, he had moved back in with Caroline to support her after Jamie's death, but – three months after the accident – he had turned up on Emily's doorstep with a suitcase and told her that Caroline didn't need him anymore. That he wanted them to make a commitment. That he wanted a future with her. Her patience and love had been rewarded: he was finally all hers.

Except, that hadn't been the truth. It was there in black and white on the divorce papers. The night he moved in with her had been the official date of his separation from Caroline. For the first few months of their relationship, he had still been married to her.

They'd had an almighty row about it. She'd felt physically sick at the thought that when they'd first kissed, he'd still been living with Caroline as her husband. That Jamie had been angry with his father because he had, in fact, been cheating on his mother.

Caroline's face was creased with disgust. 'And yet, you still married him? Knowing that he had lied to you all that time?'

She could understand Caroline's disbelief. If it had been one of her friends, she would have told them to run a mile. *Once a cheater, always a cheater.* But the feelings she'd had for him ran so deep. They had shared so much. She couldn't bear to let him go. They had been living together for over a year and she was pregnant with his child. It was too hard to give him up.

Now Caroline was pacing the floor. 'And there was me thinking that he'd moved in with a friend when I asked him to give me some space. One lie used twice. How economical. I'm sure it wasn't difficult for him. At that point, I couldn't care less where he was going to live – it was all I could do to keep putting one foot in front of the other. I had no idea that he'd left my house and come straight here to you. The whole way through our divorce, I thought he was being so generous – letting me stay in the house, accepting the list of unreasonable behaviour we had to cite to get the divorce to go through – when all the time, he was living a new life with you. We could have cited adultery and been through the whole process a whole lot quicker.' She stopped walking and looked at Emily. 'Even if you are telling the truth… even if you had your head so far stuck in the sand that you didn't realise that he'd been lying to you… you still knew the truth eventually. My husband left me for you and you've lied about it to my face for all this time? All the help I've given you and you *knew* what you'd both done.'

There was nothing she could say to absolve herself of that. Before she'd met Caroline, it had been easy to believe Pete's version of her. That she was a little cold. That their love had withered. Once she had experienced Caroline's generosity and care, it got harder to reconcile the two. 'I am sorry. Truly sorry. But I couldn't see what good it would do to tell you now. How would that have helped?' She swallowed down the tears that threatened. 'But I am sorry, Caroline.'

Caroline spun around on her foot. 'Sorry? Sorry? How can you expect me to believe you are sorry?' She seemed to rise higher in front of her very eyes. 'You said that Pete was coming home late? That you thought he was having an affair?'

She wasn't sure where Caroline was going with this. 'Yes?'

Her face hardened; her eyes were dark. 'He was with me. All those evenings he told you that he was working late he was at my house. We were spending more time together. We were,' she paused for emphasis, 'spending a *lot* of time together.'

A chill trickled down Emily's spine; she couldn't speak.

Still Caroline stared. 'And then he told me you were pregnant.'

Emily couldn't feel her legs. 'I see.'

Caroline's face was red; her eyes pierced into Emily. 'Do you know what he said when he told me you were expecting a baby?'

Emily didn't want to hear this. She couldn't cope with knowing what Caroline was about to tell her. 'I don't think—'

'He said that he wasn't in love with you. That it had been a mistake. A reaction to Jamie's death. If you hadn't been pregnant, he would never have—'

'Please, I don't want to hear any more.' Emily put both hands up in surrender. Caroline's words were knives.

If anything, Caroline's face got redder. 'You don't want to hear? How do you think I feel knowing that my husband was having an affair? And how the hell did you let me take you in, look after you, care for your son while knowing this all the while?'

Caroline stepped forwards. Emily flinched as if she was about to hit her. 'I am so sorry. If I could make it better I would.'

'Well, you can't.' Caroline strode towards the door and slammed it on the way out.

For the next hour, Emily sat in her chair while Dylan cried in her arms. Of course, Pete hadn't loved her. Of course, Caroline wanted nothing to do with her. What she had done was unforgivable. If she hadn't met him that Christmas. If she hadn't got pregnant. If she hadn't agreed to marry him. If she hadn't been such a blind and useless fool. If. If. If.

She banged on her head with her fist. It felt like her son was shouting at her. 'I know, I know. I'm still useless, Dylan. I'm still making a mess of everything.'

How the hell could someone like her ever expect to be a good mum to this helpless little boy?

CHAPTER THIRTY-THREE

CAROLINE

'What an utter, utter, pig-faced… pig!'

It was so unusual to see Gabby's eternally smiling face red with anger that Caroline almost smiled. It was just the two of them at the café that morning as David had whisked Faith away for another weekend – a hotel not a boat this time – and they'd had to sit near the door because their favourite corner table was occupied.

'I'm sorry. I know he's dead and everything. But he was seeing her the whole time? When you were grieving for Jamie, he was… visiting Emily?'

Caroline's stomach churned. It was a deeply unpleasant thought. 'He was with her. That weekend. The weekend Jamie died.'

Pete had told her that he was away on business that weekend. She'd even thought about going to visit Jamie at the time. It would have been nice, just the two of them. Out for lunch and then she could have taken him to the supermarket and made sure he had enough food to last him a while longer. When she'd floated the idea, Pete had laughed at her – laughed! – told her that Jamie needed his independence, not to have his mother fussing over him. Now she wondered if he had been more worried that Jamie might reveal what he knew.

Gabby stirred her coffee and slowly shook her head. 'I can't believe Jamie knew about it. Poor kid. He must have been really torn about what to do.'

Jamie's diary didn't sound so much torn as disgusted. There had been only one person she could think of who might be able to tell her how he had felt. Last night, she'd called Beth and they had spoken on the phone for over an hour.

After asking how she was and chatting about her psychology course, Caroline had explained why she was calling and told her that she'd read Jamie's diary; that she knew he'd discovered Pete's affair with Emily. 'Is that what you wanted to talk to me about on Jamie's birthday? When we were sitting on his bench?'

Beth's voice had been hesitant, unsure. 'Yes. Well, I was going to ask how you were. And then when I saw Jamie's dad, I just assumed...'

Caroline had understood how difficult it must have been for her to be frank. 'That we were still together?'

Beth had sighed. 'Yes.'

On that day, sitting on Jamie's bench with Pete holding her hand, Caroline had thought it was possible they could be together again, too. Her face burned at the thought of those evenings he had come to see her. How easy it would have been for her to let him return home to her as if nothing had happened.

She'd wanted to know more. Every detail. 'What did he tell you about it all, Beth? I know you were the one who encouraged him to write it all down.'

Again, Beth was hesitant. 'Well, when he told me, I thought that he should tell you. I said it wasn't his secret to keep. If his dad wasn't going to tell you, then he should. But he was so concerned about hurting you and he loved his dad. You know how they were together. He didn't want to do anything that might split you up. I think he was hoping that it would all go away and you would carry on.'

Caroline's heart had ached at the thought of the burden of truth Jamie had been carrying. She did know how much Jamie idolised his dad. The shock of seeing him cheating on his mum must have been immense. 'But it didn't all go away.'

Once Beth had started to talk about it, the words seemed to be rushing from her mouth down the telephone. The relief of confession. 'No. He couldn't let it go. Every time he had a drink, it would come up. And then he started acting different.'

Caroline had sensed a change in him those last few weeks, but she had only had hurried telephone conversations to base it on. She hadn't been there to see for herself what was going on with him. 'What do you mean?'

'He was drinking a lot. I mean, obviously a lot of drinking goes on here, but he was getting really drunk even halfway through the week.' She had paused. 'He started smoking a lot too. Weed. Marijuana. It made him so paranoid and I was really starting to get sick of it. I couldn't do anything right. We were arguing quite a lot.'

Caroline hadn't known any of this. There had been a toxicology report as part of the post-mortem but it had been inconclusive. She had been adamant that Jamie hadn't taken drugs and no one had testified otherwise. Including Beth. Had they even asked her?

She hadn't mentioned that the two of them hadn't been getting on at the time either. Had she? 'I'm sorry to hear that, Beth. That must have been really tough for you. Is that what happened that night? Is that why he left the bar without you?'

Beth had started to cry. 'It's worse than that. He was flirting with a girl at the bar. Erika. She was on one of his maths courses. I got really cross with him and I said... I said...'

She had been really crying then. Caroline hadn't wanted to make the poor girl feel any worse. 'It's okay, Beth. Don't tell me if you don't want to.'

It had taken a few moments for Beth to be able to talk clearly again. 'I do want to tell you. I wanted to tell you at the time but I was too worried about what you'd think of me. I'd had too much to drink too and I was so angry with him. He was making me look like an idiot chatting to the girl in front of everyone and I'd had enough. I said to him, "You're just like your dad." I knew it would hurt him. I knew it would. I feel so awful about it.'

Caroline could have joined in her crying, but she'd held it together. 'And then he left the bar?'

She could only hear sniffing at the end of the phone. Eventually, Beth had spoken. 'Yes. He left in a temper. His friends tried to stop him but I didn't say anything. I wanted him to leave so that he wasn't chatting up Erika anymore. She was the one who left the other bunch of flowers at the bench. I found out after you left on Jamie's birthday. She told another friend on their course and he told me. She feels awful, too.'

It was all such a terrible, terrible mess.

Beth had started crying again. 'If we hadn't had that row, I would have gone back to his room, or he would have come to mine. If I'd been there, it wouldn't have happened. You must hate me. It's all my fault, isn't it?'

'No, my love. It was not your fault. And you can ask your friend to tell Erika the same thing. It was an accident. A tragedy. But it definitely wasn't your fault.'

Beth could barely get her words out. 'I just wish I could go back to that night and tell him not to leave. Or go with him. I just keep playing it over and over in my head.'

Caroline had done the same. If she had gone there that weekend. If she had called him that night. With the revelations in the diary and this phone call, she had another set of 'what-ifs' to add to her collection. But that wasn't helping anybody. 'Jamie wouldn't want that, Beth. It was an accident. There was nothing you could have done. He wouldn't want you going over the past like that. You've got a great future ahead of you. Remember him before that night. Remember happy Jamie who loved you.'

There was still so much unsaid. Why hadn't Beth mentioned the diary at the inquest? Or even told Caroline about it before now? All the months – and experts – trying to get to the bottom of what had happened that night and this may have been a vital piece of the puzzle.

But she hadn't wanted to ask her that question. Not yet, anyway. It would only make Beth feel worse and it wasn't as if it would change anything. Jamie would still be gone.

Going into that room on the day of the inquest, months and months after Jamie had gone, had been so very difficult. She missed him every single day. A pain like a festering wound which hurt all the time, but listening to evidence, expert opinion, reliving the worst day of her life, had been like taking the bandage off and exposing the wound to the sting of the open air.

She'd closed her eyes. No. She wouldn't ask Beth why she hadn't mentioned the diary. Because she didn't want to know.

Last night, she'd finished the call doing her best to reassure Beth, just as Gabby was trying to do for her now. 'Well, at least you know that you did the right thing asking Pete to leave. You don't have to wonder about that anymore.'

It made no difference now, but it might help to be completely honest. 'I was thinking about asking him to come home, you know. I didn't tell you or Faith but – before I knew about the baby – I thought that he might… that he might want to come home.'

Gabby reached over and wrapped her hand around Caroline's fist, which clutched at a tissue. 'We suspected as much. We just didn't want to interfere.'

'Because you knew it was a bad idea?'

Gabby shook her head. 'Because no one can tell someone what to do in their marriage. Our job was to be there if it didn't work out.' She paused, tested the waters with a smile. 'And because, yes, we thought it was an absolutely terrible idea.'

Caroline's short laugh made a teardrop fall from the end of her nose. 'I can imagine the two of you talking about it. You were definitely not Pete's biggest fans.'

'It wasn't about him; it was about you. It was as if you were going backwards. You were doing so well, coming out with us, working at the children's centre. You were really making progress. The thing with Pete, well, it just felt as if you were slipping backwards again.'

Her friends were so wise. Were they right about that? Had she been trying to recreate the past? Listening to Emily describe her feelings for Pete – and his for her – had reminded Caroline how they had been in the beginning too. But it had been a long time since she'd felt like that about Pete, and if he'd been having an affair with Emily, he had clearly not been passionate about her, either. Yes, she had been considering asking him to come home. But she hadn't been looking to rekindle their love: she had been looking for someone to buffer the loneliness of her life.

'You didn't think it was a good idea, me getting to know Dylan, either, did you?'

Gabby paused. Looked her in the eye. 'That one is down to you. All we want is for you to be happy. And not to be hurt anymore.'

It was all irrelevant now, anyway. She wasn't likely to see Emily or Dylan ever again. It would be better to forget that Dylan – and Emily – existed. It was time to follow the same advice that she had given Beth last night: look to the future.

She had the interview for her new job this week. That would be the first step.

CHAPTER THIRTY-FOUR

EMILY

In the week since her conversation with Caroline, Emily hadn't left the flat. Once she had got as far as putting Dylan in the pram and standing, holding tightly to the handles, heart fluttering in her chest, in front of the open door. After five minutes of deep breathing, she'd pushed them both over the threshold into the communal hallway, walked slowly towards the main entrance, out into the dark morning. When she'd felt the beginning of rain on the top of her head, she had been relieved to have an excuse to turn back inside.

Though it piled more guilt onto her shoulders every time she looked at it, the food that Caroline had filled her freezer with and the three huge tins of baby milk powder she'd left in the cupboard meant that there was no urgent need to go anywhere. Or see anyone. Or even speak aloud.

The last person she had spoken to was Amy's boyfriend, Stuart, yesterday. He'd picked up on the eighth ring. 'Hi. Amy's phone.'

She had been just about to hang up and the sound of his voice had wrong-footed her. 'Oh. Hi. Is that… It's Emily. Amy's friend. Is she there?'

'Hold on.' She'd listened to the sound of his breath – like he was walking somewhere. Then she'd heard him speaking to someone else. A question. 'It's Emily. Do you want to speak to her?'

She hadn't heard the answer, just his breath as he was walking again. When he'd spoken again, his voice had been quiet. 'Hi, sorry, she, er, she's not really up to talking at the moment. She, ah, she lost the baby yesterday.'

Emily had closed her eyes, winded by sorrow. All she could think of was Amy's face at Pete's funeral, unable to suppress her joy, her relief, at finally falling pregnant. It was so unfair. Why was fertility such a lottery? There was Amy, desperate to have a child, and here she was, feeling...

She couldn't finish that sentence, even in her head.

Last night, she'd lain awake, staring at the ceiling, trying to make sense of it all. Amy. Caroline. Her ungrateful and incompetent self. After about three hours' sleep, she'd woken up to Dylan's persistent yell. The crying had continued. He'd now managed three hours straight.

He'd been fed, changed, walked around the room again and again and again.

He just wouldn't stop.

Caroline would know what to do. Caroline had that special walk, special pat. Caroline was a born mother. A mother without a son.

Was that her fault too? Had Jamie got so drunk on the night of his accident because he'd been upset with Emily and his father?

She shuddered, started walking again. 'Please, Dylan. Please stop crying.'

Did he miss Caroline? She'd spent so much time with him these last few weeks that maybe he thought she was his mother. What was Emily then? A stand-in? A poor copy? A replacement?

Just as she'd been to Pete.

Poor Dylan. It wasn't his fault. It was hers. She was a bad mother and there was no one to show her how to be better. No mum. No Pete. And now no Caroline.

Caroline. The mother without a son.

Dylan. The son without a decent mother.

What did her own mum used to say? *A mother will sacrifice anything for her child.*

However hard it was, Emily knew what she had to do.

CHAPTER THIRTY-FIVE

CAROLINE

Caroline's interview for the new job was Monday morning at 11 a.m. For the last five minutes, she'd sat staring at the blinking cursor on her screen, trying to see why the last two columns in the spreadsheet wouldn't reconcile. Pushing aside the pile of invoices, she picked up her mug to make herself a third cup of coffee. More caffeine might help.

It was all very well Faith telling her that she was perfect for the job, but she wouldn't be the only one getting interviewed. Faith's boss Lorna was coming down from the area office to see three candidates. Faith had refused to tell Caroline anything about them, which could only mean that they were better qualified than she was.

She called through to Michaela on reception. 'Do you want a coffee?'

Michaela looked up from the attendance registers she was working on. 'Another one? You'll spend half your interview going to the toilet.'

Caroline leaned against the doorway. 'I know. I just can't sit still. I'm so nervous.' It wasn't just nerves about the job; the last week had been awful. Reliving the last weeks and days of Jamie's life.

Michaela took off her glasses and tilted her head. 'You don't need to worry. Faith wants you and you've been a social worker. What more could Lorna want?'

In her head, Caroline knew that she was right. But everything had been knocked out of kilter this week. It was as if someone had taken hold of the floor beneath her and tugged at it, and she still hadn't got her balance. On Michaela's desk, sheets of paper stood in three important-looking piles. 'What are they?'

Michaela replaced her glasses and tapped the first pile with her finger. 'The information about each of the candidates for Lorna. The application forms and CVs. She's read them on email but she likes a paper copy to write over while she's in the interview.'

Caroline peered at them. 'Oh, really? What am I up against?'

Michaela's eyes widened. 'You can keep your eyes away from those, madam. Faith would have my guts for garters.' She frowned. 'Are you really that nervous about this?'

Was it nerves? Or full-on trepidation? When she'd woken up this morning, she couldn't quite decide if she wanted to pass the interview or fail it. Was she even up to the job?

The front door pushed open and a young woman in a smart suit and iron-straight strawberry blonde hair walked up to the reception desk. 'Good morning. Chloe Jordan. I'm here for an interview for the outreach job?'

Caroline backed out of the way, collected her make-up bag from under her desk and made for the toilet. Time to get ready.

The interview went very well. Faith had prepped her about the job so she was able to speak confidently about her previous experience working with families and supporting them. When Lorna had asked her why she'd left social work, that had been a little trickier. The skin that had started to heal over Jamie's loss had been rubbed raw again by the revelations in his diary, but she'd managed to hold it together to explain how losing him had affected her ability to cope with the pain in other people's lives. As she'd practised with Faith, she emphasised to Lorna how she was ready now to get back to a role like this – and that, actually, her experience would only add to her understanding of how life's heartbreaking twists and turns can change everything.

Although it was a relief to exit the room, which was small and hot, she did leave thinking that she'd done all she could. However, she had no idea how much experience the two women who'd gone before her might have and whether Lorna would prefer them. They'd promised a decision by the end of the day.

When she returned to reception, there was a buggy parked in the foyer which looked vaguely familiar. It even had a changing bag over the handle in the same design as the one Emily used. Behind the front desk, Michaela was holding a baby who was even more familiar. And crying.

'Oh, great, you're out. Your friend Emily just dropped the baby off – she said you were looking after him tonight? I didn't want to disturb you in your interview, but the poor little man hasn't stopped grizzling. She left some cartons of baby formula and I've tried him on one of those, but he's not having any of it.'

Instinctively, Caroline held out her arms for Dylan; his warmth and weight almost made her cry, she had missed him so much. But there had been no word from Emily since their confrontation last week. Why was she dropping him off here? It didn't make sense. 'Did she say anything else? Like what time she'd be back?'

Michaela shook her head. 'No, but she did leave a note for you.'

Just as she passed it to Caroline, the door to the interview room opened and they watched through the office door as Faith accompanied Lorna to the reception desk to sign out. They were laughing and chatting. Lorna looked up and saw Caroline through the doorway. She nodded at Dylan. 'Are you getting some practice in already?' She smiled. 'I'll let Faith tell you the good news.' She waved at them, picked up her briefcase and shook hands with Faith.

Faith watched through the window until Lorna was safely in her car before bounding into the office. 'You got it! She was so impressed with you. She kept saying how pleased she was that we would have someone with your social work experience.' She stopped short and took in the crying baby. 'Where did that baby come from?'

'It's Dylan.' Caroline waited for the penny to drop.

Faith's eyes widened. 'Emily's baby? What is *she* doing here?'

Caroline moved Dylan so that his face was against her shoulder, shushing him as she jigged him gently up and down. 'She's not here. She just dropped the baby off.'

Michaela retreated to her reception desk to sign in a couple of young mothers, so Caroline stepped forwards to press the door closed. She continued to walk up and down across the office, soothing Dylan back to sleep.

Faith folded her arms, watched Caroline pace up and down. 'Did I miss something? Why have you agreed to look after Dylan?'

'I haven't. I'm as surprised as you. I haven't even spoken to Emily since last Monday. She's left this note – can you open the envelope for me?'

Faith took the envelope from her hand, sliced it open with her finger, then passed back the letter inside.

Continuing to walk up and down, Caroline read aloud.

Dear Caroline,

You have no idea who I am. Who I really am.

When you look at me now, you can't see the smile which drew Pete to me, can't hear the laugh that infected my friends, the love of life which attracted the attention of strangers. It's not a surprise: I don't see that woman any longer, either.

Even if I could show you that part of me, your opinion would always be coloured by the things that have happened. Events that we can't alter, however much we long to. But, of all people, I

*hope that you will understand how much a person can change.
How much a life can change.*

*Still, I'm not asking for your sympathy. I'm not asking you
to help me. What I'm asking you to do, I ask for him. Accepting
that you will judge me, knowing that you won't understand,
but believing – and hoping with every scrap of me – that you
will do it. You will do it for Dylan. And for Pete. And Jamie.*

*Pete was the absolute love of my life. When he held my
hand, I was safe, I was happy, I was home. Now the possible
feels impossible, hope has become bitter disappointment and the
future is just dark. Pete is dead and I am lost and there is no
other choice but this.*

*Please forgive me. I wish I could make it up to you for
everything that has happened, but I can't. You don't know me
well enough to understand that I am not a bad person, that I
wouldn't have started anything with Pete if I'd known he was
married. I was in love with him. More than that, I think I
persuaded myself that I needed him. I was afraid of being alone.*

*I can't turn back the clock. But I know that I have brought
you a lot of misery and I am truly sorry for that. You have helped
me so much in recent weeks, but I can't do this anymore. I love
Dylan so much, but I am not good enough for him. He is so
much happier with you and I want him to be happy.*

Please look after my boy.
Emily

For a few moments, Caroline stared at the paper. When she
looked up at Faith, she saw her own shock mirrored back at her.

Faith spoke first. 'Bloody hell.'

Although she'd just read the words aloud, Caroline's brain was
having a hard time making sense of them. 'Has she just *given* me
her son?'

'It sounds like it. What are you going to do? Are you going to go round there? Do you want me to call the child services team?'

Dylan had finally dropped off to sleep on Caroline's shoulder. She moved him into a lying position in her arms, his face so peaceful in sleep. Again, she marvelled at his likeness to his older half-brother. 'No, don't call them yet. I'll try to get hold of her and speak to her.'

Faith nodded. 'Okay. Why don't you go now? Take the rest of the day off. In fact, you've had hardly any holiday since you started. If you need to take some days to sort this out, just let me know. You can even work from home if you need to.' She pushed herself away from the desk and looked down at the sleeping Dylan, reaching out to stroke his cheek. 'How could she just abandon him like this?'

Caroline wanted to agree. Wanted to join in and say that Emily was an awful mother, that she didn't deserve this perfect little boy.

But she knew how frightened Emily was, how scared that someone – maybe social services – would take her son away from her. That she'd left him with Caroline was the ultimate in trust, love and self-sacrifice. She loved her son and she wanted him to be safe. Even if that meant giving him away.

But what about her? Where was she? Who was she with? And, most importantly, was she safe?

CHAPTER THIRTY-SIX

CAROLINE

Emily hadn't answered any of Caroline's eight calls. She'd been around to the flat and there was no answer there either. Where was she?

Dylan had slept in the car on the way to the flat, and had stayed asleep when she'd lifted him out to place him in the pram. He'd slept through her knocking on the door of the flat, calling Emily's name through the letterbox and ringing the doorbell repeatedly. However, when she tried to put him back into his car seat, he woke up and demanded some attention.

'Hey, hey.' Caroline hooked her thumbs under his armpits and made a cradle for his head with her fingers. It was amazing how quickly the moves came back. 'There's no need to cry, little man. We'll get you some milk, shall we?'

She'd missed chattering away to him this week, his gurgled replies that she could interpret any way she chose. 'Is that, "yes please, Auntie Caroline, I'd love some milk"?'

There were cartons of formula in the bag, ready to be tipped into bottles. It was an expensive way to do it, but she'd bought boxes of them wholesale to make life easier for Emily when she'd first gone back to the flat on her own. Dylan clearly wasn't impressed with the idea that he should go back into his car seat so that she could take him home to feed him. There was a high street with a few cafés a short walk from here. That would be a quicker and less noisy option.

The bell on the café door jangled as she pushed it open with her elbow and backed in, pulling the buggy in behind her. A hand appeared on the door as an older man held it back so that it was easier to get in. 'Let me get that, love, you've got enough to be doing.'

She smiled gratefully and looked around for somewhere to sit. A waitress sashayed past carrying two mugs of coffee and nodded to her right. 'There's a table in the corner with room for your buggy. Get yourself settled and I'll come over and take your order.'

Once she'd stowed the buggy between the table and the wall, she picked up Dylan and held him close while she rummaged in the changing bag for the carton of formula and a bottle. It took a bit of balancing to hold him and fill the bottle, but it wasn't long before he was feasting greedily on the milk.

'You were hungry, weren't you, mister? You need to slow down or you'll get that nasty wind.'

The waitress appeared by the side of the table with her notepad. 'He's a tiny one. How old is he?'

'Six weeks. He was five weeks early so he's still catching up.'

'If he keeps drinking like that, it won't take long.' The waitress nodded at the bottle which was going down at a rate of knots. 'Now, what about you? What can I get you?'

After she'd ordered her coffee, Caroline was happy to just watch Dylan's cheeks as he sucked at the teat of the bottle. Was it muscle memory that – over twenty years after she'd fed her own baby – made this feel so familiar already? The weight of him on her forearm, the warmth of his head on her inner elbow, the faint smell of milk. There was something so natural, so… primal about this.

She was jogged out of her thoughts by an older woman at the next table. 'Isn't he a lovely boy, what a lucky mummy you are.'

Caroline opened her mouth to explain that Dylan wasn't hers. But that's not what came out. 'Yes. He's a really lovely boy. I am lucky.'

She hadn't exactly lied. She hadn't said that he was her son. What did it hurt if she just enjoyed this moment a little longer?

The teat of the bottle hissed as Dylan let it out of his mouth and a dribble of milk ran down his chin. She wiped it with a muslin cloth then rested his chin in the crook of her hand while she rubbed his back.

His burp was loud enough to wake him from his drunken stupor and his eyes flicked back open. For a second, it looked as if he might cry, but the older lady covered her face with her hands and peeped out from behind them. 'Peekaboo!'

Dylan seemed fascinated by her. Watched her face intently. Jamie had been like this, too. Strangers would gravitate towards him and he'd love them back. She'd lost count of the times old ladies in supermarkets had told her what a 'heartbreaker' he was going to be when he grew up. They couldn't have predicted how much.

The waitress arrived with her coffee. Sliding it onto the table, she stood back and watched the woman entertaining Dylan. 'It doesn't seem five minutes ago that my big lumps were his age. Is he your first?'

Caroline swallowed. 'No. No. My first one was born more than twenty years ago.'

The waitress raised an eyebrow. 'Crikey, that's a big gap. Still, I think you appreciate the second one more. You know how quickly it goes, don't you?'

Yes, she knew how quickly it went. How quickly the suckling baby became the chubby toddler who changed into the gap-toothed nine-year-old and then the sullen teenager. How the days and the months and the years were like sand slipping through your fingers and, try as you might, you couldn't hold onto them.

The older lady continued to pass her hands back and forth in front of her face to entertain Dylan as she spoke. 'If you're lucky, they bring you grandchildren and you get to do it all over again.'

The coffee Caroline had sipped seemed to harden in her throat and she gulped it down. She hadn't even thought about grandchildren. None of her friends had children old enough to be thinking about that yet. But when they did, she would be a spectator of their happiness again. That's the thing with loss. You don't just lose someone once. You lose them again and again, over and over.

She moved Dylan to her other arm, rubbed his back again to be sure that there was no more wind to come up. For the last twenty minutes she had been someone again, she had been the mother of a small child. People had talked to her, been interested in her. Even if it was only because of Dylan. For the last two years she had felt like a balloon with a cut string, floating around with nothing to anchor her, gradually deflating and becoming smaller; less and less significant. Today she was useful, interesting, necessary, needed. It was intoxicating.

Maybe it was right that she look after Dylan for a while. She had time, she had love. Emily needed space to heal, to find herself. Caroline was doing her a favour, really. She could take Dylan back to the house now and try again to get hold of Emily. If she wanted to stay away for a while, Caroline wouldn't judge her. She would tell her to do what she needed to do; Caroline would make sure that Dylan was okay. A prickle of pleasure bloomed in her chest at the thought of taking care of him on her own.

The older lady got up slowly from her chair, reaching for the walking frame she had hidden behind her seat. As she hobbled past the table, she stopped and placed a pound coin beside Caroline's coffee cup. 'Put it in his money box.' She tapped Caroline's hand. 'You're a lucky lady. Boys always love their mums best.'

'Thank you. That's so kind of you.' Caroline smiled at her retreating back, then looked at the coin. Her vision blurred.

Boys did need their mothers. And mothers needed their sons. She knew that better than anyone.

She took out her purse to pay the bill.

CHAPTER THIRTY-SEVEN

CAROLINE

When she returned home, the first person she called was Faith, who was still at work.

Faith's voice was both reassuring and challenging. 'You've still not found her? What did the police say?'

Caroline was glad she was having this conversation on the phone so that she didn't have to deal with the disapproval on Faith's face when she admitted her failing. 'I haven't called them yet.'

Faith was one of those friends who would go to the guillotine for you but also hold you to account like a high court judge. 'Why not?'

To be fair, she had a point this time. Not that Caroline wanted to admit that. 'I am worried what they might say. About Dylan. If they think she's abandoned him, they'll get child services involved and then—'

Faith cut through her excuses. 'But she *has* abandoned him. She has abandoned her son and that means she could be in a really bad way, Caroline.'

Caroline shuddered. She knew this, of course. But it had been surprisingly easy to not think about it for the last couple of hours. Again, she was grateful that Faith wasn't there to see her blush. 'I know. But she hasn't exactly left him in a bag at the fire station. She gave him to me. To look after. She knew I would keep him safe.'

There was a pause at the end of the line before Faith spoke, her voice softer this time. 'Caroline, honey. He's not yours. He's not your baby.'

It was easier to talk to tough Faith than kind Faith. The sympathy in her voice was all it took to tip Caroline into tears. 'I know that. I know he's not mine. But I do love him, Faith. I know you warned me about getting attached, you and Gabby. You told me to be careful, but I couldn't help myself.'

'Oh, love, of course you couldn't. You've got the biggest heart of anyone we know, that's why we were concerned about you. And losing Jamie… that's not something you get over, is it?'

No. Losing your child is not something you ever get over. She had learned to live with it. The loss. The pain. Some days she would even laugh and enjoy herself. But it was always there, opening the closed door, sitting on the empty chair, lying beside her on the empty side of the bed. Dylan wriggled in her arms. He was life. He was the future. The two things she had been lacking for so long.

But Faith was right. Emily needed help. 'If I can't get hold of her soon, I will call the police.'

'Do you want me to do it?'

'No. I'll do it.'

'Okay. If you need me, I'm here.'

Calling the police was the right thing to do, but as soon as she ended the call to Faith, Caroline's nerve wavered. What if they wanted to take Dylan from her until they found Emily? Caroline had no right to him, no claim. They weren't related in any way. If she tried to explain that he was a half-brother to her son, she would imagine that would only make them more likely to want to take him away from her and into custody.

Plus, would the police even take her seriously if Emily had only been gone for a few hours? She was an adult, after all. Wouldn't they just assume that she needed some time out? In fact, maybe that was all that she needed. Some time to rest, to sleep. She'd been through a lot.

Dylan started to fidget in her arms; she'd need to feed him again soon. 'Well, whatever we decide, you're going to need something to sleep in tonight, little boy. As luck would have it, I've still got your big brother's crib, so let's prepare you some lovely milk and then we'd better get to the shops before they close and grab some more formula for you.'

Between feeding him, changing him and getting to the shops to pick up some more vests and a tin of formula, Caroline convinced herself it was pointless to call the police so late that evening. She'd also managed to pick up a baby gym just like the one Jamie used to have. Dylan would love it when he got a bit bigger, she was sure.

The next morning, Caroline woke to the sound of Dylan's cries. He had been an absolute angel, only waking once in the night for a feed and then going straight back to sleep. She couldn't help but wonder if he'd been fractious around Emily because she was so nervous. Once she had some time to get herself well again, it would be so much easier for both of them.

Making tea and breakfast was far more pleasant now she had him for company again. It wouldn't be that many months before he would be reaching out for her toast. Jamie used to love sitting in his high chair with a toast soldier in each hand, stuffing them into his mouth alternately and squeezing them into a bready pulp. Maybe she could go back to the shop where she'd bought the baby gym yesterday and see what they had in the way of high chairs.

Her phone buzzed with a message and she held her breath as she picked it up. Would it be Emily?

Faith.

What did the police say?

I haven't called them yet.

What? He was left at the children's centre. That makes him my responsibility. If you don't call them right now, I will. I mean it!

I'll call them now.

Good. Call me straight after.

Irritated by Faith's interference, she tried Emily one more time. When it clicked immediately to voicemail, she kept it brief. 'Emily, it's me again. I'm worried about you so I'm calling the police.'

If only Emily would just let them know she was okay, she could get on with looking after Dylan. She tapped her fingers on the kitchen counter, giving Emily five minutes to reply, then dialled the non-emergency number for the police which she found online.

'Hi. I need to report a missing person.'

'How long have they been missing?'

'Since yesterday lunchtime.'

'Do you think that they are at risk in any way?'

Was Emily at risk? It certainly wasn't normal to leave your baby behind. She didn't want to mention this unless she absolutely had to. 'I don't know. She is currently on medication for postnatal depression, so maybe.'

'Does she have her baby with her?'

Caroline squeezed Dylan a little tighter. 'No. He's with me.'

'And what is your relationship to the baby?'

'I'm his,' Caroline crossed her fingers, 'aunt.' It didn't feel like a lie. He was Jamie's half-brother. Her ex-husband's son. Surely that made them related in some way?'

'And do you often take care of him?'

'Yes. They have been living with me. I am used to looking after him. He's fine with me.' That part, at least, was a hundred per cent true.

'Okay. Well, let's take some details and work out what to do first. If you have a recent photograph of her, that would be useful, too.'

Caroline answered the questions to the best of her ability. Address, mobile number, physical description. Some of them – date of birth, for example – she didn't actually know. And she didn't have a photograph, either.

The police officer was very patient. 'Is there anyone who might have a photograph? Or who might have more information about where she might have gone? Someone who knows her well?'

Emily had lived in her house for three weeks; how come she didn't know about these things? What had they even talked about in that time? It was amazing how consuming a small baby could be. Most of their conversation had been about him. And about Jamie. It had been wonderful to be able to speak about Jamie with someone who wasn't worrying that she might be slipping backwards. The only time she had mentioned a friend was Amy, who had come to visit. Caroline knew that they'd worked in the same building and that the building was close to Pete's office, but there were a lot of office buildings at the bottom of Victoria Street, so that wasn't a lot to go on. She had no idea how to contact Amy. 'No. There's no one that I know of.'

'Okay. Well, I'll get this uploaded onto our system. We will send someone round to Emily's address and make some enquiries in the local area and the hospitals. In the meantime, if you think of anything that might help, or if you hear from her, please let us know.'

'Of course. Thank you.'

Now she had called the police, everything began to feel more real. They would check the hospitals. The thought of Emily requiring medical help was frightening. What the hell had she been thinking, sitting in a café with Dylan when Emily could be…

She didn't even want to think about what might have happened. It didn't matter how angry she'd been, she wouldn't want to see any harm come to her.

'Oh, Dylan, where is your mummy? Where might she have gone?'

He looked up at her, blissfully unaware that his life might be about to change forever. These were the moments; the hairpin bends in the road which you didn't see coming. Hurtling onwards until a sharp left or right sent you over the edge.

What must have been going through Emily's mind in the moments before she'd left Dylan at the children's centre? When she had been writing the letter? As she'd walked away? What dark path had she taken in her mind that had made her feel that this was her only avenue? And was that path so dark that she might have done something even worse? She'd lost her mother, her husband and now her son. What did she have left?

If only she'd pick up the phone. She didn't need to come back; Caroline was more than capable of looking after Dylan for as long as she needed. She just needed to call and say that she was okay.

On the subject of calling, she suddenly remembered that Faith was waiting to hear from her. It only took a second to find her in her phone favourites and Faith picked up after one ring. 'Have you notified the police?'

'Yes. I just spoke to them. Not that I could tell them very much. What do I do now?'

'Is there anyone you can think of that she mentioned to you? Any friends? Relatives? Places she liked to visit?'

'There's no one.'

She'd already said as much to the police officer on the telephone. But repeating it to Faith made her realise it again: Emily had no one.

'Then I guess all you can do is stay home and sit tight. Wait to hear from her. Or the police.'

Caroline closed her eyes. The last thing she wanted was another call from the police. 'Okay. I'll call you if I hear anything.'

When she ended the call, she sent another text to Emily.

Where are you? I've called the police.

This time, Emily called back.

CHAPTER THIRTY-EIGHT

EMILY

After leaving Dylan with the receptionist, Emily had walked away from the children's centre as quickly as she could, half expecting Caroline to come running after her. For an hour, she had walked the streets, not wanting to go home, not able to stay still. It had taken every ounce of strength she had to leave Dylan there and walk away. It was the best thing for him. One day he would understand.

Had she expected to feel relieved? Looking after him for the last few weeks had felt an insurmountable task. The relentless cycle of feeding, changing, getting him to sleep.

And the crying. She'd never known how the cry of a baby could twist your insides until you thought you might explode. Loud and sharp and painful; her need to make it stop had been so overwhelming at times that she'd been frightened about what she might do.

She shuddered. Leaving him with Caroline was safer for all of them.

But she didn't feel relieved. In fact, the further she got away from him, the more difficult it became to put one foot in front of the other. Almost as if she was joined to him by a length of elastic and she was getting to the point at which it wouldn't stretch any further. When she got back to the flat, she had to force herself to put the key in the lock and open the door. She closed it behind her and stood in the tiny entrance hall.

Silence.

The hall was tiny. A mere nod at a room, a pretence of space. Each wall only a large pace in length. In that tiny square, she had learned of Pete's accident, discovered the bleeding after her fall from the bath, revealed to Caroline that she had been the unwitting end of her marriage and – worse – the catalyst that may have ended her son's life.

She dropped her coat and phone and keys on the floor and stumbled through to the bedroom. Falling onto the bed fully clothed, she dragged the quilt over her head and lost consciousness.

The next morning, when she woke, the flat was eerily quiet. It had been so long since she'd been completely on her own that she had no idea what to do. She had no urge to eat breakfast, but she made herself a black coffee – more for something to do than because she wanted it.

Picking up her coat and keys from the hallway floor, she realised that her phone was dead. Not that it mattered. The only person likely to call her was Caroline and she didn't want to speak to her yet. Still, she stuck it on charge anyway. Ten minutes later, she was still staring at it as the unread texts and missed calls from Caroline stacked up on the screen. As soon as it had a thirty per cent charge she unplugged it, stuck it in her pocket and headed out the door.

Drizzling rain meant the park was empty when she got there, but the wide branches had kept the ground at the bottom of her favourite tree dry. Emily sat with her back to the rough bark, knees pulled up to her chest to avoid getting them wet. The moody grey sky was strangely calming and she closed her eyes and let her head rest on the thick trunk.

She'd counted five texts and seven missed calls from Caroline on her phone, but she didn't want to read them or listen to the voicemails. Caroline would just try to get her to come back, offer to take her to the doctor again. Possibly, she'd be angry, tell Emily that she didn't deserve to be a mother. Like she didn't know that already. Either way, she couldn't face it. She was so tired. If only when she shut her eyes she could go to sleep and wake up to something different. Or not wake up at all.

Another text message alert. Caroline again. This time she saw the message as it appeared on the screen.

Where are you? I've called the police.

Emily's heart thudded in her chest. This was exactly what she didn't want. She'd left Dylan with Caroline so that he would be safe. If Caroline had called the police, did that mean she was thinking of giving him to them?

With shaking fingers, she pressed Caroline's number and called her. She picked up immediately and Emily didn't give her a chance to say more than hello. 'Why have you called the police?'

'Why do you think? I've been worried sick. I needed to find you.'

'I don't need you to worry about me. I need you to look after Dylan. Is he okay?' It sounded so quiet at the other end. An icy fear pressed its nails into Emily's spine. Where was Dylan? *Please don't say she's called social services.*

'He's absolutely fine. He's lying in my arms looking at me right now.'

Emily tried not to picture it. 'Did he have you up all night?'

'Only once. And he went to bed really well. I think he must have turned a corner with the colic. It can just stop like that, apparently.'

Of course, Emily was pleased that Dylan was content. But the confirmation that he was better off without her was another stone in her pocket. 'That's great. Look, please call the police and tell them to stop looking for me. I just need…'

What did she need? To be alone? To go to sleep? To disappear?

'You don't need to worry about Dylan. He is absolutely fine. Look, why don't you just have a few days to yourself. Rest, see some friends…'

Caroline clearly had no idea what this was like. Emily couldn't rest for a minute and she had no friends here to see. 'What about the police? You need to call them *now*. Say it was a mistake. A mix-up. If they think I've abandoned him, they might take him. You know that.'

There was a pause at the other end. 'I'll call them. And I'll take care of Dylan. But you need to take care of yourself, Emily. You need help.'

She'd had help. She'd been to the doctor. She'd taken the pills. It hadn't worked. There were no other options. 'I'm going to stay with a friend. She'll look after me,' she lied.

It worked. She could almost hear the relief in Caroline's voice. 'Good. Well, I'll call the police and tell them it was a false alarm. Will you call me when you're settled?'

Emily breathed out. Dylan was safe. He would be okay. 'I will.'

As soon as she ended the call, she turned off her phone.

The bark of the tree was rough on the back of her head. If only what she had said were true. If only there was a friend she could go and stay with for a few days. Someone to tuck her up in bed like a child and just let her rest.

And then it came to her. She might not have a friend like that, but her mum had.

CHAPTER THIRTY-NINE

CAROLINE

Now that she knew Emily was fine, Caroline could enjoy her time with Dylan with a clear conscience.

Faith had already offered her a few days' holiday if she needed some time, but she was relieved that Faith was in a meeting when she called to say she'd be taking a whole week. Michaela took the message and said she'd get Faith to call her later.

It was a shame she had to go back to work at all. Even with the promise of the new outreach job, it would be a wrench to have to leave Dylan to go and help other families.

Of course, that was assuming Dylan was still staying with her by then.

It would have been nice to take Dylan to Crystal Palace Park, but the weather was dull and wet so, instead, she unpacked the baby gym she'd bought yesterday and laid it out in the lounge. The mat was designed like a huge leaf and the frame like vines. Hanging down were jungle animals: a giraffe, an elephant and a monkey.

She laid Dylan gently underneath. He was too small to play with it yet but he might enjoy looking at the animals. She sat on the floor next to him, her legs curled underneath her. 'Your big brother used to love his baby gym. He used to kick his little legs and...' She stopped speaking when her voice started to tremble.

Would she ever get to a place where she could talk about Jamie without getting upset?

It was so lovely having Dylan here; she had missed him so much. Her anger had been so fierce that day at Emily's flat that she'd wanted to leave and forget that she'd ever existed. But it had been impossible not to think about Dylan. Not to wonder if he was okay. Not to miss him.

How had Emily left him? When Jamie had been this small, Caroline couldn't bear to be away from him. She could still remember clearly the day Pete had insisted that they leave Jamie with her mum so that they could go out for dinner. She'd inhaled her sweet-and-sour chicken so fast that she'd given herself indigestion. Then, when Pete had refused to do the same, she'd called her mum three times to check that Jamie was okay.

But Emily had been gone nearly twenty-four hours now and she hadn't even said when she'd be back. Clearly she needed more help; she needed to get better before she could look after her son.

Well, that's what she was here for. She would look after him as long as she was needed.

CHAPTER FORTY

EMILY

'Emily? Oh my word, what a lovely surprise!'

Emily had spent the fifteen minutes from Sydenham Hill to Victoria, the two stops to Oxford Circus on the Victoria Line, the six stops to Liverpool Street on the Central Line, the hour and twenty minutes on the train to Ipswich and the eight minutes in the cab thinking of nothing else but getting to this house. Now she was here, in front of Auntie Julia, she had no idea what she was going to say.

Thankfully, with Auntie Julia, that was never a problem. 'Come in, come in, love. Your Uncle Phil was just about to make a cup of tea. Phil!' she shouted back through the hallway. 'Make an extra cup, Sue's Emily is here.'

Sue's Emily. Just the mention of her mother's name tugged at her insides. *Sue's Emily.* If only she did still belong to her mother.

Julia wasn't her real aunt, but she had been Emily's mother's best friend since they'd worked together at Barclays in the centre of Ipswich at age sixteen. Julia had met Phil at about the same time as Emily's mother Sue had met Gary – Emily never referred to him as her father, even in her head – and they had spent time as a foursome before Gary had shown his true colours and Julia wouldn't even be in the same room as him. Julia was the friend who had taken Sue and Emily in when they'd finally been able to leave him. Now she was here, Emily wished she'd come sooner.

The last time she'd been in their lounge had been her mother's funeral when Julia had insisted that they have the wake here rather than a hotel. It looked different now. The blue-and-white colour scheme had been replaced with hot pinks and lime greens. Emily could still remember Julia's advice to her mother when they'd moved into their little house: *Have neutral walls and furniture, Sue. Then you can just change your cushions and you'll have a whole new look.* Julia and Phil had been there with them the first week, wielding soap and buckets, paint and paintbrushes to help them make it into a home.

'Here you go, love.' Phil put a cup of tea on the coaster in front of her. 'How are you? How's that baby of yours? Our Grace said she'd seen an announcement that you were pregnant, but we haven't heard anything since. You know she's got two of her own? Twins, would you believe? A right pair of rascals.'

It felt like a million years ago that she had excitedly posted the picture of her and Pete grinning like loons on her Instagram. She saw Julia dart her husband a warning look and he paled as he realised his potential gaffe. *They must think I've lost the baby.* 'He's fine. Dylan. We called him Dylan.'

Phil breathed out with relief. 'Well, that's great. Where is he today? With his dad?'

Emily didn't want to lie, but she couldn't cope with rolling out the horror of the last few months just yet. It was easier to avoid it. 'Actually, my friend is looking after him.'

Julia smiled. 'Well, that's lovely. You must bring him to see us. Oh, your mum would be so proud. A grandson. She'd have doted on him.'

Emily chewed at her lip. Julia nudged Phil and he got up from his seat. 'It's good to see you, love, but I'm halfway through mowing the lawn, so I'll leave you two to it.'

As soon as he was out of the room, Julia got up and came to sit next to Emily on the sofa. 'Right. Much as I'm pleased to see you, how come you're here out of the blue? What's going on?'

Like a wave, everything welled up inside Emily and she burst into tears. Julia pulled her into a hug. 'Oh, love. What is it? I can see you're not right.'

Still, Emily cried. She couldn't speak yet. Julia rocked her gently in her arms. 'Is it Pete? Has something happened between the two of you? Or is it being a mum? It can be pretty overwhelming in the beginning. Are you finding it all a bit too much?'

Eventually, Emily's tears subsided and she, slowly and haltingly, told Julia everything. Pete. Caroline. Jamie. Dylan. The marriages, the divorces, the deaths, the births. She didn't leave anything out, not even her shame at realising that she and Pete had been having an affair. She finished by describing her depression, the trip to the doctor, her argument with Caroline and the fact that she had abandoned her son.

Julia sat and listened. Didn't interrupt once. When she was finished, Emily sat back and waited for soothing words. Or advice. But Julia's words were not what she had been expecting. 'Your mum had depression, you know. When you were little. It's not surprising. She had that waste of space husband to deal with as well as a young child. Did you know that you came to stay with me for a while?'

Emily just stared at her. How had her mother never mentioned this? 'No. I have no memory of that at all.'

Julia smiled. 'Well, you won't. You were only tiny. But, oh my, that little mouth could yell the house down. Your mum wasn't getting any sleep and she still had to go to work the next day: she was like the walking dead. And *he* was no help – your father. So, I told her to let me have you for a bit. It was only a couple of nights and then we did it once a week for a while. Sunday night she would drop you off and then I'd take you home on a Monday afternoon, as soon as Phil got in from work and could watch our Grace. Just one good night's sleep a week made all the difference. She could cope again.'

Emily couldn't remember the last time she'd got a whole night's sleep. Actually, she could. It was the night after she got soaked at the park. When Caroline had slept on the floor of her bedroom. But that was too simple an explanation for what she was going through. 'It's more than just not getting enough sleep.'

Julia patted her hand. 'I know that, love. You've been to hell and back these last few months, but you could have had the easiest time in the world and still have had postnatal depression. It's chemical, isn't it? Or hormonal, or something? I don't know the science, but I know what it is. What I'm saying is, having it – depression – it doesn't make you a bad mum. It just means you need some help. We all need that sometimes. I had to have some counselling a little while after your mum died. I just wasn't coping. I love the bones of Phil, but he's not very good at the *emotionals*, as he calls them. That's what I had your mum for. When I lost her, I… Well, I don't need to tell you, do I? You know how great she was.'

The ache of longing within Emily answered that question. With all the rubbish life had dealt her, her mother had been strong and kind and warm. When someone like that dies, you can't fill the hole they leave behind. You just learn to live with it. 'She was a wonderful mum.'

Julia nodded. Her bottom lip wobbled and she pressed it down for a moment before answering. 'Yes, she was. And a great friend.'

Emily realised why she had been drawn here today and also, perhaps, why she hadn't come before. 'I wish Mum could be here.'

Julia put a hand to her chest. 'Oh, me too, love. There's no one who can fix things for you like your mum, is there? I know it doesn't feel possible right now, but that will be you one day. You'll be the one that your Dylan will come to for help.'

Emily couldn't look that far into the future. It was too frightening. 'What if I'm not up to it? What if I don't have the answers?'

Julia chuckled. 'You think I had all the answers? You think your mum did? We all just did our best. All you have to do with children is keep loving them. Do you love him? Do you love Dylan?'

Emily thought about that little boy. His dark, serious eyes that looked at her as if he'd been here before. Who could fail to love him? 'Yes. Yes, I love him very much.'

'Right, then. How about you stay with us tonight, and then tomorrow we'll take you home to get that boy and the two of you come here for a while?'

Emily tilted her head to one side. Had she misheard her? 'Sorry?'

'We've got plenty of room and your mother would never forgive me if I didn't look after you. It's kind of this Caroline to look after Dylan for you, but she's practically a stranger. We're your family. Come and stay with us. You can register with my doctor and we'll get you some help, and Phil and I will be here to look after you both until you're feeling better.'

This was where her mother had come when she'd needed help. Why hadn't Emily thought of it before? A glimmer of hope lit inside her. 'Are you sure? Do you need to check with Phil?'

'Check with Phil? He'll be made up that I've got someone to talk to instead of chewing his ear off. Since Grace moved to Bristol with the twins, it's been pretty quiet around here. I'd love you to come. And I can't wait to meet that little boy. I'll go out to the garden and tell him now.' Before she stood up, she leaned over and kissed Emily on the cheek. 'Why don't you call your friend and tell her we'll be there in the morning?'

Left alone in the room, Emily put her hand on her chest and waited for her heart to calm back down. Julia was right. She loved Dylan. She missed her son.

Caroline's phone went straight to voicemail. She'd try her again later.

CHAPTER FORTY-ONE

CAROLINE

'I think his colic is getting better. He's much more settled at night now.'

Faith had her arms folded and her voice was stern. 'Right.'

Caroline chose to ignore Faith's eyes boring into her and continued to fold and refold Dylan's blankets and romper suits. She was beginning to regret asking her and Gabby to come over. 'She said she's fine. She just needs some time out. You know what it's like being a new mother. How overwhelming it can be.'

Faith was still watching her. 'She's not all right, though, is she? I mean, yes, there were times when my two were young when I wanted to run away, but I didn't do it, did I? That's the difference. She is *not* okay.'

This situation was not as stark as Faith was painting it. It wasn't as if Emily had run away and left Dylan alone. She'd asked Caroline to care for him. 'Lots of people leave their children with someone if they go away. Grandparents. Or friends. Or they hire a nanny. No one bats an eye at that. That's all I'm doing. Looking after him.'

Faith narrowed her eyes. 'A nanny? That's how you see yourself? Honestly?'

Gabby shuffled on her seat. 'When you spoke to her on the phone, she told you when she was coming back, did she?'

This was a little more difficult to explain. Caroline had just been relieved that Emily was safe. They hadn't made a formal plan or anything. 'I guess it's open-ended for now. She needs to see a doctor, recover.'

Faith wasn't about to let up. 'And she's doing that, is she? Going to see her doctor? Didn't you have to practically force her there last time? How is she going to sort this out for herself?'

Maybe she should have just invited Gabby. 'She's going to stay with her friend. I'm sure she'll help her get everything sorted out.'

'What friend? Where? And why hasn't this friend been around before now?'

Faith was worse than the police. 'Why are you interrogating me like this? I haven't done anything wrong, Faith. I'm just helping her out. Don't I get any credit for helping out the bereaved wife of my ex-husband?'

Faith put her hands in the air and Gabby took over. 'Of course, you do. And, of course, you have to think about baby Dylan. But we're worried you're not thinking this through rationally. When you were a social worker, how would you have reacted to this situation? Emily has postnatal depression. She's left her baby with a virtual stranger and disappeared. You've got to see that this isn't right?'

She didn't have to see anything. Dylan was the helpless victim of all this. Emily said she was getting it sorted out and she had to believe her. What other option did she have? 'There are plenty of unofficial adoption arrangements out there. Like I said, grandparents, aunts—'

Faith's eyes bulged out of her head. 'Is that what you're thinking this is?'

Gabby spoke before Caroline could. 'Faith. Calm down. This is Caroline. She's not going to do anything stupid. We just need to help her figure this out.'

Irritation itched at Caroline from the way Faith was speaking. She loved her friends, but this was really none of their business.

'This is the best thing for Dylan. You know what will happen if his mother can't cope. Child services will get involved. We know what happens to kids in the system. And she knows I can look after him, but they might not think so. I can't risk… I can't risk…'

Faith folded her arms. 'His mother? Do you mean Emily?'

Caroline frowned. 'Of course, I mean Emily.'

'This is the woman you were falling over yourself to invite into your home a few weeks ago, and now you're not even using her name.'

This was getting ridiculous. Faith was not the world authority on dealing with this. 'I don't want to talk about this anymore. I can look after Dylan. *Emily* can get herself back on her feet. Maybe go back to work. Get her life together again.'

'And meanwhile you're being… what? The nanny? The doting aunt? The foster mother? You can hate me for saying this if you want, but you cannot do this, Caroline.'

Caroline stood, anger trembling through her body. 'Do what? Look after a child? Let his mother have some rest? I'm not doing anything wrong, Faith. Why can't you understand that?'

Gabby had started to cry. 'Oh, honey, I know it's been tough for you. But this is not the way—'

'I have no idea what the hell you both think is happening here. What am I doing that is so bad?' Caroline had swivelled around to face her friend. Faith was opinionated and frank, but she hadn't expected Gabby would side with her.

Gabby stood and joined her. 'It's not bad. It's just not… Oh, Caroline, we should be here for you more. We've let things slide…'

'No! No, it's not that. You've both been incredible, I don't need you to do more.'

It was true. They had done everything they could. But they couldn't be there all the time. Couldn't hold her close in the dead of night. Couldn't be what she needed.

Faith was nodding. 'Gabby's right. We'll be around more. You can come and stay with me if you like and—'

'No!' Caroline realised that she'd almost shouted at Faith and took a moment to start again. 'I'm sorry, but you're not listening to me. I don't want you to do more. That's not what I need.'

Gabby tilted her head. 'What do you need, love?'

Her mind reeled off a filmstrip of memories, of feelings, of love and pain. She squeezed her eyes shut to try to stop them filling with tears. 'I need... I just need... I need to look after him. I need to keep him safe.'

They were interrupted by the ding of a text message. Emily. It took her a while to scroll through the essay-length text. And another couple of minutes to understand what Emily was telling her.

'What is it, Caro?' Gabby's voice was gentle. 'Is it Emily?'

'She wants to come and get him. Tomorrow. She wants to pick him up and take him back with her to stay with some friend of her mother's. It's ridiculous. How can I let her do that?'

Faith's voice had softened, but it was still firm. 'You don't have a choice, Caroline. Dylan is her son. She can take him wherever she wants. He's not yours.'

Gabby held up a hand. 'Faith. Slow down.'

The fight slipped from her body and Caroline sank down into the armchair again. 'You're right. Of course, you're right. But you don't understand. I need to do this. If you knew...' How could she explain to them that she had been lying for so long?

'Maybe we do understand.' Faith was looking her dead in the eye. Gabby perched on the arm of the chair and took her hand again.

They thought she was talking about Pete. But it was something much worse than that. A secret. A secret she had kept for a long time. 'But you don't. You don't know.'

Gabby stroked the back of Caroline's hand with her thumb. Her eyes were full of tears. 'We do know, honey. We do.'

CHAPTER FORTY-TWO

EMILY

The next morning, Caroline must have been watching for her through the window because she opened the door before Emily even rang the bell. She was strangely formal. 'Hi. Come in. Are you okay?'

Even though she'd told them that she'd need a day at home to get her things together, Julia had still insisted that she and Phil drive her to Caroline's rather than let her get the train back. They'd arranged to drive on to Bristol and stay the night with their daughter, Grace. Tomorrow afternoon, they'd drive back, meet her at the flat and take her and Dylan back home to Ipswich.

Emily felt better than she had in a while, but 'okay' was still a vast overstatement. 'Where is he? Where's Dylan?'

'He's in his cot. Asleep. It took a while to get him off for his morning nap, so we shouldn't disturb him. Why don't you come through to the lounge so that we can talk?'

For the last half hour, Emily had been itching to see him. In the car, she'd shown Auntie Julia pictures of him on her phone. Whether Julia had been truthful or not, Emily had been thrilled when she'd said she could see her mum in the shape of his mouth. She was still apprehensive about whether she could be the mother he deserved, but with Julia's support, and maybe different medication, she was hopeful for the first time that she might get there. 'I'd really like to just go up and see him first. Can I go up?'

Caroline looked reluctant, but she obviously couldn't deny her seeing her own child. 'Of course. His cot is in my room. Go on up. I'll make us a drink.'

When Emily pushed open the door to Caroline's bedroom, she couldn't help but feel like an intruder. But when she saw Dylan, his chest rising and falling with his sleeping breath, looking so tiny in that huge cot, it was all she could do not to sob.

She knelt down by the side of the cot and reached her hand in to place her finger in his palm. In his sleep, he clenched his fist and squeezed it. Her heart did the same thing. 'I'm sorry. Oh, Dylan, Mummy is so sorry she left you.'

She sat with him as long as she needed to, just listening to him breathe. Once she'd reassured herself that he was okay, she gently pulled her finger free. It was time to face Caroline.

Caroline had made them both a hot drink and was sitting waiting for her. Maybe Emily was being paranoid, but it felt as if Caroline was sitting in judgement. She probably deserved it. 'Thank you, Caroline. For looking after him. I'm sorry that I just left him like that. I was… I just felt like I'd run out of options.'

Caroline smiled, but there wasn't a great deal of warmth in her face. 'It's okay. And he's fine, Emily. It's you that I'm worried about.'

The tone of her voice reminded Emily of a stern headteacher. 'You don't need to worry anymore. I am really grateful for everything that you've done, but I know what I need to do now. I think we're going to be okay.'

Caroline didn't look convinced. 'I don't even know where you've been.'

Emily wanted to remind Caroline that she was an adult, but she could understand that her recent behaviour might not reflect that. 'I've been to Ipswich, where I'm from. I went to visit my aunt.

Well, she's not my actual aunt but that's neither here nor there. She said I can stay with her. *We* can stay with her. Me and Dylan.'

Caroline's mouth tightened. 'In Ipswich?'

The more Emily thought about going back to the town she grew up in, the better she felt about it. She could take Dylan to the park she'd loved as a child. Even introduce him to her favourite tree. She'd avoided going home because the memories would be too painful. If only she'd realised that it was the best thing she could have done. 'Yes. Aunt Julia has a three-bedroom house. There's plenty of space for both of us. Even with all Dylan's kit and kaboodle.' She smiled weakly at her attempt at humour. She wanted Caroline to see that she was doing better.

But Caroline's face didn't change and she didn't reply. Emily pressed on with her explanation. 'I'll take him back to the flat today. And then, once I've packed everything up tomorrow, I'll call Julia and her husband Phil and they'll pick me up. Phil said he doesn't mind doing two trips if we can't fit everything in. But they've got a cot and a lot of other baby stuff already from when their grandchildren were small.'

Caroline frowned. 'Won't you want to leave some things at your place for when you come back?'

Emily shook her head. 'I'm going to rent out the flat. Or even sell it. There are too many bad memories there. I'll stay with Julia for a while and then, once I'm feeling up to it, I'll decide whether to come back to London or stay in Ipswich and find a job there. I've got the rest of my maternity leave before I need to make a decision.'

Caroline's face paled. 'You're not coming back?'

Emily shrugged. 'I don't know yet. Julia said I shouldn't think too far ahead. I need to get well first before I'm ready to make any big decisions.'

'Selling the flat seems like a big decision.' Caroline's voice had a hard tone she'd never heard before.

They were interrupted by a familiar cry from upstairs. Before Emily could get up, Caroline was on her feet. 'You stay there. I'll go and get him and bring him down.'

Emily listened to Caroline's tread on the stairs, then across to her bedroom, her soothing tone as she spoke to Dylan, although she couldn't make out the words. After what seemed like forever, she heard her walking carefully down the stairs.

There was something in her posture as Caroline walked in the room which made Emily uncomfortable. The closeness of her hold. It was possessive, even. Emily stood to take her son, but Caroline didn't offer him up. 'He was pulling his legs up when I got there. I'll just walk him up and down a bit, see if I can get any wind up.'

Emily held out her hands, desperate to feel his warmth and his weight. 'I can do that.'

Caroline was already pacing up and down, rubbing Dylan's back, in the way Emily had watched her do many times. 'You rest. You've had a long journey. You don't want to push yourself too fast too soon.'

Two weeks ago, she'd been more than happy to let Caroline take control, but not now. Not when she had seen the possibility of a better future. 'Actually, I've had a good day. I know that I'm not well. I know that I'm going to have to sort out my medication, counselling, anything I need to do to get better. But I really feel that I can do it.'

Caroline's face didn't change. 'Today you do. But what about tomorrow? Next week? Next month? No. You can't take him.'

Her words were like a punch to the stomach. Emily could barely breathe. 'What do you mean?'

'What if you can't cope? What if it all gets too much again?'

Emily didn't need Caroline to ask those questions. They were pretty much on a loop in her own head all the time. 'Julia will be there to help me. She's retired. She'll be there all the time.'

Caroline's hand fluttered to her throat. 'I'm sorry, but I can't let you just take him. It wouldn't be responsible. You left him, Emily. If I just let you take him now and something happened – if he got hurt or you left him again – I would never forgive myself.'

Emily froze. She felt sick at the very idea. 'I would never hurt Dylan. I love him.'

'Of course, you do. But you've been struggling and that's not going to go away overnight. I don't want to be unkind, Emily. I'm just worried about Dylan. Why don't you leave him with me a while longer? Go to stay with your aunt. Get better. You can visit him whenever you want.'

Emily's heart thumped in her ears. What was happening here? Was Caroline seriously suggesting that she keep Dylan? She'd been a social worker. She would have contacts in the police and with social services. What was she willing to do?

Fear strangled Emily's voice to a whisper. 'He's my son, Caroline. He belongs with me.' She stood up and held out her arms. 'Give me my son.'

Caroline stopped walking. She stood in front of her. 'You've got to think what's best for Dylan.'

Something deep inside Emily rose up, pushing aside her fear, her anxiety, her uncertainty. Her voice sounded deeper when she spoke next. 'Give me my son, Caroline. He's not yours. He's mine.'

CHAPTER FORTY-THREE

CAROLINE

Handing Dylan over to Emily felt like cutting off her arm. Shouldn't she be trusting her instincts? If the hell of the last two years had taught her anything, surely it had been that?

Emily had all but ripped Dylan from her arms, but now she sat on the chair cradling him, kissing him, her love for her son was there for anyone to see. But love wasn't enough, was it? Not enough to keep him safe. He was too precious to take a risk.

'You shouldn't rush into this, Emily. It was only two days ago that you left him behind and didn't look back. How can you have changed your mind so quickly?'

She knew that her words would hurt, but she couldn't think about that right now. Her only concern was Dylan. It was all she could do not to reach out and take him back.

This wasn't just about her personal feelings. A career in social work had taught her that she had a duty to put the needs of the child first; he was innocent and vulnerable and needed protection.

Emily didn't take her eyes away from Dylan as she spoke. 'That day, I was in a fog. I couldn't see my way out. Leaving him with you was the only way I could guarantee that he'd be safe. I was so low, Caroline, so unbelievably low, that I couldn't imagine ever feeling worse.'

Now she looked up at Caroline, her eyes bright with tears. 'But not having him with me? That was worse. That was much worse. And I have a plan now. I will go to my aunt's. She will help me. We won't be alone anymore.'

Caroline pressed a fist into her chest, where her own loneliness lived; she wouldn't wish that on anyone. Even though she'd tried to be there for Emily the last few weeks, she knew that another body in the house wasn't enough to keep at bay the cruel fingers of isolation. She could understand Emily's longing to return to somewhere that felt like home.

But that was another thing: she'd never heard Emily mention this aunt before – she could have even made her up. It was like a switch had been flicked in her brain. 'How come you didn't go to your Aunt Julia before this? If you are so close, why wasn't she the first person you thought of when Pete died? Why wasn't she at the funeral?'

Emily's hesitation before she answered made her even more suspicious. 'I don't know. Now that I've seen her, I can't understand why she wasn't the first person I called when Pete died. If I had called her that first night from the hospital, I know she would have been there. We haven't spoken properly since I met Pete because I was so wrapped up in my life here and I didn't want to go back to Ipswich when my mum wasn't there. But that still doesn't explain it. I didn't even think to call her and I don't know why.'

Caroline could have told her why. Depression and anxiety are both liars which keep you from seeing the truth. Hadn't they done the same to her? Still, she wasn't ready to take that risk. 'It's just very strange that you should suddenly decide to go there yesterday.'

'I know. But I can't explain why because I don't know myself. I'm just really glad that I did.' She paused and looked at Caroline again. 'You can meet her tomorrow if it would make you feel any better?'

How would that make her feel any better? Even if this woman existed, she had no idea what she was like. Whether she would make sure Emily got the help she needed.

Begrudgingly, she had to admit that Emily did seem more balanced, more positive than she had since Pete's death. But she'd thought that before. Thought that things were on the up, only to find out she'd made a terrible, terrible mistake. How could she let Emily just take Dylan away to who knew where? What was her state of mind?

Now Emily was talking to Dylan, although her words were for Caroline's benefit. 'Mummy has been poorly, Dylan, and Auntie Caroline has been looking after you. But it's time for us to go home now. Mummy is going to see the doctor and she is going to get better. I promise. I am going to get better for both of us.'

It was too quick. Too soon. 'Mental health isn't like a broken bone, though, is it? We both know that. Some days you feel like you can cope; others you can't get out of bed. I've been there, Emily. I've had the dark days, when you would do anything not to think, not to know, not to feel. *Anything.*'

The more she thought about this, the more the potential horror of this situation became a possibility. Her heart started to beat harder. If she let them walk out the door, she might never see them again. Miles away in Ipswich, she would have no way of knowing whether they were okay. What if it didn't work out with this mysterious aunt? With no flat to come back to, what would Emily do? Would she, could she, do something truly awful, to both of them?

Emily looked horrified at her words. 'You think I might *kill* myself?'

Is that what she was saying? She remembered her training. If you think someone is suicidal, you should ask them the question: *Are you having suicidal thoughts?*

'I don't know, Emily. But I do know how quickly those thoughts can be triggered sometimes. How they can come out of nowhere. At least, as far as everyone around the person is concerned.'

Emily stood up as if she was going to leave. Her face flushed with anger. 'That's enough, Caroline. I know you think you are trying to help me. That, with all your social work experience, you think you know better than I do. But you don't know me. You've only seen me at my worst. I will get through this. I'm grateful for all you've done for us. But I have to go now.'

Caroline's heart was beating so hard it felt as if it might burst out of her chest. 'Listen to me! Please, Emily, just listen to me. I know what I'm talking about. I'm begging you. Don't walk out that door.'

Emily's eyes flashed. 'I know that you were a perfect mother, Caroline. When Pete spoke about you, he would say what an absolute martyr to motherhood you were. Running around after Jamie, pandering to his every whim. I know you think that I'm not good enough, but I am Dylan's mother, not you.'

Caroline flinched at her words. They were like knives and she held up her hands to shield herself. 'No. No, I was not the perfect mother. You don't understand at all.' Suddenly her legs didn't feel able to keep her standing, and she sank down onto an armchair. There was nothing else for it. She needed to tell Emily everything. 'I'm not just talking about you, Emily. Or about Dylan.'

Emily paused in picking up her bag from the floor. 'What do you mean?'

Caroline sighed. Suddenly she felt very tired. 'What did Pete tell you about Jamie's death?'

Emily tilted her head. Frowned. 'He was in his room at university, he was smoking with his head out of the window, but he was drunk and he fell…'

Caroline pressed her lips together. Took her time before she spoke. 'That's almost true. Except he was on his own at the time and… and the police report said that they thought he jumped.'

CHAPTER FORTY-FOUR

CAROLINE

Was it easier saying it aloud for the second time in twenty-four hours? No. It wasn't. It was unlikely that it would ever get easy to say that her beautiful, perfect boy had taken his own life.

The look of shock on Emily's face was what she'd expected – but not seen – on the faces of Gabby and Faith. Although she'd never told them what the police had said, and they hadn't attended the inquest, somehow they had known for a long time what had happened. True friends that they were, they'd waited to be told by her. And how could she have told them her secret when she hadn't wanted to believe it herself?

Emily's face was grey with shock. 'I don't know what to say. I thought… Pete said…'

'That it was an accident? Yes. That's what we told everyone. What we told each other. What we told ourselves.'

It required physical effort for Caroline to wrench her mind back to the day of the inquest. The description of Jamie's last moments. Beth's tremulous testimony when the coroner had asked her – more than once – about Jamie's state of mind before his death.

She hadn't been able to even look at Caroline and Pete when she'd spoken. *He was pretty down*, she'd said. *There was a lot on his mind.*

Every word was another flagstone on top of Caroline's chest. Why was he so down? What was on his mind? How had she not known? Now she said the words she had never spoken aloud before yesterday. 'Jamie's death was recorded as suicide.'

Emily shook her head as if to bat away the idea. 'I don't understand. Pete said it was an accident. He said that he was drunk. That he was leaning out of the window to have a cigarette. Because of the smoke alarm in his room. Pete said…' She trailed off in response to Caroline's sad smile.

'Pete said what we both said all the way through. What we believed. What we had to believe. But the coroner didn't agree.'

From the evidence given by his friends, Jamie had been on a night out. He had drunk a lot. Had had a row with Beth and was back in his room.

His room was on the eleventh floor of a tower block. The window of his room looked out on a tarmac path which led down to a lecture theatre. According to the CCTV, Jamie had climbed out of his window at 2.15 a.m. He'd been drunk and had fallen from the window. With no witnesses, it was surely inconclusive whether he had intended to jump or whether he'd fallen? For the last two years, Caroline – and Pete – had chosen to believe the latter. The coroner believed otherwise.

Emily's hand fluttered to her mouth. 'But why? Oh God, was it because of me? Because he saw me and Pete?'

Caroline took a deep breath. This was the question that had been circling in her mind ever since she'd read Jamie's diary. They would never really know the answer, so what was the point of torturing Emily further? 'I don't think you can blame one event. He had struggled with his mental health before. During his A-levels, he'd become overwhelmed. It didn't seem to matter what we said, he put so much pressure on himself. His school was great – they sorted out some counselling for him and it really seemed to help. After that, we thought it was all totally fine. That it had been a blip. He went off to university and he made friends and there was Beth. I had no idea…'

Was that true? Or was that just the way she remembered it now? She had gone over and over it in her head for the last two years. Could she have done anything different? Should she have insisted he see her in those last few weeks when he was always rushing off somewhere whenever she called?

You're fussing, Pete had said. *Leave the boy alone.* And she had believed him. She had ignored her instinct and believed the man who had known exactly why Jamie wasn't returning her calls. Her anger towards Pete rose up inside her, but she tried to push it down. It wasn't Pete in front of her, it was Emily.

Emily was trembling. Words tumbled from her mouth. 'Oh, Caroline, I am so very sorry. It is all such a horrible mess. You've been a great help to me since Dylan was born. I honestly don't think I would have coped without you. I did feel guilty knowing that Pete and I had been together when you were still married, I did. But I didn't do it knowingly. And I really believed that you had ended the marriage anyway. That's what Pete said. But now this… Jamie… I just can't believe that…'

Caroline couldn't watch her suffer like this. If an affair meant that you knowingly had a relationship with someone who was married, then Emily had not had an affair. Caroline believed that much. 'It wasn't your fault.'

Pete, on the other hand, *had* been having an affair. Was Emily the first person he had done this with, or had there been others who she knew nothing about? Hadn't their marriage been a good one? In the beginning, it had been passionate. Then Jamie had been born and her love for Pete had deepened further. She couldn't have imagined ever being without him. When had that changed? Because it had. 'Our marriage had problems before you, Emily. Don't misunderstand me. I'm not excusing Pete's behaviour. He cheated on me, plain and simple, and I didn't deserve that. But

I'd be lying if I said we were happy, even before Jamie's accid—'
She swallowed. 'Before Jamie died.'

When had they gone from being unable to keep their hands off each other to going to bed at different times, watching different TV programmes in different rooms, only going out to dinner if they were invited by someone else? It hadn't been a huge event; it had been a thousand tiny forgotten gestures which had put so many tiny holes in the hull of their marriage that, when the big wave had hit, it had sunk without a fight.

Emily shook her head. 'I just can't stop thinking what if? What if I'd never met Pete? What if we hadn't kissed in that bar that night? What if we hadn't gone away and—'

Caroline held up a hand to interrupt her. 'We can't live our lives with "what if" though, can we? We've both done things wrong, Emily. But we can't keep looking back. We can't live in the past. I realised that today, looking at Dylan – he is the future. He's your future. And, if you'll let me, I'd... I'd just like to be a part of that.'

Emily shook her head again. 'I still don't understand. Why would you want to help me?'

A single tear ran down Caroline's cheek. She struggled to keep her voice steady when she spoke. 'Because finding someone who needs you is just as important as finding someone to help you. I wouldn't be doing you a favour; I need you and Dylan as much as you need me. I know you are going to your aunt's tomorrow, but is there any way you could be persuaded to make it a short visit? You have a job here, a flat, a life. I know that I'm asking a lot, and I know that Dylan is your son, but I do love him so very much. When I ask you to stay, I'm not just offering to help; I'm really asking you to give me a second chance. Please come back.'

Caroline held out her hands, palms upward, much in the same way you might offer help to a child who is learning to walk. But also in the way that you beg for mercy. With every inch of her, she was desperate for Emily to understand, to give her another chance, to let her be a part of Dylan's life.

For a few unbearable seconds, Emily looked at Caroline's outstretched hands, then at Dylan, then she looked Caroline in the eye and, with Dylan safe in her left arm, she placed her right hand into Caroline's. 'I'll come back.'

CHAPTER FORTY-FIVE

CAROLINE

The café was busy for a Saturday morning. Maybe everyone was hitting the shops early so that they could spend the rest of the day enjoying the warm September weather. Emily had opted to leave the buggy at home and carry Dylan in a sling on her front. Caroline noticed the way she wrapped her arms around him as they approached the entrance. She wasn't sure who was most comforted by the closeness.

After staying with Aunt Julia for a week, Emily had moved back to her flat. Together, in the month since then, she and Caroline had seen a solicitor and sorted out Pete's estate. As expected, life insurance policies paid off both the house and the flat. There was enough money for Emily to start looking for a small house with a garden when she was ready. For now, the flat was fine.

As Caroline pushed open the door to the café, Emily asked the same question she'd voiced at least three times that morning. 'Are you sure they won't mind me coming, too?'

And Caroline gave her the same answer. 'Of course not. They're looking forward to meeting you.'

It wasn't a complete lie. When she'd checked with Gabby and Faith whether they were okay with her inviting Emily along for a coffee, Gabby had expressed her interest in 'getting to see what she's actually like after all this time'.

Faith had been less keen. 'I am sorry for her and I understand-ish why you are supporting her. But why do *we* need to be friends with her?'

It wasn't that Caroline wanted them to be friends with Emily exactly. More that she wanted them to accept her as part of her life. Because she *was* going to be a part of her life from now on. She'd brought out her trump card. 'You'll get to meet baby Dylan.'

Faith was a sucker for small babies. 'Well, now you're talking.' She shook her head at her friend. 'You are amazing, you know. How many women would look after the woman who slept with her husband? How can you do it?'

Caroline preferred not to focus on that for too long. She could argue that Emily hadn't known that Pete was still married, but she knew that wouldn't wash with her staunchly loyal friends. To be honest, she tried not to focus on anything negative from the past for too long these days.

She'd reached out for Faith's hand and then Gabby's. 'Because I've got you two. And when you've got a lot, you can afford to be generous.'

Now, they were walking towards Gabby and Faith, other customers scraping their chairs closer to tables so that Emily and her precious burden could squeeze past. There was something about babies that brought out the best in people. Perhaps it was their newness, their vulnerability. Or maybe it was their hope for the future.

That's what Dylan had given Caroline: a future. Being part of his life gave her something to look forward to at last. On a Wednesday evening, when Emily was seeing her counsellor, she would drop Dylan to Caroline's house and it was the highlight of her week. It wasn't the only time she saw him. Many evenings she would visit Emily at the flat or they would go for a walk together. Who knew how their relationship would develop over time? She understood that once Emily was feeling better, she would need

Caroline less. Right now, she chose not to think about that. It didn't do to look too far into the future, either.

Caroline had gone back to her counsellor too. This time she was able to be more honest with her about what had happened to Jamie. More honest with herself. Giving up the secret she had carried for so long was going to take time to work through. But she'd made a start.

On her last shopping trip in this area, she had spotted a tiny pair of soft football boots in the gift shop on the corner. If Jamie had been around, it was the exact kind of thing he would have bought his baby brother. She talked about him to Dylan all the time. And about Pete. He had hurt her, but he was Dylan's father and she would be here to tell him all the good things about him. About both of them. Enough to give him roots from which to grow and be his own self.

Finally, they reached the table where Gabby and Faith were waiting for them. She felt Emily tense beside her; she knew how close Caroline was to her friends and must have known that they had spoken about her in the past.

'Morning, ladies. This is Emily.'

Gabby smiled and Faith nodded, pushing forward a small plate. 'Hi, Emily. Would you like to help us save ourselves and take one of these cakes?'

'I'd love one, thank you.' Emily slipped onto the chair that Gabby had pulled out for her and unhooked the top of the baby carrier, passing Dylan to Caroline.

Caroline could hear the love in her own voice as she turned his tiny body around to face her two dearest friends.

'And this is Dylan. Dylan Jamie Simmons.'

EPILOGUE

It was the first Saturday in May that had been warm enough for a barbecue. Caroline – and her partner Chris – had just had a detailed tour of Dylan's Lego models, and she had sneaked away to the kitchen, where Emily was chopping salad.

'Do you need any help?'

Emily turned, a small bump pushing at the middle of her apron. 'I think I'm okay, but you can stay and chat to me for a bit? Amy was keeping me company, but baby Alice woke up and she had to go and feed her.'

'She's a cute little thing. Has the adoption finalised yet?'

'Next week. It's just a formality, but Amy is on tenterhooks until everything is signed and sealed. Thank goodness she's got Alex beside her for the whole process. If she'd stayed with Stuart, she'd have been the one doing it all.'

'I can understand her nerves.' Caroline nodded at Emily's midriff. 'Your little girl will have a ready-made playmate.'

Emily smiled. 'If Dylan lets her out of his sight. He tells everyone that will listen that she's his baby. "My baby is a sister. My baby is going to play. My baby likes cars." Heaven help her if she doesn't fit his plan.'

Caroline grinned. 'He'll make a lovely brother.'

'He will.' Emily looked down at the carrot she was grating. 'I've started to worry a bit.'

Caroline leaned forwards. 'Regular worries or more serious?'

'I don't know. What if it happens again? The depression? I don't want to go back there. Especially as I have Dylan to look after this time.'

Caroline nodded. 'Of course, you don't. But you're prepared this time. You can get help more quickly. And you have John now, too. Have you spoken to him about it?'

Emily nodded. 'Yes. I told him all about what had happened as soon as we started talking about having a baby. He said the same.'

Caroline liked John. He was a great dad to Dylan already. 'Well, there you go, then. You've got John and you've got me. We'll get you through it, whatever happens.'

Through the kitchen window, they could see Dylan running around the garden, both Chris and John giving chase. 'Chris is great with him.'

Caroline smiled. 'I know. His girls are grown up now so I think he misses the rough and tumble.'

Emily nudged her. 'And how are you finding it being a wicked stepmother?'

Caroline laughed. 'I don't think they think of me like that. But they're nice girls. I like it. Maybe I'll get to be a step-grandmother one day. Who knows?'

'Well, Dylan loves the Lego ship Chris brought today, so he's definitely continuing to be a firm favourite with him.'

Outside, Dylan was screaming with delight. Caroline couldn't believe how fast he was growing up. 'He looks so much like Pete.'

Emily nodded. 'I know. And like Jamie?'

Caroline put a hand to her chest. 'Yes, just like Jamie.'

They stood there for a few moments, two women who had loved one man. And who both now loved one boy. Then Caroline jumped. 'Oh, I just remembered. I have something for you.' She darted into the lounge and came back with a flat, round parcel wrapped in tissue.

Emily frowned. 'For me? But it's Dylan's birthday, not mine.'

'Just open it.'

Emily tore off the tissue to find a wood slice, varnished in such a way that she could see the concentric circles running through it. She looked up at Caroline for an explanation. 'Is this because I like trees?'

'Partly.' Caroline pointed at a darker circle, about an inch from the edge. 'Every line is a year in the tree's growth. Some years the tree thrives and grows a lot; other years it doesn't and it hardly grows. But it keeps going, through the bad years. It keeps going and it survives until the good times come back.'

Emily's eyes filled and she reached out for Caroline's hand. 'Thank you. And not just for this. You saved me, you know. You helped me to survive.'

Caroline swallowed and squeezed Emily's hand in hers. 'And you saved me, too.'

A LETTER FROM EMMA

I want to say a huge thank you for choosing to read *His First Wife's Secret*. If you did enjoy it and want to keep up-to-date with all my latest releases, just sign up at the following link. Your email address will never be shared and you can unsubscribe at any time.

www.bookouture.com/emma-robinson

Suicide in young men has been on my mind for the last couple of years since I heard that a young man I used to teach ended his life at the age of twenty-five. According to figures released in 2020, male suicide rates are higher than they have been in twenty years. As a mother of a young son, this has preyed on my mind and led to the story you've just read.

Similarly, Emily's struggle with pre- and postnatal depression is something that affects thousands of women each year. In researching this book, I asked an open question on my personal Facebook page and was overwhelmed by how many women, who I knew personally, had been affected by this in some way. Again, I believe that the more we read, write and talk about these subjects, the more people can be helped.

Caroline and Emily's story is my small contribution to that dialogue.

I hope you loved *His First Wife's Secret* and if you did, I would be very grateful if you could write a review. I'd love to hear what you think, and it makes such a difference helping new readers to discover one of my books for the first time.

I love hearing from my readers – you can get in touch on my Facebook page, through Twitter, Goodreads or my website.

Thanks,
Emma

      motherhoodforslackers

      @emmarobinsonuk

      www.motherhoodforslackers.com

ACKNOWLEDGEMENTS

Grateful thanks to my brilliant editor Isobel Akenhead – I hope we can meet in person to celebrate soon! Also, to Kim Nash for all her PR wizardry and for all the FB lives and chats, and to DeAndra Lupu for copy-editing, Laura Gerrard for proofreading, Carrie Harvey for final checks and Alice Moore for a gorgeous cover – you are all amazing!

The more books I write, the more I have to rely on the generosity of other people sharing their life experiences with me. This time, I have so many people to thank for helping me out with my questions on a variety of topics from pre- and postnatal depression to baby colic to the role of the police after an accident. Thank you so much, Kerry Kay, Louise Hoskins, Emma Tallon, Lorraine Giroud, Nicole Fayers, Charlotte Hellis-Gilbert and Louise Dorling. Any mistakes are mine.

Trevor Colton, we had had quite a few wines when you asked me to put Captain Trevor in a book someday, but I hope you enjoyed his cameo in this. Dr Fayad Ayoub, you can start speaking to me again. And Chloe Jordan, Michaela Balfour and Lorna Corbin – I hope you were paying attention in Chapter Thirty-Five!

My friends and family deserve to be thanked after every book as I couldn't do it without their faith and encouragement. During 2020, juggling life and work and writing was a particular challenge and I could not have done it without my mum – in our bubble – looking after the kids and dog, and Dan for letting me disappear to the loft with my laptop.

Lastly, to everyone who has bought, read and reviewed one of my books, I am truly grateful. I hope you enjoy this one too.